Sign up for our newsletter to hear
about new and upcoming releases.

www.ylva-publishing.com

OTHER BOOKS BY FIONA ZEDDE

HOUSE
OF
AGNES

FIONA ZEDDE

ACKNOWLEDGEMENTS

Lee Winter, thank you for saving Agnes. That's all.

DEDICATION

For my family, my loves, my friends.

CHAPTER 1

"YOU KNOW, ALL WORK AND no play makes Queen Agnes a very dull girl."

Agnes saved the spreadsheet on her computer and looked up, masking her irritation at being interrupted. A glimmer of light fell over the bare shoulders of the woman walking into her office unannounced, the emerald minidress a complement to her slim but curvaceous figure. The woman's high heels teased the marble floor, and her smile said she wanted a lot more than a talk.

"It's a good thing I'm not a girl then." She sat back in her leather executive chair, giving Rox the attention she obviously wanted. "The evening went well?" Although if it hadn't, one of Agnes's security people would've let her know long before now.

"Just as expected." Rox gave her trademark smile, the one that regularly had men and women offering up thousands of dollars to spend a few hours with her.

She pulled a small stack of bills from her cleavage, all hundreds and all miraculously dry, and laid it on Agnes's desk. "It went *very* well, actually. And I kept the tip." Her cheek dimpled and her red mouth glistened in the soft golden glow from the Tiffany desk lamp. "Care to help me celebrate?"

Before Agnes could accept or refuse the offer, Rox shrugged off her dress. It slithered from her body and pooled around her feet in a puddle of green satin.

Agnes drew in a breath. The lamplight played over Rox's curves, showing off her high breasts with nipples stiff from the arctic air-conditioning. Her belly was tight with muscle and her hips rounded and smooth. The V at the joining of her thighs was completely bare of hair.

Bald vaginas had never been Agnes's thing.

She sat back in her chair and rolled her favorite pen between her fingers, leisurely appreciating all the ways Rox had taken care of her body.

The woman was beautiful. Truly. From the loose waves of hair around her fashion model face to her long legs and every worthwhile stop in between. But Agnes didn't fuck any of the women who worked for her. Never had, never would.

They all knew that and, Agnes was well aware, still tried to make a game of seducing her. She'd seen plenty of naked women before though, had touched enough of them, had made them come. There was nothing special she could have by drinking from that particular well.

"I've already had my dinner for the night," she said with slightly pursed lips, finally smiling when Rox huffed out a sigh of frustration and picked up her dress.

They'd done this dance too many times before for Agnes's refusal to come as a surprise.

"Look at you," Rox went on. "With your gorgeous face, all that flawless skin, those tits and legs any girl here would kill for, you're perfect. But you might as well be a statue for all the use you make of what some of us go under the knife to get. It's a waste."

Even for Rox, this was a little far. She usually only took it as far as a little flirtation, flashing bare breasts or sending suggestive texts. However, her attempt at cruelty was nothing compared to what Agnes had suffered on a daily basis at the hands of the man who'd raised her.

"Are you quite finished?" Agnes didn't hide her amusement at the pathetic stab.

It made her glad, these flashes of meaningless challenge she saw in Rox and some of the others. Before, with her father, they'd been too terrified to do more than breathe around him. Now, they felt safe.

Rox made that frustrated sound again. "Fine, but you can't sit here untouched in your glass tower forever. One day, you'll have to let someone in, let them touch you, and feel what it's like to be a real woman instead of a queen of air and broken dreams." Rox draped the three-thousand-dollar dress around her neck like a scarf and turned on her stilettos, her nude body again shimmering faintly in the light. "Good night, Queen Agnes."

"Good night, Rox."

Agnes went back to what she'd been working on before the interruption, paying scant attention to the petulant stab of high heels into marble as Rox walked away. She barely glanced at the stack of hundreds, content enough to know it was there.

"Oh, God, I'm so sorry!" Her assistant, Clare, rushed in, slight color in her cheeks despite the level tone of her voice. "I tried to stop her from interrupting you, but that woman who keeps trying to see you called again." She swept up the cash Rox left and sat down on the nearby leather sofa to count it.

"Next time our persistent mystery woman calls, just put her through to Whit." Whit was Agnes's personal security. "As for Rox," she said with a faint quirk of her mouth. "I can handle a woman trying to seduce me."

Clare acknowledged the order about the mystery woman with a nod. "Was that a seduction? It looked like an ambush to me."

"To certain wildcats and other prey animals, it's the same thing."

Clare snorted and tapped the neat stack of hundreds she'd just counted. "It's all here. Five thousand." She made a note on the iPad she always carried and put the money in the floor safe hidden underneath a waist-high bronze statue of Oshun. "By the way, Rox requested the next week off."

Agnes mentally consulted the schedule. "Of course. She's earned it. Give her two weeks if she needs more."

"You know she won't." Sitting once again on the sofa, Clare started doing something on her iPad that involved lots of fast but silent typing. "She'd want to get back to work as soon as whatever is keeping her away gets sorted."

The "whatever" was probably a woman, maybe even someone Rox met on one of her recent assignments. Incredible. Sometimes Agnes was surprised at the stamina Rox had for someone her age. Agnes liked sex as much as most, but she couldn't understand doing it for work then running off and doing it for fun too. Which was probably why she wasn't having any sex at all.

"I just sent her the approval of the next week off and your offer for the one after that." Clare interrupted Agnes's useless musings on her sex life. She darkened the iPad's screen and put the device face down on her lap.

"Perfect." Agnes tapped the mouse to wake up her own screen. A reminder to herself that she still had work to do even if a part of her wanted to step out and breathe different air. "Thank you. You can head home now. I know it's late."

"I don't mind staying." Clare gave her quick smile, hands tucked in her lap. A trick she used to seem vulnerable and compliant when she was anything but. It also was a trick she didn't need to use with Agnes. But habits were hard to break, especially ones painfully learned.

"I know, but you need to go home so I can have a clear conscience." Agnes made a shooing motion toward the door. It was already half past five on a Friday afternoon. Although Clare's cat wouldn't be calling the cops to find out where her human went, Clare still needed some time away from The House. Even if she didn't want to admit it.

"Fine. I'll go, but only if you do too."

Agnes raised an eyebrow, giving her assistant a single glance.

"Fine. I'll stay out of your affairs." Clare stood up, smoothing down her skirt. "You should leave, though. I'm sure there's someone out there who wants your company."

Agnes smiled at that not-so-subtle way of trying to find out what was going on in her life. They'd worked together for over five years now, the entire time this current version of The House had been in existence. Despite that, Clare—and most of The House's employees—knew nearly nothing about Agnes's personal life, and she preferred it that way.

She'd made The House of Agnes from the ashes of what it had been and created an image for herself—deliberately remote yet fair, untouchable, and just a little bit dangerous—so their competitors didn't get any foolish ideas. That cultivated persona wasn't easily worn, but she kept it up in all areas of the business. She didn't become or stay Queen Agnes by allowing everyone to know intimate details about her, such as whether or not she had a family and, if so, where they lived. Not that many people even knew where she lived.

Her business details, though, were more public. It was common enough knowledge that the top three floors of this twenty-story building housed her offices plus a pair of penthouse apartments for her exclusive company use. H Holdings, the name The House of Agnes did business under, quietly owned the whole building and rented the rest of it out to other businesses.

"Thank you, Clare. I'll only be here another hour or so anyway."

"All right. I'll keep my cell phone close if you need me." Then, with another apologetic smile, her assistant was gone.

Agnes waited until she heard Clare's footsteps disappear down the hallway toward the elevator before she stood. Her bones hurt. She stretched her long body and sighed at the sensation of moving muscles held too long in one place. The outer glass walls of her office, tinted and bulletproof, reflected her figure against a background of the night's darkness. High heels, matching gray skirt suit, white blouse with the high collar held closed by a diamond brooch. Cool. Professional.

Clare was right, though. It had been a long day, and this suit she wore, both the face and the outfit, were pulling tight now over her skin. She ached to get rid of them.

So, she did.

She slipped out of her suit, the matte heels, her boring blouse. Unpinned the stern updo. Her reflection this time was very different from the one everyone saw. Her nearly six-foot body, nude except for the plain black bra and G-string, straightened hair loose around her face and brushing the AC-hardened tips of her breasts. As Rox had so charmingly stated, not bad for thirty-six.

The freedom of being nearly naked and away from the scrutiny of others made her close her eyes for precious seconds. Then she shook herself. It wasn't as if she had all night.

In the closet, she chose pink. A knee-length pencil dress with three-quarter sleeves and a high neck. It looked good, softened her usually remote-looking features, and hinted at an innocence she no longer had. She stepped back into the matte heels. An attempted smile in the mirror looked more like a snarl, but that was all right too.

After setting an alarm on her phone, she took her private elevator down to the garage. There, she climbed into one of her anonymous-looking cars and drove toward her private club, where she usually ended up at least once a month. It was a routine Whit repeatedly warned her to break.

But she didn't want to.

CHAPTER 2

THE HALCYON CLUB WAS SUITABLY discreet, its facade nameless with only a numbered address above the thick metal door that managed to look both secure and elegant. It had pretensions to those centuries' old members-only British gentlemen's clubs, except membership was limited to women. Agnes loved it.

For her, it was a place where she could blend into the background and observe other people—not something she was free to do as Queen Agnes—and occasionally take someone upstairs to one of the private rooms for sex. If she was in the mood.

"Good evening." The woman outside the door greeted her with a respectful nod as she scanned her membership card on the handheld device. "Welcome back."

There was no name tag attached to the breast of the woman's dark suit, but Agnes remembered her from the last time. "Thank you, Nicole." Though Nicole was obviously trained to keep her face neutral, something akin to the guards at Buckingham Palace, her thin lips twitched with pleasure. Not quite a smile but just enough.

Nicole opened the tall, heavy door for her and stepped back to let her pass through.

She made a note to leave Nicole a tip before she left.

Colder air washed over Agnes's face as she walked in from the late September evening. She took a table in a darkened corner that placed her back to the wall and gave a view of the circular, high-ceilinged room. As expected, for a Friday evening, it had a decent crowd. With the tables spread far apart, the mostly low-voiced conversations were light background noise, leaving the members tucked away in their own private bubbles. On the second floor, ringed by a dark steel balcony and accessible via a winding staircase, were more private tables, more hidden corners. The next floor up were the meeting rooms, some outfitted with desks and computers, others with beds and safe-sex paraphernalia. All the rooms were soundproof.

Faint longing throbbed inside her, to touch someone, to make them cry out with pleasure. Maybe she'd make use of one of the rooms before she left.

A woman in the club's crisp uniform—black trousers and matching suspenders worn over a burgundy long-sleeved shirt—appeared at Agnes's table. She already had a single glass of golden liquid, along with a nearly full bottle, balanced on her tray.

Agnes nodded her acceptance of the eighteen-year-old single malt scotch whiskey.

"Would you like the bottle as well, madame?"

"Just the glass for now, thank you."

Once the waitress placed the drink gently on the table and melted away, Agnes took a sip and sighed at the fragrant burn. A slow stroke of her tongue along her lower lip caught any lingering drops of the precious liquid. The purely physical pleasure from the whiskey's heat spread through her chest and down into her belly.

After a moment, she felt a prickle of awareness and noticed a nearby table of well-dressed women discreetly lapping her up with their eyes. Agnes didn't mind. She liked to watch too. It was a completely human impulse after all. Although sometimes, like tonight, she'd much prefer—

"May I join you?"

A low voice shook her from her musings. Standing near her table, close but still at a respectful distance, was a young woman. At a guess, in her early to mid-twenties. She wore her thick, natural hair twisted and fastened at the back of her head in an elegant bun. Her face looked young yet interesting, with its confident eyes and a smiling mouth painted with nude lipstick.

A sudden image came to Agnes of the young woman on her knees, smearing that lipstick all over Agnes's clit. Her thighs squeezed together, and she almost moaned at the resulting zing of pleasure.

Luckily, the young woman seemed oblivious.

She was dressed appropriately for the club in a loose yellow blouse that bared one shoulder and showed off the fact that she wore nothing underneath it. Dark high-waisted slacks clung to her lush hips, and she wore bright yellow stilettos. She looked good in the simple yet objectively alluring outfit, but there was something about the way she stood that gave the impression of a child playing dress-up.

Maybe that was something that did it for Agnes then, because there was no denying the stirring of interest in her lap.

At Agnes's appraisal, the woman put her glass of wine on the table but didn't make a move to sit down. Which was fortunate. Agnes didn't deal well with people who presumed too much. Even one as intriguing as this.

Between the girl's youth and Agnes's own time constraints—she'd need more than an hour to properly appreciate a woman like that in her bed—she made the only logical decision she could. "I'm not looking for any company tonight," she said. "But thank you."

The woman's confident expression leached away, and her lower lip slid out in a pout. "It's only a shared table, you know. I didn't say I'm on the menu."

"Still, no."

Eyes that had been warm only moments before took on a more calculating edge. Before the young woman could say anything else, the server who'd brought Agnes's drink appeared.

"Miss, there's a free table over there if you want a place to sit." The server's voice was low yet authoritative, and something in her tone reminded Agnes of Whit. No nonsense. Dangerous.

Panic flicked across her would-be companion's face, and she backed up a step.

Oh for God's sake.

"It's all right," Agnes said to the server. "She's not bothering me."

"Are you sure, madame?"

"I am. Thank you."

The server looked between Agnes and the young woman, then backed away with a slight nod in Agnes's direction. Agnes wouldn't be surprised if the woman was being tracked by cameras and investigated right now. Despite her presence in Halcyon, the girl didn't seem like a member, especially not with the way she was just treated.

Once the server walked away, the stranger gave Agnes a wide smile. The relief on her face didn't seem quite in proportion to what almost happened, though. "Why do I get the feeling you saving me from getting put on my ass wasn't an invitation to sit and enjoy the rest of my drink with you?"

"Because you're as smart as you look." Agnes raised an eyebrow.

The woman pursed her lips, then, with her head slightly tilted Agnes's direction, she picked up her drink from the table. "Then I guess I'll see you around then."

"Perhaps."

The woman paused. "That sounds like a challenge."

"Let me guess. You love a challenge."

"Something like that." The woman shifted, but it seemed like strategy rather than nervousness, a movement designed to show off her thick thighs in the clinging slacks and to incite the jiggle of her full, high breasts. Her perfume smelled light and sweet. "Now it's my turn to make guesses," she said, not smiling. "You love to be in control. On top of everything and everyone at all times, like a queen in her high castle."

Agnes drew in a quiet breath. The woman definitely knew what buttons to push. Agnes had come here to escape who she was in her glass tower and had even put on different clothes, but here she was still trapped in that persona she wore like a suit of armor.

She could step out of that suit, though, just like the other one she'd left behind.

Temptation blew its warm breath at the back of her consciousness. This wasn't one of her employees. She could take what this woman offered, guilt-free, even if it was just to share a drink and conversation. Her lips parted, the invitation to stay for a drink—and maybe more—just there on her tongue.

The phone in her purse vibrated, a burst of three sharp tones.

A kick of relief straightened her spine, and she forced a regretful smile. "Excuse me. I have to get this." She took out her phone.

A red light blinked next to the name on the screen. One of her assets was in trouble. Fingers moving quickly, she sent a text to an extraction team on standby near the woman's location. Agnes never second-guessed her assets. She'd promised to keep them safe when they came to her house, and that was exactly what she did.

ExTeam6: En route. Four minutes.
Agnes: Let me know the situation when you arrive.

She tapped the button next to the asset's name, changing the blinking red light to blue, letting her know help was on the way. The extraction team would handle it, but Agnes made a note to have a debrief with her asset in the morning and flag that client as one they wouldn't work with again. Once done with the phone, she put it away and turned her attention back to the woman.

"What's your name?"

"Delores."

"That's your real name?"

"Yes. Why? Don't you like it?"

"It just seems like a bit of a mouthful for someone like you."

"Trust me, I've never had any complaints about being more than a mouthful." A teasing smile flashed. "But since you object, you can call me Lola."

"Lola." Agnes rolled it around on her tongue a couple of times and found that she liked the taste. And speaking of taste… "Would you like another drink?"

While Agnes had been paying attention to her phone, Lola had drained her wine. Only a smear of red remained at the bottom of the glass.

Lola seemed to consider her. "As much as I'd love to help spend your cash, I think I need to keep sober around you."

"A sparkling water then?"

"Sure."

Agnes signaled for the server while Lola sat down opposite her. The girl leaned forward, her forearms resting on the table and shoulders back, a pose that bared the heavy weight of her breasts in her blouse the color of sunlight. Her nipples had hardened in the club's cool air, and the pleased curve of her mouth said she knew Agnes was watching.

It was a beautiful sight. That curvaceous body. The knowing glint in her eyes. A private amusement.

"Here you are, ma'am." A new glass of red wine and a fresh whiskey appeared, courtesy of the very efficient server, while Agnes was busy ogling Lola.

"And a sparkling water, please."

"Of course." The server sailed off toward the bar.

With the whiskey a hot caress on her tongue, Agnes allowed herself the luxury of a thorough look while the heat of attraction moved slowly through her veins and settled between her thighs like an impertinent tongue. The muscles in her belly jumped. Aching now for some kind of relief, her sex thickened and soaked the thin crotch of her underwear.

This *child* was pushing all her buttons.

Although she didn't live like a nun, it was rare that a woman, a stranger, had such a strong pull on her. Sure, Lola was sexy, but Agnes worked every day with women gorgeous enough to appear on movie screens. This was the first time in years—maybe ever—that the urge to touch snaked under her skin and pushed her toward a hasty decision.

Exhaling a sigh of equal parts pleasure and chagrin, she put the heavy glass down with a gentle click against the wooden coaster. Would it be that much of a shame in taking this thing as far as it could go?

"So now that we're sharing a table," Agnes murmured, "what do you have in mind for us to do?" She put the metaphorical ball in Lola's court, intrigued to see what she would do with it.

"What, is this some sort of audition?" Lola took a sip of the new wine, ignoring the water the unobtrusive server had brought, and Agnes licked her own lips at the smear of red that clung to Lola's mouth. "Should I dance for you now?"

Okay. Agnes could play with this hand. "No audition. You just do whatever you want."

"Whatever I want..." Lola playfully tapped her lower lip with two fingers, dragging Agnes's attention back to that hot mouth and what she wanted to do to it. Agnes shifted her thighs, stirring the heat between them. "Even if I want you to sit in my lap?"

Surprise felt a lot like desire, and Agnes swallowed it down with a mouthful of scotch. Normally people wanted to sit in *her* lap and have her tell them what to do, now and even back a thousand years ago when she dated men. Well, maybe the men didn't want to sit in her lap, but they'd

11

always deferred to whatever she wanted, and she'd been only too happy to take the reins.

This new development was *intriguing*. It was all too easy to imagine it, draping herself over Lola's lap and letting Lola take charge of her. Not that Agnes would ever allow it to happen, but still... She squirmed then and drew in a silent breath at the sweet ache the movement stirred inside her core. Yes, she was definitely into Lola, into this moment and whatever it promised.

"While I'm not sure you could handle me, it's not an *idea* I would be opposed to," Agnes finally said once her brain stopped its little short circuit.

"Really?"

The comical widening of Lola's dark eyes and the way she leaned into Agnes with a smile that was almost childlike in its glee, so different from the poised, overtly seductive creature she'd first presented herself to be, made Agnes think she was actually seeing Lola, who Lola really was, for the first time. Until that moment, it didn't even occur to Agnes that Lola was being anything but genuine. Pushy, yes. Flirtatious, absolutely. But the idea that Lola had been putting on a front twisted something in Agnes's stomach. Despite the low-grade desire threatening to take Agnes over like a fever, it raised an alarm in the parts of her above the waist.

She took a mental step back and forced her body to calm down. Lola was a stranger, even with a casual fuck lurking on the horizon, Agnes wasn't about to break her years-long habit of constantly being on guard. No matter how interesting the potential fuck was. "Yes, really. For now, let's just enjoy our drinks, shall we?"

Disappointment stilled Lola's face, and Agnes silently cursed, instantly wanting to bring back that joyous flirtation. Maybe she was being manipulated, but this felt too good to let go.

She slid a hand over Lola's. "Can I interest you in—?"

A familiar chime on her watch sounded. And stopped her in her tracks. Quickly, Agnes drew her hand back, or at least tried to, but Lola grabbed it.

"Can you interest me in what?" Lola asked.

But Agnes didn't have any more time to waste.

The alarm she'd set before she left the office chimed again.

"It doesn't matter, because now I can't." Agnes allowed the regret to touch her voice. "Real life calls." She pulled her hand away and stood, taking one last sip of whiskey before picking up her purse. "The bill is already settled. Enjoy another drink or two if you like, and have them put it on my tab."

A pang of disappointment tightened her throat. This was the first time in years she'd felt something this delicious, this powerful. And she wasn't fool enough to think it would happen again anytime soon.

"Enjoy the rest of your life," she said to Lola and headed out the door.

It wasn't until she was in the car and speeding toward home that she realized she hadn't given Lola her name.

As usual, it was quiet in the underground garage and long passageway between the H Holdings high-rise and the other glass and steel tower where Agnes lived. She parked her car in its spot among three other vehicles, still wrestling her regret at leaving Lola in the club without a way for them to contact each other again.

Whit could make some discreet inquiries, a traitorous part of her whispered. *After all, how many twenty-something Deloreses could there be in New York?*

The walk in the underground passageway, about two city blocks, gave her plenty of time to recall each intriguing moment she'd spent with Lola. Soon enough, a steel wall stopped her from going any farther. Agnes pressed her hand to the palm print reader built into the tunnel wall, then the retina scanner when prompted. The massive steel door opened with a gentle rumble, releasing a breath of cool air.

"Welcome home, Agnes," the computer said.

"Thank you," she said, responding to the prompt for voice-ID.

At the elevator beyond, she went through the same security measures again, then pressed the button for the penthouse. The doors opened and the smells of home greeted her—the lavender room freshener Whit insisted on, furniture polish from a recent cleaning, and the faint scent of something with cardamom from the kitchen. Right on time, her stomach rumbled.

"Honey, I'm home," she called out and imagined the resulting frown on Whit's face.

Her high heels clattered and fell to the floor just inside the door when she kicked them off with a sigh. From behind her came the delicate chime letting her know the apartment's alarm had reset behind her. Her keys and purse went on the narrow pedestal by the elevator door.

"Whit won't like that." Bare footsteps sped across the marble in the long hallway, and a young girl appeared, running toward Agnes with a wide, gap-toothed smile. She skidded to a stop. "You should put your shoes in the closet like you always tell me to do."

"She can ground me if she wants." Agnes crouched in time to catch the girl leaping into her arms, gasping out a laugh at the five-year old's weight. "Hey, sweet pea." Gretchen smelled like Dove soap and mint toothpaste, fresh from a bath.

"Nessa!" The girl giggled. "You know Whit won't do that. You're too big."

"Whit doesn't care how big Nessa is," someone else said softly.

Agnes turned with Gretchen in her arms—Lord, her sweet girl was getting heavy—to see her bodyguard and friend making a more sedate way down the hall. "You know it's creepy to talk about yourself in the third person."

Whit wore her typical "relaxing at home" outfit of mid-height pumps, A-line skirt, and lacy blouse under a light sweater. All in shades of beige. At one point, someone might have told her the look and color choice helped her blend in, but it did the opposite. A six-foot-tall woman with a puckered scar down one cheek and the habit of wearing purple lipstick could only blend in so much.

"You have no idea just how creepy I can be," Whit said with a smile in her low, smoky voice. Her warm eyes crinkled at the corners. "Did you brush your teeth, Gretchen?"

"Yes, I did!" Small arms tightened enough around Agnes's neck to pinch skin as Gretchen leaned toward Whit, her mouth wide open. "Smell." Agnes winced and adjusted Gretchen's grip.

Smiling wider now, Whit took her up on the challenge, sniffing at Gretchen's mouth. The movement exaggerated the already dramatic line of her jaw and graceful shape of her head under her low-cut, natural hair. "I suppose that's good enough." Whit drew back. "You know it's past your bedtime, little one."

"I know," Gretchen whined, her charmer's smile on full wattage, making Agnes smile right back. Gretchen was so precious. "But I was waiting for Nessa to come home and tuck me in."

Which was why Agnes had set her alarm. No matter how much fun she was having at the club, Gretchen remained her first priority. She lightly squeezed the child in her arms. "Come on. You can tell me all about your day while I tuck you in." As she headed toward Gretchen's bedroom, she felt more than saw Whit melt away to another part of the house.

"You have to tell me a story!"

"Okay, one story. A short one."

When Gretchen had come into Agnes's life, one of the things the parenting coach had stressed was how important routine was to a child. Five years ago, as well as now, Agnes arranged most of her life around Gretchen. The rewards of making that decision were clear every day.

"Your hair looks nice." Gretchen tugged Agnes's loose hair and leaned in to smell it. "Like a princess!"

Agnes chuckled. "Thank you, sweet pea."

"Did you have a date?" The way Gretchen said the last word sounded as if she was parroting someone. Probably Whit.

"No, darling. I did meet a nice woman after work, though."

"Ooooh. Did she have princess hair too?"

"She did. It was very beautiful. Like a cloud."

"That's nice. Will you bring her home so Whit and I can meet her?"

Agnes imagined Lola in her home, spread across the living room couch, drinking wine while Gretchen peppered her with all kinds of questions. The thought wasn't as ridiculous as it should have been.

"Maybe one day, sweet pea."

Satisfied with that, Gretchen settled down in her bed and was already yawning when Agnes started to read the requested bedtime story. It wasn't long before she fell asleep, and after kissing her smooth forehead, Agnes turned on the night-light and closed the bedroom door behind her.

Just as the door clicked shut, Whit stepped into the hallway. Her previous smile was gone. "We may have a problem."

CHAPTER 3

She almost had her.

Cursing under her breath, Lola called herself a thousand kinds of blazing idiot.

Queen Agnes was right there in her sights, practically eating out of her hand—or about to eat something—and she just *fucking* let her go.

"Shit."

"Is there something else I can get for you, miss?"

The waitress who basically offered to toss Lola out on her ass earlier glided up to the table like some kind of vampire, and Lola nearly jumped out of her skin. How the hell was she going to slip under the queen's skin if a normal woman made her lose her shit?

"No, thank you. I'm fine for now." She waved the waitress off.

Lola's hands vibrated against her thigh, and her leg was shaking so hard it was as if she were tap-dancing with one foot. As much fun as she was having at this crazy playground for rich women, she couldn't stick around to enjoy all the snobbery. She had to get the hell out of Dodge and follow the reason she'd come to Club Halcyon in the first place.

The whiskey Agnes left behind on the table was tempting. God, was it ever. She needed something strong after finally confronting the woman responsible for her sister's death.

Her hand twitched toward the whiskey, but she reached for the wine instead and nearly choked on the tasteless crap.

What she really wanted was a beer. But a Bronx girl who'd rather chill on the couch with a Red Stripe beer and a plate of homemade sweet potato fries wasn't about to snag someone like the queen. If Lola had to drink an ocean worth of overpriced grape juice, she'd do it to get close enough to Agnes Noble, the notorious New York madam. Close enough to ensnare her. To seduce her. Then bring her entire house tumbling down.

If Lola could help it, Zoe would be the last innocent young girl Agnes lured into her trap.

Fuck it. She grabbed the glass of whiskey and downed it, choking as a path of kill-me-now fire raced down her throat.

"Can I help you, miss?" The waitress appeared out of nowhere with that calm look on her face that most likely hid a sneer.

"No." Lola coughed again. "I'm good."

After giving Lola a disbelieving look, the waitress left her alone again. Lola dragged the glass of red wine closer. The merlot wasn't beer, but at least she could handle it.

Unlike the whiskey.

Unlike Agnes Noble.

When she and Jamika first came up with the idea to dig into The House of Agnes and expose it to the world, Lola was sure Agnes was just a normal woman, overrated and easy to trick with a quick smile and an offer of sex from a hot young piece. Although Lola wasn't vain enough to think she was necessarily hot, she *was* younger and had been around the block enough to know that most rich old people were either trying to fuck the wrinkles away or bury their aging bodies into something young and fresh so they could forget they were one birthday away from collecting social security.

From Jamika's research, they'd found out that Agnes was one of those older women, nearly forty, probably wrinkled as fuck up close, and easy to tumble into bed. Easy to bring to her knees with a few hours of hot sex, some wiretaps, a juicy newspaper article, and the right word to the cops about her very illegal business.

But they had been dead wrong.

The pictures Lola had looked at when she was doing her research should have prepped her, but the reality of Agnes was nothing like any of the photos Lola had seen. From the moment she invited herself over to Agnes's table and caught Agnes's eyes, it felt as if she'd been trapped by some kind of spell. Agnes was surface-of-the-sun blazing hot.

Her skin was flawless. Absolutely smooth without a single laugh line. At first glance, she could easily pass for a woman in her twenties or early thirties. But a more thorough inspection would catch that sharp and dangerous gaze, a gaze that shattered the illusion of Agnes being a youthful and carefree twenty-something.

That perfect skin said Agnes wasn't the laughing type.

Somehow that made Lola—well, not *sad* exactly, but…almost empathetic. A wrong emotional step. She wasn't going to win this thing by feeling sorry for the woman who'd basically killed her sister. The woman whose cool façade couldn't hide the dangerous fire in her dark eyes.

Jamika was right. She had to be careful.

After drinking the rest of her shitty wine and sending a "thank you" text to Maddie, the woman who'd helped her get into Halcyon, she left the club.

"Would you like me to call a cab for you, miss?" The woman at the door asked Lola as she stepped down the short steps and onto the sidewalk.

"No, thank you. I'll be walking." She slipped the woman a twenty-dollar bill. "You have a nice night."

"You too, miss."

The wind was brisk out on the street. Lola shrugged on her jacket, making sure her apartment keys were still in the zipped inside pocket.

"So, how did it go?"

Jesus fucking Christ!

A skinny girl suddenly appeared at Lola's side, nearly giving her a heart attack. The girl, her lips skinned back from her teeth in a smile that looked disturbingly like a shark's, laughed and huddled deeper inside a fake fur coat. "You got in all right, didn't you? No trouble?"

"Yes, I got in fine, Maddie," Lola said, trying to get her rabbit heart under control. "Uh, thanks for the connect."

"Glad to help." Maddie fell in step with Lola, and Lola had to keep herself from groaning out loud. She definitely wasn't in the mood for company right now. But if it hadn't been for Maddie, she wouldn't have gotten this far, so Lola sucked it up and kept walking toward the subway.

"What're you doing out here, anyway?" Lola asked.

"I got your text."

"And you just happened to be near here?"

"Nope." Maddie flashed her teeth. "Was waiting for you to be done. I want to know how it went." The all-business glint in her eye said she was actually hanging around for some cold, hard tip money in case Lola got what she wanted out of the evening.

The too-skinny twenty-something escort had a connection who'd not only found out Agnes's hang-out spots, but also had access to them.

Lola had met Maddie by accident in the lounge of one of the high-end hotels known to be trolling grounds for call girls and rent boys. Her search for clues about Zoe's life and what happened to her led there and she'd been getting discouraged, exhausted from weeks of fruitless searching. Lola had been at the bar, on the edge of giving up for the night and going home, when Maddie, looking nineties heroin-chic in a tight white dress, sat next to her.

Maddie was a paler version of early-'90s Naomi Campbell, all long legs and longer weave, her tilted eyes cunning and narrowed as if she were seeing right through Lola's clothes to count exactly how much money she had in her pockets.

Of course, she'd propositioned Lola.

And once Lola had said she was only looking for information but still willing to pay, Maddie became a gushing fountain of information.

Yes, she knew Zoe, Maddie said that night. Word on the street was that she'd hooked up with the vicious director of The House, an old guy so hopped up on Viagra that he personally "tried out" every woman who worked for him.

This same man had once promised Maddie herself a place at his escort agency but ended up screwing her instead, then screwing her over. He had a daughter who took over after he died. This daughter, Agnes, was just as bad as he was. She also had a taste for the ladies.

No, she didn't know what happened to Zoe, Maddie said the last time they'd talked, but she could help get Lola close enough to Agnes to find out.

All this Maddie had said in a voice as sweet as buttercream.

"So, if you're out here, I guess the bitch didn't take you up on the offer of your fine self." The look Maddie skimmed over Lola's body now hinted that she'd never do anything as stupid as turn her down for sex.

"She didn't turn me down."

But hadn't she, though? One minute, Lola and Agnes had been flirting with the sweet certainty of sex in one of the upstairs rooms between them.

And the next… Well, Lola wasn't exactly sure what happened. Agnes's phone had gone off, but even before that she'd started to pull away.

"Well, hope you didn't expect her to be as easy as all that to get into the sack."

Lola flushed because obviously that was exactly what she'd thought.

"She has a hundred and one hot properties she can take anytime she wants," Maddie continued. "You can't just expect to show up with some firm tits and have her lose her shit over you."

Well, if that didn't give Lola the ultimate reality check… "Fuck."

Maddie's laugh was loud and mocking. She threw her whole body backward, braying like a skinny, hairless donkey. Nobody near them looked their way, but that was just New Yorkers for you. Maddie could've knifed her on the sidewalk, and the most Lola would've gotten was some teenager taking a video to post online for likes.

The girl's laughter cut off as suddenly as it began. "Sorry to break it to you, but that house didn't stay on top just because of luck. Agnes runs a tight operation. Even if you did somehow get into her pants, that doesn't mean you'd get to wander all over like a happy little bloodhound." A manic giggle bubbled up from Maddie and, doubled over, she pressed a hand to her belly. She was probably an only child, or just somebody really good at entertaining themselves. "Only someone who works at The House can bypass all that security and get the kind of info you're looking for." Her laughter trailed off, but her smile stayed put. "I mean, you seem like a real go-getter and all, but I doubt you'd have the stones to get in there and bust that place wide open."

"Excuse me?"

"Oh, come on." A sudden cold wind whipped by. Maddie sank her chin down into the collar of her thick coat, jammed her hands into the pockets. "You're a college girl who barely knows about real life. You probably never stole a single thing. Never had to back up your girls in a fight. The world Agnes lives in would chew you up and wouldn't bother spitting you out."

It was on the tip of Lola's tongue to tell Maddie all about her investigative reporter credentials, that she wrote for some big papers under a pseudonym even Maddie would recognize. She didn't waste her breath, though. The point wasn't to impress a girl who was obviously only interested in the money Lola gave her in exchange for information.

An idea prodded at her, begging for notice.

Lola had the experience. She'd gone undercover in shady restaurants, banks, the offices of government officials. Would infiltrating an escort agency be any different?

She'd done all kinds of dangerous things for a byline. Finding out what happened to Zoe was worth more than that. If it wasn't for Zoe, Lola wouldn't have made it to college, much less have the career and the life she had now.

"You have no idea what I'm capable of," she finally said to Maddie.

Maddie puffed out a breath of disbelief. "Sure."

Hiding her annoyance, Lola said her good-byes when they got to the nearby subway station. Maddie disappeared down the steps to catch a train, and Lola, after turning over the crazy idea that wouldn't go away, called a Lyft to take her back up to the Bronx.

Her thoughts were still buzzing when she let herself into the fifth-floor walk-up she shared with her best friend and tossed her keys on the bookshelf near the door.

"That doesn't sound like the key toss of a returning conqueror," Jamika called out. "Did you fuck up and fall face-first into the queen's lap?"

"Shut up! I almost had her," Lola shouted back as she kicked off the painful high heels she'd borrowed from Jamika. She wriggled her toes to get some circulation going. "How the hell do you wear these fucking things?"

"*Fucking things* is right, so be careful with them. They're the keys to my sex life."

Their apartment was small, though bigger than the shoebox Lola had shared with her mother and sister growing up, so it only took a few steps down their short hallway to get to the living room where Jamika lay sprawled on the sofa with a small plate of the Nutella crunch cookies Lola had made that morning sitting on her belly. A glass of chocolate milk was within easy reach while some sci-fi show with hot girls in tight clothes murmured from the TV screen.

The gray light from the small set flickered over Jamika's round-cheeked face, her T-shirt with NYPD over the boobs, and gray sweats. Her blond-streaked dreads were pulled back in a long ponytail. She bit into a cookie, scattering crumbs all over her chest, and slowly chewed while keeping her eyes on the TV.

It would be easy to think Jamika was relaxed, the way her long body was almost liquid on the oversized couch they'd both loved on sight at an estate sale. But her deep-set eyes were intent, and lines of tension etched the sides of her mouth. "You found her. What happened?"

Between squirming out of her cougar-trapping clothes and grabbing a pint of ice cream and a spoon from the kitchen, Lola gave Jamika the highlights.

"And she wasn't even that scary," she finished, sinking down beside Jamika on the couch. Jamika moved aside to give her some room. "I had her sniffing up my skirt without even really trying. She has a big and bad reputation, but she's just another woman who likes to get her snatch scratched."

Lola wetly licked her spoon, intentionally being gross. If she didn't do something to distract herself from her sweating palms and pounding heartbeat, then she'd be taking them—and Agnes—far too seriously.

Jamika's eyes narrowed, and the look she gave Lola felt as if she were seeing far too deeply under Lola's carefree surface. "What else?"

Lola bit back a sigh. This was what she got for having a best friend who knew her better than anyone. "I ran into Maddie on the way home."

"You know I don't trust this chick, but keep going."

"You were right. Seducing my way into The House isn't going to do it. I need a better plan, and I think Maddie has the perfect one—although she doesn't think I can do it." She dug her spoon into the ice cream and left it there.

"Which is?" Jamika looked worried.

Lola outlined the plan she'd come up with in the simplest terms: infiltrate The House as one of their escorts, metaphorically burn the place down from the inside, collect her Pulitzer Prize by writing a blazing exposé while Jamika got her high-profile bust.

Easy. Right?

The details of the plan had come to her during the car ride home, and although her stomach had sloshed unhappily at the thought of what pretending to be an escort meant, she was determined to go through with it.

"Are you out of your mind?" The plate of cookies on Jamika's stomach almost fell as she quickly sat up. "That's the craziest thing I've heard you say—ever. This is a dangerous businesswoman, not some overhyped celebrity chef with an inflated ego you can stroke with a few words and a smile."

"No, no. It's going to be so easy. After meeting her in the flesh, honestly, she's not that intense."

Lies.

Although Lola had gone into the club fully intending to go through with fucking Agnes if she could, she'd never expected to feel the sharp jolt of attraction, the melting at her core that told her having sex with Agnes would be no hardship. Actually, becoming one of Agnes's escorts and sleeping with strangers for money was a big, uncomfortable leap. But it shouldn't be. Although Lola was only twenty-three, sex hadn't been a big deal for years. Working for The House—assuming she could get on their payroll— should be nothing.

Jamika's plate scraped across the coffee table as she abandoned it to pin Lola with one of her serious stares. "Let's say I believe you, and you finally get into The House as one of their escorts. What are you going to do when she asks—no, excuse me, when she *pays*—you to fuck somebody?"

"I'll do it. It's just sex, Jamika, not my soul." But Lola didn't feel as certain as she wanted to.

"I know you like sex, but allowing strangers to use your body isn't like taking home a random hottie from the club. It's dangerous. You don't get to say what happens to you once they pay."

Lola found a smile from somewhere, determined not to show Jamika how much her words worried her. She had to do this. For Zoe. "It'll be fine, J. You'll see."

Jamika made a sound filled with doubt and resignation, then knocked back her glass of milk as if she wished it were something stronger. "This is crazy," she said again.

Triumph turned Lola's fake smile into the real thing. She plopped her melting pint of ice cream next to Jamika's cookies and stretched out to take up more room on the sofa. Even though Jamika hated the plan, at least she accepted it. That meant she'd have Lola's back, no matter what.

All was right with the world.

Lola snagged a cookie and bit into it, humming at the rich flavor of the Nutella and crunchy pieces of hazelnut. This was a pretty good batch. Better than the ones she'd made before.

"It's no crazier than you chasing bad guys around New York in your designer pantsuits, *Detective*," Lola said.

"I have to gain respect somehow." Jamika rolled her eyes, a sign that she was giving in to Lola's diversionary tactics, and everything else, for now.

"Come summertime, you'll basically be a walking sponge, dripping sweat and funk. No one's going to respect you then." Lola reclaimed her ice cream.

Jamika snorted out a laugh. She was a new detective, barely eight months in with her spanking new badge and partner who kind of hated being stuck with a twenty-four-year-old, and a woman at that. Jamika's words. That was part of the reason Jamika had gone all in with Lola on the mission to bring down Queen Agnes and every rotten thing she stood for. Few of the people at work took Jamika seriously. Sure, she'd graduated from high school at fifteen and finished college before she could vote, but that just made them think she was too booksmart to do real police work. Jamika wanted to prove them wrong, and what could be a better way than bringing down Queen Agnes, the Madam of New York?

All that was true and as real as the glass ceiling, but the main reason Jamika had involved herself in this whole operation was because of Lola. Best friends forever since they met in Mrs. Miller's Pre-K class a million years ago. They'd been ride or die through Jamika's abusive ex-girlfriend, the death of Lola's mother, Jamika's fear she wouldn't pass the detective's exam, and Zoe's disappearance.

Jamika was amazing, and sometimes Lola didn't think she deserved her.

She shoved a spoonful of the mostly melted chocolate brownie ice cream in her mouth and forced herself to chew then swallow as she looked away from Jamika's worried face to the TV screen. Her vision blurred, but she blinked the stupid tears away.

"Anyway, I'm going to her office on Monday," Lola said.

"That soon?"

"There's no point in waiting. The sooner I get in there and start investigating, the better. God knows how many women are trapped in The House and too scared to look for help. We can be that help." Even though it was too late to save Zoe, they could rescue women like her who had been caught in a bad situation.

"I'm just nervous *you'll* be the one needing rescue down the line," Jamika said. "Agnes didn't get to be this powerful because she nicely *asked* the competition to stop existing."

"I know that." The steel in Agnes's gaze had more than hinted at her ruthlessness. "Neither of us is going into this blind. Trust me, I know what I'm getting into."

Maybe that was the problem.

As much as Lola tried to pretend with Jamika that Agnes didn't scare her, Lola's knees were knocking together like sticks in a storm. She was going to confront Agnes again, talk with her, lie to her and get her to implicate herself on tape. Maybe even on camera if she could pull it off. Lola was nervous as hell. But the part of her ruled by the hungry ache that made her want to hunt under Agnes's skirt and eat what she found there was weak. Lola wanted to see Agnes again and not just to bring her to her knees in the way she'd first planned.

Lola's mouth longed to taste.

Her hands ached to touch.

The muscles of her thighs trembled to clench around Agnes's face and never let go.

And that scared Lola out of her ever-loving mind.

Which was probably why, that night, she dreamed about the news she'd gotten nearly seven months before. Five years, eleven months, and one week after Zoe went missing.

With fear and nausea dueling in her stomach, Lola had huddled against her best friend in the medical examiner's office, waiting for the doctor to come back in. Jamika had squeezed her hand but didn't bother with any unnecessary words. One of the reasons she and Lola were best friends. She understood what Lola needed.

"Sorry about that, ladies." The medical examiner came in, eyes radiating sympathy under round-framed glasses, her apple-shaped body clad in a boring, comfortable-looking pantsuit. She'd given her name earlier but for some reason, it kept falling out of Lola's brain. "This office is too busy when I don't want it to be, then dead otherwise." She winced. "No pun intended." The chair behind her desk sighed as she sat down. "Now, where were we?"

"You were telling my friend that her half sister is dead," Jamika said, and sickness churned in Lola's stomach. It was the same sickness that had sent her rushing to the bathroom earlier that week when she'd first gotten the call to identify what the ME's office had determined were the remains of Zoe's body.

In the nearly six years since Zoe had left, Lola had lived in a dream world assuming Zoe had just taken off because she was sick of whatever she had been doing to keep Lola out of foster care and a roof over their heads.

"Young lady…" The ME gently scolded Jamika, although she couldn't have been much past thirty. Lola eyed the boring pantsuit again, the low heels. Okay, maybe forty.

"I'm not that young," Jamika pulled herself straight in the chair. "I just made police detective this year."

The woman brightened, even if it did seem a little artificial. "Congratulations!"

When Lola felt Jamika's uneasy look aimed her way, it was her turn to give a reassuring squeeze. Despite what was going on right now, Jamika didn't have to apologize for being proud she'd arrived at the goal she'd been racing toward since they were kids.

Lola straightened in the uncomfortable plastic chair and steeled herself for what was to come. "I'm ready."

The ME cleared her throat. "All right then." After a quick search for what turned out to be a baby-sized box of tissues, she produced a manila envelope from a drawer. Several photos came out. "Are you sure you're ready?"

"As I'll ever be. Don't worry. I had my freak-out before we came over." Still, the sickness moved around in her stomach, and Lola had to swallow a couple of times to make sure it stayed down.

With her look of sympathy amped up to the point where Lola almost worried about her, the ME slid three large photos across her spotlessly clean desk. Facedown.

"Although a dental record match wasn't possible and her fingerprints aren't on file for a match, we're confident who we found is Zoe Anders. It would be pointless to show you any photos of the body because, frankly, there's nothing there you'll recognize." The ME paused, and Lola felt the woman's eyes on her face although she couldn't bring herself to tear her gaze away from the backs of the labeled photos. "What I have are photos of items that were with the victim, in her handbag, on her person." Another pause. "Do you understand?"

"Yes." The words scraped from her throat in a whisper.

Jamika gripped her hand. "We can do this later if you want. Tomorrow. Next week. Never."

"No. I already waited this long to find out what happened to Zoe. I can't be a coward now."

"Okay." Jamika blew out a breath. "Okay."

Her hand shaking, Lola quickly turned over all the photos, Band-Aid-ripping style.

The first photo was a close-up of an oversized burgundy leather purse, designer like the type Zoe had taken to carrying around the last year or so before she disappeared. Laid out side by side in the second photo were a matching burgundy wallet, Zoe's driver's license, a couple of faded receipts with dates Lola could barely make out, a tube of expensive lipstick, and what looked like a brushed steel pen.

The ME reached over and tapped the third photo. "These are the clothes she was wearing." Size four designer jeans, a cropped blouse that might have once been white, and black high-heeled sandals.

"That's it?" Zoe always carried a bunch of random stuff in her bags—candy, a change of clothes, a book or three because she loved to read. Once Zoe had even reached into one of her endless purses and taken out a mini first aid kit when Lola had cut herself messing around in the park.

"Were you expecting something else?" The ME's eyebrows rose.

"She—was a little bit of a hoarder when she had those jumbo purses, like she had to fill them up—you know?—since there was so much room." Lola tore her eyes away from the photos to look at Jamika for confirmation. "Right, J?"

"True." The hand on her shoulder migrated to her back, a warm and settling weight. "But maybe somebody robbed her before the—uh—before she was found."

Lola swallowed like crazy, fighting the rising lump in her throat and the tears that burned her eyes.

A few days before, after the police had called her and told her there was a strong likelihood her missing sister had been found, Jamika went digging. Lola almost regretted knowing what Jamika had stumbled onto. Zoe had been found in an old suitcase, her body folded up like origami and left to rot near a dumpster in Jersey. No clues about the actual site of her murder or why the body had turned up now.

Everything in the photographs the ME put out for her said the woman they found was Zoe. Her strong, bullheaded sister who never gave a second thought to taking care of Lola when their mom checked out.

The tears spilled out of her eyes and down her cheeks, her fight to keep them at bay lost. Her head felt cotton-thick, and she wanted nothing more than to go home and curl into a ball in her bed.

"The police did some investigating, but—" And here, the ME's eyes flickered to Jamika, as if to silently communicate something with her. Apparently the ME was speaking in a language Jamika didn't know because Jamika just stared back at her. "It's an old case and as a suspected sex worker…"

Shock raced up Lola's spine. "Don't say shit like that. You don't know anything about my sister." Fingers pinched her hip in warning, but she ignored them. "She was a waitress."

The ME braced her hands on the desk. Sympathy still warmed her face, but there was a bit of impatience too. "During the preliminary missing person investigation six years ago, the officers found credible evidence that suggested Zoe Anders was a prostitute—and I'm sure you're able to verify that." She nodded at Jamika. "Sad to say, and as awful of a truth as it is, Ms. Osbourne, cases of missing prostitutes aren't investigated quite as rigorously as they should be. And one this old…" Regret took the place of sympathy on her round face. "I'm sorry."

Unpleasantness twisted Lola's insides. This time, it wasn't nausea; it was a truth she didn't want to see. Like realizing her mother was an addict after watching her grow more and more hooked on the drugs a boyfriend had given her, seeing the drugs eat her alive until there was nothing left of a mother, nothing left for Lola and Zoe to love. Their mother's addiction forced Zoe into a role she never wanted—trying to mother a teenager when she was still a child herself.

Once their mother had died of an overdose, barely seventeen-year-old Zoe kept them both fed and clothed and sheltered in their cramped one-bedroom apartment. Gradually, Zoe had become distracted and absent, disappearing for long stretches of time and reappearing with more money than her waitressing job could ever earn.

The three years between them had seemed like an ocean.

When Zoe did eventually come back to the apartment, she'd smelled like a stranger, of designer perfumes and expensive silks and leather. Then one day, not long after Lola had graduated high school and was accepted to college on a full scholarship, Zoe had just disappeared.

And had apparently ended up being murdered and tossed in an old suitcase along with her useless designer clothes and matching leather accessories.

"Do you want them, Lola?"

What?

While she'd fallen into the well of memory, things had kept on going without her. The ME held out a large paper bag while Jamika looked at her with worry pressed between her eyes.

Lola shook her head. "I'm sorry. What did you say?"

"Your sister's recovered personal effects." The ME put the bag on the desk.

"I can deal with this if you don't want to," Jamika said quickly.

"No, no. It's okay." She would rely on Jamika for the support because it was something she needed like air right now, but she wasn't about to use her friend's presence to avoid doing what she needed to do. Zoe didn't raise her to be a coward.

With the bag in her lap, she slowly opened it. The brown paper crinkled in her shaking fingers. Somehow, she'd expected the inside of the bag to smell like death, rotten meat and old blood, or maybe even like the dumpster near where they'd tossed Zoe. But only the scent of old leather drifted up from it. Something metallic glinted from inside, and she picked it up. A pen. It was the one from the photograph.

The slim barrel was cool between her fingers. Pressed into the top part of the pen was a small logo no bigger than the tip of her index finger. The logo, etched on a royal blue background, was a stylized H and A printed in the same shade of silver as the pen and intertwined to form a crown. The pen was heavy and felt expensive.

Lola twisted the cap, expecting to reveal the nib—wasn't that what they called the part that did the actual writing?—but instead a thin, deadly blade gleamed in the light. Breath rushed from Lola's mouth, and all her muscles tensed.

Danger! That was what the knife seemed to shout.

"What's HA?" Jamika peered at the penknife's logo, frowning.

Lola had no idea, but she intended to find out.

Lola swam up from the dream with tears burning twin paths down the sides of her face. Zoe was dead. And Agnes Noble had something to do with it. The queen was as much her enemy as was Lola's attraction to her. She had to destroy them both.

CHAPTER 4

AGNES'S NIGHT HAD BEEN FILLED with dreams of sex. Of falling into a trap made of soft thighs and slick flesh while a symphony of moans rose and fell in an overheated room. The trap tasted sweet, and she'd been helpless to stop her tongue from lapping up dripping nectar, her fingers from plunging into a tight and eager sex while sharp nails dug into the back of her neck and urged her on.

Agnes woke up gasping, her center a profound, wet ache. Only an early appointment prevented her from slipping her hand between her own thighs and finishing what the dreams had started.

So, there she was. At work. Frustrated. Aroused.

Thoughts of Lola danced at the forefront of her brain, distracting her enough that Clare had to call her name a few times to get her attention. Finally, she'd just waved Clare away to get her own work done while Agnes sorted through something mindless.

Three hours of the workday wasted.

After barely an hour of looking through the company financials, something she'd already gone over before with the accountant, she pushed away from the desk with a sound of impatience. She'd finally managed to put Lola from her thoughts, but what replaced her was something even more dangerous.

Movement against The House.

Some unknown entity had been savaging their legitimate investments, burning down a few small buildings they owned in different parts of the country, and making more aggressive attempts at hacking into their financial accounts. Whoever it was hadn't done any significant damage—it was almost as if they wanted Agnes to know they were out there and set to do something bigger.

Agnes stalked from her office, aware of the ominous sound her high heels made on the marble.

Clare looked up expectantly from her computer.

"Schedule a meeting with my security team, please. Sometime this week would be best." She paused. "And add Malcolm to the list." He was in charge of their investments.

"Face-to-face or…"

In person would make the most sense, but the week was already busy, and Gretchen's school had a fundraiser she couldn't miss. "Not face-to-face."

Clare made a quick note on her iPad. "I'll let you know what time."

"Thank you." She turned to walk away as Clare's phone rang.

"H Holdings, how may I help you?" Clare paused. "No, I'm afraid that's not possible. We've already had this discussion." The conversation went on, but halfway down the hallway, something in Clare's voice made Agnes turn around.

"Who is that?"

Eyes narrowed, Clare tapped the mute button without telling whoever it was on the other end to hold on. "The woman who's been trying to see you for the past few weeks." Then her assistant tilted her head, a birdlike motion. "Now, she's saying she's met you and has something of yours that you forgot in a club of some sort."

Club? The only club Agnes had been to recently was…

"Put her through." She headed to her office, leaving the trail of Clare's obvious surprise behind her.

Clare, though, was the consummate professional. "Of course," she said briskly. "One moment, please," she told the woman on the line.

So, despite not giving Lola a single hint about who she was, the girl had found her. Not a good sign. Whit was going to very cheerfully strangle Lola with one of her argyle sweaters. The thrum of excitement in Agnes's belly, though, couldn't be denied.

She picked up the call. "How may I help you?"

"You forgot something when you left the club the other night." Lola's voice spilled warm and teasing through the phone and into Agnes's ear.

The sensation in her belly spread lower. Flashes of last night's dream spilled like sun-warmed honey into her thoughts, but she couldn't allow them to affect her. Much.

Lola wasn't all she seemed, that much was obvious by the end of their little impromptu date, and Agnes needed to remember that.

"What is it that you think I forgot?" she asked.

"Me."

Agnes knew better, but she allowed the smile anyway. After all, there was nobody here to see it.

"So," Lola continued. "I'm calling to give you the chance to fix that mistake."

But Agnes wasn't in the mood to play games. "How did you find me?"

"Lucky guess?" Lola's voice lilted up at the end, sounding innocent and cute.

Agnes wasn't buying it. "Try again."

An impatient huff came through the phone. "How about I come over in person and tell you what you want to know?"

Agnes drew in a sharp breath. Bringing Lola here would be an absolute mistake. She was very obviously up to something, and Agnes knew she should leave the encounter back in the club where it belonged.

"Yes, come to my office." Apparently, her mouth wasn't listening to her brain.

"When do you want me?"

A shudder of want rippled down Agnes's spine, and she bit the inside of her cheek at the images those simple words sent cascading through her mind. Lola, on her couch, naked, offering up her ripe and young body in exchange for whatever it was she wanted.

"I'd like you to come now."

"Oh good. I'm already downstairs."

Of course she was. If she were the eye-rolling type, Agnes would've done just that at herself. She'd chosen quite the time to let her sex drive do the thinking for her. But *God*, it had been so long since she felt that primal connection with someone, that sensual craving to the exclusion of anything sensible. Had she even felt that with her first girlfriend...?

Now was *not* the time to open that can of worms.

She sent security to escort Lola up. When the girl appeared in the doorway of her office, flanked by two of her most efficient members of her office security team, Agnes sat back in her chair and watched her, trying to pretend she hadn't been waiting with a hitch in her chest since they'd gotten off the phone.

Lola held a small cake carrier in her hands. The carrier was a clear plastic, just wide enough to cover both her palms, and had four shot glass-sized parfaits inside.

What was *this* about?

For a moment, Lola's face was lively, eyes devouring every detail of the office, of Agnes, the panorama of New York City spread out beyond the slightly darkened glass. Despite the distance between their ages, this was no girl, Agnes realized. Lola was a grown woman, one who moved through life with an energy and hunger Agnes envied.

Then a mask fell over Lola's face, and she became someone else. A woman perfectly composed. Pretty in fuchsia heels, tight jeans, and a cropped blouse telling the world how much she loved Brooklyn. Her one concession to the October chill was a leather jacket, also fuchsia, draped over her arm.

Today, she wore her hair straightened and in loose curls that bounced around her shoulders. With her hair down and her casual clothes, she looked even younger than she had in the cool intimacy of the club. Fresh as a daisy ready to be plucked.

She didn't seem dangerous at all. In fact, with her slow smile and the way she ran her eyes over every part of Agnes she could see, it seemed as if she was ready to pick up right where they'd left off on Friday night. But danger often lay in the most innocent of facades, the ability to lull the victim into a stupor of relaxation and mental ease before striking, deadly and true.

Agnes nodded at the pair who escorted Lola in. "Thank you. I'll take it from here."

The two dipped their heads to Agnes and slipped out of the office with nearly silent footsteps, closing the door behind them. She waved Lola toward the chair on the other side of her desk.

"I made you a present." Lola bypassed the chair and stretched to set the doll-sized cake carrier on Agnes's side of the desk, adjusting it just so.

"These are cherry cheesecake whiskey shots, since you were really into your whiskey the other night." She bent and Agnes couldn't stop her hungry eyes from latching on to the enticing weight of her breasts under the white T-shirt as she settled and resettled the cake carrier on the desk.

Agnes subtly squirmed in her chair, her body reacting against her will to the imprint of large nipples against the white cotton of Lola's shirt. "You didn't have to bring me anything," she said.

"I know, but I wanted to." Brown eyes peered up at her through a thick screen of lashes. Lola took the top off the cake carrier, and the scent of heated cherries wafted out. She touched the outside of one of the shot glasses. "This is a layer of crushed shortbread cookies. Here is homemade whipped cream." The tip of her finger slowly moved up the slender shot glass, indicating each level. "And this one is a cherry reduction cooked down with American whiskey. Not the fancy stuff you're used to, though."

The reduction was red, sticky, and surrounded by whole pitted cherries. Agnes's mouth watered a little. Although her thirst could very well be attributed to the lush breasts straining against the white cloth so temptingly close to her face.

The three other glasses in the cake carrier were more or less the same, although two had fresh whipped cream as the final layer, a thick and stemmed cherry on top.

"Thank you." Agnes cleared her too-dry throat. "I'm sure I'll enjoy them."

"I hope you will." Lola covered the shot glasses and straightened with an impish smile.

"Tell me," Agnes said once Lola sat down, "what do you really want from me?"

Lola took a breath. Even though it would be easy to think it was just to bring attention to her breasts, plump and high under the "I" and "Brooklyn," Agnes got the fleeting impression that Lola was actually *nervous*.

"I want to work for you," Lola said.

Agnes ignored the prick of something cold and unpleasant in her chest. She didn't want to call it disappointment. Or a feeling of betrayal. "If we'd slept together at the club, was the plan to charge me for it afterward?"

The mask slipped. And its loss briefly animated the youthful face across from hers—showed the clear "oh my God, no!" before the real emotion got tucked away and Lola sat up straighter in the chair. Breasts out. Chin up.

"Would you have paid?" she asked.

"We'll never know, will we?" Elbows braced on the arms of her chair, Agnes pressed her fingertips together.

Lola was dangerous. Agnes didn't need any of her security people to tell her that. But there was something else about her, something beyond her flirtation and kissable lips.

Agnes made a split-second decision based on nothing more than a feeling. "Do you have any experience for the kind of work you're here for?" She ignored the faint gasp that came from the intercom on her desk that should have been off.

"No," Lola said with a cheeky smile. She didn't hide her relief as well as she thought. "But I can make up for it with enthusiasm." She shifted in a way that shimmied her breasts under the thin shirt. It was the same trick she'd used at the club, but the repeat performance didn't make it any less effective. Agnes didn't bother trying to keep her eyes above Lola's neck.

"All right then. We'll get a nondisclosure agreement for you to sign, then get started." Agnes raised her voice. "Do you have one ready, Clare?"

"Yes, ma'am."

Lola visibly startled when Clare's voice came through the intercom's speaker and squirmed in the comfortable leather chair as if it was suddenly filled with biting ants.

Moments later, Clare came in with the NDA and Lola gave what was probably meant to be a charming smile, but Clare ignored her, putting the paperwork in Agnes's hands before sweeping back out of the office and closing the door behind her.

"I don't think she likes me." Lola's smile said she didn't really care.

"Clare doesn't feel one way or another about you. Give me your driver's license, please." Agnes scanned the license, then gave it back to Lola along with the NDA and a pen. "Read and sign this."

Lola's bright smile faltered when she saw the pen, brushed steel and bearing The House's logo.

Second thoughts, already?

Her hands that grasped the documents and pen were trembling. "Okay!" The cheer in her voice was a little overdone, but Agnes said nothing, only allowed her those second thoughts and third, watching the mask shift and stretch over Lola's features, although it never completely fell away.

Lola focused her attention on the papers in front of her while Agnes ran the scanned ID through her computer's database. By the time Lola finished reading the agreement, Agnes had looked through all the background information available on one Delores Osbourne.

The sound of a pen scribbling quickly across paper pulled her gaze from the computer screen. A smile firmly in place, Lola pushed the signed NDA across the desk and sat back in the chair, legs crossed, hands resting on her knee. Her bouncing knee.

She was nervous. Good.

"Now what?" Lola asked.

"Now you answer some questions for me."

"Okay. I'm ready." That too-wide smile came again.

Agnes looked down at her blank notepad before lifting her eyes to coolly regard Lola.

She was nothing like Rox or any of the other assets who worked for The House. Which was...unfortunate. The beautiful men and women who offered themselves to Agnes whenever they were bored or craved a challenge were easy to ignore. Looks and attitudes like theirs, the transparent attempts at seduction, were as common as leaves in a forest. Every magazine had a similar pair of breasts, the same type of eyes, symmetrical faces, and gym-hardened bodies. They never excited Agnes.

But Lola, with her round face, soft-looking body, and suspicious ways, did.

"Tell me, what do you want more than anything else in this world?" Agnes asked.

Surprise once again tipped the mask off Lola's face, and it was a look Agnes wanted to see more of. "What?" Lola's bouncing knee stopped moving.

Agnes leaned back in her chair, sure she didn't need to repeat herself. Lola had heard very clearly what she asked.

"Look, I know I started this game or whatever it is we're doing right now, but I *really* need the work." Lola slid to the edge of her chair and put both feet firmly on the floor, earnestness taking over her face.

With a shiver of distaste, Agnes wondered if she was about to get a version of the "law student putting herself through school" line.

Lola continued. "I've heard good things about your place and thought if I'm going to…whore myself out, I might as well do it the right way."

"And how did you learn that being with H Holdings would be the *right way*?" Lola was flattering her, slicking her up for a shafting that she probably thought was a sure thing.

Women had come to Agnes before, men too, wanting things and willing to trade the use of their bodies for them. As Lola had done under false pretenses at the club. And Agnes had been so very close to giving in.

"I've heard things," Lola said. "Nothing I've seen here today says what my sources told me was wrong."

Sources. Interesting word choice.

Agnes slipped the signed NDA into her desk drawer, deciding suddenly that they were done. Here in front of her was a woman of masks and make-believe. She wriggled around truths and dared Agnes to invite her into her life.

Exhaustion pressed down on Agnes's shoulders. "Thank you for your time. Someone will be in touch," she said.

"That's it?"

"For now, yes."

Desperation flashed in the pretty, dark eyes. "But I didn't answer your question."

"Yes, I noticed that." Agnes stood up and invited Lola to do the same. "Good luck on your second interview."

With obvious reluctance, Lola got to her feet. "If this is the way you attract new girls to this place, it's a miracle you have anyone working for you."

"The people who work for me are here for the money and safety, not my charm." Agnes stepped from behind the desk but kept her distance. The few feet separating them were just enough to give Agnes a hint of the perfume Lola wore. It was the same one from the other night.

"Cold, hard cash is pretty miraculous." Lola stuffed her hands in her back pockets. The move pushed out her breasts, showed off the narrowness of her waist, the loving and tight caress of the jeans around her hips and thighs.

Everything about the way she stood there, temptingly close, seemed to say *take take take*, but Agnes was no mindless idiot ruled by sex. She cleared her throat and inclined her head toward the door. "Clare will see you out."

Showing once again she was worth every penny the company paid her, Clare appeared as if by magic. She opened the door, then stood back, patiently waiting with a neutral expression for Lola to leave.

Agnes stood with the desk behind her, and when Lola left her office with an unsmiling backward glance to meet the two-man security team already waiting for her, Agnes took a step back to brace her hands against the edge of the desk. Her legs were *not* trembling.

Clare, still poised in the doorway, looked down the hall toward Lola's disappearing figure and waited for the distant chime of the elevator before speaking. "If you don't mind my asking, ma'am, what was that about?" A frown settled between her clear brown eyes. "You never interview...anyone."

Agnes couldn't deny the truth in that statement. Despite its reputation, H Holdings wasn't that kind of escort service. As to the answer to Clare's question, she wished she had a good one.

"She's up to something," Agnes finally said and went back to sit behind her desk.

"Yes...?"

Despite her unease, she almost smiled. An obvious statement like the one she'd just made did deserve a snarky answer. "I want to know what that something is. As the saying goes, keep your enemies closer." Although the kind of close she wanted to get to Lola probably wasn't what Sun Tzu had in mind when he came up with that bit of advice. "There's been some suspicious activity going on recently, as you know, and she may have something to do with it." Unlikely, but maybe if she said it enough, one of them would start to believe it.

"Of course." Clare fiddled with the fastening of her watch before, with an apologetic look at Agnes, she stopped. She clasped her hands neatly in front of her. "Your meeting has been set up. A video call on your secure line tomorrow morning. The only time they could both agree on that lines up with your schedule is five o'clock."

"In the evening?"

"The morning. I've blocked off two hours for the meeting, and that will give you time for your later obligation."

Every weekday morning, Agnes took Gretchen to school. "Thank you."

"Of course." Then Clare let herself out.

The door closed behind her, and Agnes leaned back in her chair, her eyes drifting to the statue of Oshun guarding the floor safe, then to the cherry and whiskey shots on her desk. She teased the corner of her mouth with her tongue, anticipating the sweetness of the cherries tempered with the flavor of the whiskey. She imagined what it would be like to kiss Lola and suck the taste of fruit, cream, and liquor from her lips.

A quiet groan spilled from her.

For weeks now, she'd felt a change coming. Chaos riding astride a whirlwind. And now, here was Lola. A challenge, a mystery, a liar.

True, Agnes had opened her door and invited Lola inside. But what else could she have done?

She was, after all, her father's daughter.

CHAPTER 5

"I think I'm in." Lola flopped down on the empty side of Jamika's bed, her whole body buzzing with relief and the sweet smell of near-victory. It was ass o'clock in the morning on a Saturday, but she was too wired to sleep in. The doctored information Jamika's tech geek had planted for Agnes to find during a background check on Lola had worked like a charm. "We got this."

"Seriously? Are we doing this right now? It's early as hell, and I have to get up for work in—" Jamika groped for her phone on the bedside table, then groaned. "—in less than an hour."

"Last night, you got in too late for me to give you the good news."

"Cell phones exist. Pen and paper. I hear that even text messages are a thing." Jamika grumbled some more, then flopped onto her back to give Lola the evil eye. Her night bonnet sat drunkenly on top of her head.

"This is some good stuff. You're going to change your grumpy grumps when you hear it."

"Then spill already because my grumpy grumps aren't going anywhere right now."

"Well, I told you how it went at her office yesterday."

"Yes. You sent me a text like a normal person."

Lola poked her friend in the ribs, and Jamika squirmed away but only far enough to grab a pillow and smack Lola in the face.

Snorting out a laugh, Lola batted the pillow away. "Anyway, before the end of the day, I got a text from the assistant or receptionist or whatever that woman is."

Jamika's head popped up, the sleep abruptly clearing from her eyes. *Now* she was paying attention. "And...?"

"They scheduled my second interview. The actual fucking part of the interview." She thrust her hips back and forth a couple of times just in case Jamika missed what she was talking about. "I'm supposed to show up there after the results of my STI tests come in."

"And you're going to go through with it?" Jamika's cascade of frowns made her look a little like a Klingon. "For real for real?"

Lola rolled her eyes. Of course she'd have sex with whoever she had to for this investigative story and the takedown of The House. It wasn't ideal, but she'd do what she had to.

"I *am* going through with it." Why wouldn't she after they'd come all this way?

The mattress shifted as Jamika sat up and propped herself up against the headboard. She pulled the bonnet off her head, and her thick, blonde-streaked dreadlocks tumbled around her shoulders and down her back. "So, we're really doing this. We're really going after one of the most powerful women on the East Coast."

"Yup. We are."

During those few minutes in Agnes's office, Lola felt as if she were about to vibrate out of her skin. She'd been there, the place where Zoe had been and had probably spent her last days. It had taken everything in Lola to pretend she wasn't about to fly apart. Oh my God—when Agnes took out that pen, the one identical to the one the cops found with Zoe's body... Lola's stomach churned at the memory.

After the way their interview ended, she'd half expected not to hear from Agnes or anyone in The House again. The security goons with their stone faces watched every move she made and escorted her all the way downstairs and out of the building as if they were worried she'd try to steal something. And then, when she was halfway down the block, she'd gotten that text from Clare telling her to come in. The moment she saw the text on her burner phone, the one she'd bought and activated just for this assignment, her pulse tripped with excitement. Her second gambit had paid off.

The idea of having anonymous sex for money made her knees shake a little. She knew, though, that it was a small price to pay to bring down Agnes Noble and her corrupt house that destroyed lives and families.

Families like mine.

The bed shifted as Jamika got up. She scratched a butt cheek just visible under the oversized T-shirt she wore to bed and headed for the bathroom.

"I'm going to need coffee for the rest of this discussion." The bathroom door clicked shut behind her.

Over coffee and homemade cranberry chocolate chip muffins courtesy of Lola, Jamika and Lola talked strategy. Discussed what-ifs. Created contingency plans.

"What about bugs?" Lola asked, breaking her second muffin in half before taking a bite. "Do you think I should try to plant one in the office or wherever I end up?"

"Too risky." Jamika shook her head. "With as much security as she has, I'm sure she sweeps for bugs every damn hour. It would point right at you if they found a bug just a few minutes or hours after you—the only new face in the place—were there. You'd get tossed out before you even get the chance to bend over for your first client."

"Nice one, J." Lola wrinkled her nose.

"Don't get fussy on me now, Miss Sex-Is-No-Big-Deal." Jamika spoke around a mouthful of muffin. "This is a good batch, by the way. Perfect cranberry-to-chocolate chip ratio."

"Thanks. Glad my stress paid off for you."

"You stress the best of anybody I know. It's delicious." Jamika finished off the last piece of her muffin with an annoying smack of her lips.

"Can we get back to the plan, please?" Lola said through her laughter. Her friend was ridiculous.

"There isn't much to plan. You get in there and—uh—do your thing. Be convincing and show her she'd be letting grade A pussy slide through her fingers if she didn't hire you."

"It has been said before." Lola waggled her eyebrows.

Jamika rolled her eyes. "Anyway. Just do what you need to do—leave the bugs here! They'll probably search you real good before letting you anywhere past public spaces."

Lola hadn't thought of that. Would Agnes do the search herself? Her inner slut wriggled a little at the thought before Lola brought her under control. Agnes probably didn't do any of her dirty work herself. Not to mention, she was a terrible person, someone who took innocence and turned it into money, then left regret and broken bodies behind.

"Okay, *fine*. No bugs. But you have to help me pick out something to wear. I'm not up on the latest hooker chic."

"Don't be a dick. A lot of escorts this high up on the food chain dress like you and me, only a lot richer. Elegant and fuckable. People you can take to a corporate company party or charity ball. We're not talking clear heels and crotchless leather pants here. I've busted enough of them to know."

"Do you—?"

Just then, Lola's phone vibrated with a new e-mail notification. She grabbed her cell off the kitchen table. Although it was a little early, she'd been waiting for a reply to one of her recent clients about getting paid. The promised two thousand dollars was now a week late.

"Gimme a sec," she said, opening the e-mail app on her phone.

But it wasn't a reply from the magazine.

It was her bank.

"This is weird."

"What? Another of your old hookups stalking you again?"

"That was one time, J. *One* time…" Lola replied with only half her mind on what Jamika was saying. She had to blink at the information on the screen again. It had to be some kind of mistake.

"So, what's got that look on your face?"

The notification of deposit from her bank stood out glaringly on the screen. And no, that client who owed her the cash didn't have access to this account.

"Someone just put twenty-five thousand dollars in my checking account a few minutes ago." She scrolled through the rest of the information, her mouth dropping open. "It doesn't say anything here about who it's from."

Jamika's chair shrieked across the floor as she pushed back from the table to stand behind Lola. Her hot breath smelled like cranberry chocolate chip muffins and coffee. "That's a lot of damn money!"

"It has to be some kind of mistake." A really nice mistake, but still.

"What kind of mistake is this, though?" Jamika pointed at the phone's screen with a buttery finger. "Whoever did this has to have your name *and* account number." She pulled back, a smirk lifting the corners of her mouth. "Do you think Agnes wants your ass that badly?"

"I don't think it's her. From what happened today, she barely wants me in there at all, and if that Clare person had any say in it, I wouldn't even be allowed back for the interview."

Jamika's smirk slid away. "Yeah." She settled back on her side of the table. "Then what's this about?"

"I'm going to the bank to find out."

"Good call," Jamika said. "Although they'll probably think you're weird for saying you *don't* want a huge deposit in your account."

"I mean, my Nigerian prince could've *finally* delivered on all those e-mail promises, and I'm just worrying for no reason."

"Nice thought but that's doubtful. It's somebody's mistake. When they realize they gave the money to the wrong person, I sure as hell don't want you to repay twenty-five grand with a bullet to the kneecaps."

Lola shuddered. "A little dramatic, don't you think?"

Maybe not, though. The biggest bank balance she'd ever had in her life stared back at her from her phone's screen, a temptation and a warning.

"I bet you don't know a soul who'd want to give you this kind of money," Jamika said.

That was sadly true. Some of Lola's clients barely wanted to pay her the few hundred dollars they owed.

"This is weird as fuck, and I'd rather you return the money before some gangster comes after you for it." Jamika gave her a stern look. "As a cop, I support that move."

"Fine, fine. I already said I'll go to the bank."

"To give the money back, right?" Jamika's eyes narrowed. "I'd rather you keep your kneecaps right where they are, thank you very much."

"To give the money back," Lola confirmed. Shaking her head at her friend, she put her phone away. This afternoon, she'd make some time to go to the bank and sort everything out. "Now, where were we?"

CHAPTER 6

"We practice our letters today." Twisting in the grip of her seat belt, Gretchen stretched past Agnes and squinted out at the rain through the Lincoln Town Car's window. The chilly fall morning, which mostly yielded views of other cars lumbering along with them through traffic, drifted slowly past. "I can write my name already, though."

"Good girl. I'm glad our lessons didn't go to waste." With a practiced move, Agnes quieted the phone vibrating in her dress pocket but didn't take it out. On their rides to school, she always gave Gretchen her complete attention. "What's your plan for class then since you already know what to do?"

"Maybe help other kids." A frown pulled down the corners of Gretchen's mouth. "But nobody likes a know-it-all."

"Especially the people who don't know anything at all," Whit agreed from her seat on the opposite side of the car. Today, she wore all gray. Heels, slacks, pale blouse, and a fussy little sweater. Her lipstick was a matte dark violet.

Gretchen stuck out her lower lip, looking thoughtful. "Maybe I'll just pretend."

"No, love. Don't diminish yourself for other people." Agnes could see Gretchen wrinkle her forehead at the unfamiliar word. She waited for Gretchen to ask what it meant before answering. "It means to make yourself seem smaller or less-than just to make somebody else feel better."

"Oh! Nope." Her lips made a popping sound, and she looked up from the lap desk where she'd been scribbling her name with different-colored crayons, trying to write it in the cursive she and Agnes had practiced weeks ago. "I *don't* want to do that, Nessa."

"Good. You could ask Mrs. Parran to give you some different work to do, something else to practice."

Gretchen frowned, and Agnes laughed. Like her, Gretchen wasn't interested in doing more work for no reason. "You could just practice like you're doing right now." She gestured to the lap desk and the various versions of Gretchen's name that looked like something a child twice her age would write. "Make it pretty for yourself."

"Okay," she said. "I'll do that." She grinned over at Agnes while Whit stifled a smile. Water splashed up against the window in a rippling wave as the car glided through a puddle. Gretchen giggled. "Splash!"

Gretchen was such a mix of mature and childlike that Agnes was never bored. Sure, she'd often been caught off guard and even charmed out of giving a deserved punishment, but it seemed to go with the parenting territory. With Whit by her side, along with an army of trusted bodyguards, the last six years had gone better than she'd expected. Agnes loved Gretchen, and she'd do whatever it took to protect her.

The car pulled up to the school and slipped behind the others waiting to unload their precious cargo.

Agnes smoothed back the baby hairs from Gretchen's soft forehead. "You ready?"

"Yes!" With her big smile on display, Gretchen tucked away her crayons and stowed them in her backpack. "Are you coming home early tonight?"

"At the usual time. Maybe a little earlier but I'm not sure. Why?"

"Whit wants pizza."

A cough was all that came from Whit on the other side of the Town Car.

"Really?"

"Yes." Gretchen nodded vigorously.

Agnes turned to look at Whit. "Is that so?"

"Apparently." Whit replied dryly.

Although the play was as transparent as the Town Car's tinted windows were from the inside, Agnes didn't see anything wrong with giving Gretchen what she wanted. It was a Friday, and every report she'd gotten back from the school said Gretchen was doing very well. She was a lot precocious, sometimes too chatty, but always respectful and ready to help the teacher.

How she'd managed to escape the label of "teacher's pet" among the other children showed how likable she was. Already a better person than Agnes. She just sometimes worried that Gretchen might turn into a bit of a people pleaser. Humans were often a disappointment, and she didn't want her child to be hurt by expecting too much.

"In that case," Agnes said with a straight face. "I'll do my best so Whit can get what she wants."

The car rocked slightly as Gretchen jumped up and down on her knees on the seat. "Whit will love that."

"Oh good."

After they dropped her off, the car slid away from the curb, following the slow traffic of minivans and improperly named SUVs out of the school's semicircular driveway.

"I'm glad she's using her powers of manipulation for good." Agnes looked back at the school steps where a teacher stood making sure the children ended up where they were supposed to. "God knows her father never did."

"She's fine," Whit said. "*You*, though, are distracted."

Agnes almost sighed. "No more than usual."

"No. Actually more than usual. What's on your mind? Oh wait. Don't tell me. It's that girl who came into the office a few days ago. The one who somehow found out what H Holdings really is and wants to work under you." Whit didn't crack so much as a smile.

One day, Agnes would ask Whit how she knew so much about her business. Then again, that was part of the reason she was there. To see things Agnes missed. To know what Agnes also knew but have a different perspective on it. At times, she wondered if Clare and Whit weren't ganging up on her, determined to control both her home and office life.

"It's nothing."

"I doubt that very much," Whit said. "If some young thing is trying to get close to you and you're already suspicious, wouldn't the sensible thing be to push the trouble away before it gets the chance to take root?"

Sensible, yes.

"If she's part of the trouble that's been coming at us lately, it would make more sense to let her think she's getting in and use her to find out what's going on."

"Is that what you're doing? Seems to me you're going with your gut instead of making a plan." Whit's penetrating stare narrowed. "You never go with your gut."

In her lap, Agnes's hand twitched. She didn't fool herself into thinking Whit didn't notice. "I've got it under control."

Whit breathed out a laugh. "No, you don't. That's why you have me. And Clare."

"Just watch from a distance. Don't get involved too closely."

"You know I can't do that. I'm not here to cosign bad decisions."

This time, Agnes *did* sigh. "Very well."

Whit, Agnes sometimes forgot, wasn't just family. She wasn't just the sum of her vast weapons collection, practical advice, and J. Crew-approved wardrobe. She was also the girl Agnes had known nearly all her life. The one who'd burst into the room, no hesitation, and shot the man holding the blade that had just slit Augustus Noble's throat. That murderer had been Whit's own father. Her own abuser.

Whit was hard because she had to be. She protected what and who she loved by absolutely any means necessary. Even by being a pain in the ass.

Today was supposed to be Lola's so-called second interview. Agnes had made that up on the fly. The assets who approached H Holdings about working there were usually professionals with months or years in the game, no second interview required. These men and women usually wanted a reputable, exclusive agency that kept them safe and ensured they made an excellent wage. H Holdings was many things—feared, respected, but also fair. And it rarely took in newbies who wanted to give whoring the old college try.

"Don't act like I'm taking away your new toy." Whit looked down to rearrange the lines of her sweater over her gun holster. "You have plenty of leeway to see what this woman is up to without putting the business, yourself, or Gretchen—" She emphasized Gretchen's name with a significant look. "—in danger."

"I'm not new to this, you know. My priorities have always been clear."

"If anyone knows that, it's me, but I don't think I've ever seen you this distracted by a woman before."

"I may be a little distracted, yes, but I'm not totally stupid."

Whit made a sound full to the brim with doubt. "I've seen what this woman looks like. And I notice your body's reaction when you talk about her. The drool practically drips down your chin."

"My *body's reaction*? Really, Whit?"

Agnes's phone vibrated again, snagging her attention and saving her from seeing Whit's expression. This time, she slid it from her pocket and read the message there.

Clare: The penthouse is ready for Delores Osbourne's interview this afternoon.

A flush of jealousy rolled through Agnes's belly, up her chest and into her face. She tried to ignore Whit's interested gaze.

Agnes: Who'll conduct the interview?

They'd agreed to take this as far as a real audition of the type other houses had. Find a client or a client stand-in. Let the asset work, then do an assessment at the end of the encounter. When she'd agreed to it, Agnes had half-expected Lola to back out.

Lola had spouted that foolishness about wanting to make money, but there was a layer of lies there. Easy to spot, hard to penetrate to see what was beneath.

Lola hadn't changed her mind, though. Instead, she'd confirmed the interview time and place with Clare, sending along the message that she was ready to be an excellent new asset.

Since getting the message, Agnes had grown agitated, felt the irrational jealousy that someone would get to taste what she'd wanted so badly on her tongue during that night at the club.

Clare's reply to her question buzzed her phone. The one scheduled to "interview" Lola was Nestor. Another of their assets. A beautiful man who, in a suit, gave off "hot billionaire" vibes, even though he'd been born in the slums of Jamaica.

When asked, Lola had said she didn't care if her interview was with a man or woman. Agnes's jealousy boiled. Did that mean even if she was the one waiting for Lola in the darkened penthouse with her core aching and her empty arms waiting to be filled, it would have been the same for Lola as any other woman, any man?

Agnes's jaw tightened. This was business. For her to keep a clear head, it needed to stay that way.

Although the "clear head" thing might be one of those "closing the barn door after the horse had bolted" type situations.

Agnes thanked Clare and put the phone away. She tapped the glass to get the driver's attention. "To the office, please, Taj."

"Of course, ma'am."

Whit said nothing.

The Town Car dropped them off at the front of the building, and they took the private elevator up. Images of the two of them reflected back at Agnes from the steel doors. Whit in her head-to-toe gray with her unsmiling purple mouth. The three-quarter-length coat she'd added after leaving the car made her look taller, both more elegantly feminine and more dangerous.

Except for a quick check to make sure she looked presentable in her slim-fitting burgundy dress, black heels, and coat, Agnes deliberately looked away from her own reflection. What she looked like didn't matter. She snuck a peek at her watch. Almost eight o'clock. She had a lot of time before four this afternoon.

"Do you think she'll go through with it?" Whit asked as the elevator rushed skyward.

No need to clarify who she was talking about.

"Yes. She says she hasn't done this before, but whatever the reason she's really here, using her body in this way is something she's apparently willing to do."

And that was the rub, right? That night at the club, attraction to Lola had turned Agnes into a drooling, slow-witted version of herself. It rubbed her raw that the attraction hadn't been mutual. Lola had been planning how to get into H Holdings, not Agnes's panties.

That stung.

People used people. People got used. In Agnes's world, that was the norm. People employed whatever means at their disposal to get what they wanted.

In her own case, she had needed her father's connections and his part in a vast network already in place. She'd needed his spiderweb to get her own goals accomplished. She'd used him, used his network, then eventually had taken it for herself. So, she shouldn't have been hurt that Lola, a stranger, was willing to use her to get what she needed. Whatever that was.

"You'll find out this afternoon just how far she's willing to go." Dark amusement pulled up the corner of Whit's mouth. "And hopefully, what her end game is."

"Yes, I will."

The elevator doors slid open. "By the way," Whit said as they both stepped out. "Everything is set for the Vegas meeting. Hotel, security, airport arrangements. I'll send the info to your phone later today."

The big annual meeting with the other houses in North America had almost slipped Agnes's mind. She was more distracted than she thought. "Thanks. What would I do without you?"

"Lucky for you, you don't have to find out." Whit gave her arm a quick squeeze, then went left at the elevators while Agnes went right. Time to start the workday.

Agnes worked with a countdown ticking away at the back of her mind. The closer it got to four o'clock, the farther her mind drifted from her work. Whit left to pick up Gretchen from school. Agnes's two meetings came and went. Finally, at twelve minutes to four, she pushed away from her desk, unable to fake it for one second longer. She tapped the intercom button. "Is Nestor already there?"

"Yes," Clare said. "He arrived about thirty minutes ago."

Thirty minutes.

The leather of her chair sighed as she dipped back. Of course. Even though he was playing the role of the client this time, Nestor was a professional. He would be the one to rate how Lola fulfilled her role as an escort, from the moment she appeared at the designated place to the moment she left.

Punctuality. Performance. Pleasure. These were the key things he had to pay attention to and report back to Clare. Or Agnes.

"Thank you, Clare."

"You're welcome, Agnes."

Clare's voice was scrubbed of all emotion, which was how Agnes knew she was absolutely bursting with curiosity, and concern.

Agnes stared at the phone for some minutes, her mind tracing over things it shouldn't be, imagining. What Lola would look like pinned under Nestor's muscled body. If she would fake an orgasm or reach true pleasure. Would she imagine it was Agnes making her come instead of a stranger?

No.

Agnes's chair flew back from her desk as she stood up. She grabbed her phone, shoved it into her pocket, and left the office. Clare looked up as she passed.

"Hold my calls, please." Then she thought of Whit and the promised pizza. "If Whit or Gretchen call, tell them I'll be home at the usual time."

Clare's lips pursed, but she only said, "Of course."

Her assistant's disapproval was rancid in the air but no worse than Agnes's own. It was almost like an out-of-body experience, taking calm and measured steps to the elevator, then waiting the few seconds for it to take her one flight up to the penthouse level.

Why are you doing this? some sane part of her questioned.

No answer came.

At the door marked P4, she took the key card from her pocket and let herself in. It was eight minutes until four.

From the short hallway, she stepped down into the sunken living room where soft music already played. Some 1980s power ballad. The bare floor-to-ceiling windows showed off the city, the skyscrapers and the river. A savage blue sky.

Nestor had placed himself in a low leather chair facing the patio, his back to the door. The suit jacket of his navy blue Armani was unbuttoned, his arms spread along the back of the chair. He sat, a dramatic silhouette against the backdrop of the city. Just the way a client would, eager to make a powerful impression on the woman about to get on her knees for him.

Sunlight slashed through the room, providing the only warmth in the cold space decorated in shades of bone, gray, and black.

"You're early," Nestor said without turning around.

"And you're not paying attention."

At the sound of her voice, he jumped to his feet and abruptly turned around. "Ms. Noble."

"Nestor."

His handsome face showed his surprise, then she could see the switch flip, and he turned on his natural charm, a smile blossoming. His dimple flashed. "Do you need me to do something differently?" he asked.

A knock sounded on the door.

It was exactly four o' clock.

"Actually, I won't be needing you tonight after all," Agnes said. She took out a hundred-dollar bill and passed it to him. "Thank you for making yourself available."

"Of course." He gave a sort of old-world bow and tucked the money away. "It wasn't something I did, was it?"

"Not at all. As always, you're perfect. There's simply been a change of plans."

"Of course," he said again, putting on his suit jacket with conscious grace. "Have a good rest of your evening."

"Thank you, Nestor."

He slipped past, leaving her with the faint, citrusy kiss of his cologne. Quietly exchanged greetings came from behind Agnes as Nestor spoke with Lola in the hallway. Even in the few words, Lola's confusion was obvious.

"She's waiting for you inside," Agnes heard before the door closed, and finally, slow footsteps made their way toward where she waited.

Instead of posing for dramatic effect, Agnes poured herself a desperately needed glass of whiskey. She was going off her own script, so she wasn't exactly sure what her next move was going to be. Winging it had never been her strong suit.

"Come in," she said when Lola appeared from the hallway. She waved Lola toward the dark gray leather sectional. "Would you like a drink?"

Lola looked at her, wide-eyed. "No thanks."

Agnes tried but failed to ignore how Lola was dressed. A figure-hugging dress, electric blue and low-necked, that bared an impressive piece of costume jewelry. The necklace was a spiderweb of finely strung crystals that closed around the entire length of her neck and flowed down to shimmer over bared collar bones and rest on the plump rise of her cleavage. In the cold of the room, her nipples pressed against the thin material of the dress, likely proof that she wasn't wearing a bra.

The whole effect made her look a bit like a royal whore. A sacrifice fit for a queen.

At the thought, Agnes smiled, but she wasn't amused.

"What are you doing here?" Eyes darting around the luxurious space, Lola stepped down into the sunken room. "The guy that just left, he was hot enough. I wouldn't mind him being my first test. Or are you taking his place?"

She turned, and the skirts of her dress flared out around her legs. Sunlight caught the crystals in her spider-necklace and threw arrows of light all around the room. Her pretty mouth curved up while Agnes gawked at her.

"That's fine by me too. Sex, no matter the body, is sex. Pleasure is pleasure." That smile of hers became absolutely wicked. "Or are you just planning to watch?" She continued without waiting for an answer. "I've done that before. It's a bit kinky." Now, Lola sounded intrigued. "I'm surprised someone like you is into that."

Lola moved across the space separating them, her stilettos tapping against the marble with every step while her dress swept over the floor in a sensuous whisper. Her eyelashes had been darkened and lengthened with mascara, lids painted with subtle color. She looked up at Agnes through these new lashes, and her mouth, painted a deep red, parted to allow a single swipe of her tongue.

"You might be in for a lot more surprises where I'm concerned." Agnes clamped her mouth shut, too late, over the sly words she hadn't meant to say. Damn, Lola was gorgeous like this.

A smile bloomed on Lola's sensual mouth. "Oh, I hope so. Very much."

Still smiling, Lola reached behind herself as if she were scratching her back. The dress loosened and slithered down her body to pool around her feet.

Agnes nearly choked on her next breath. She stared at the ankles the dress revealed and nothing else, not wanting to look up and feast her eyes on what she knew was waiting for her. Then Lola moved, stepped out of the dress on towering yellow high heels to stand just a little bit closer.

Agnes's eyes moved up without her telling them to. Sliding over rounded legs, the coy indentation of knees, and thick thighs. Good God… A delicate strip of yellow cloth that was nothing more than a wish—because surely there wasn't enough of it to qualify as underwear— hugged Lola's mound and her hips. The yellow G-string, a perfect shade to match her shoes, showed off the enticing curve of her belly just below the surprisingly narrow lines of her waist. Her breasts were perfect. Heavy and round, with nipples hardened from the room's chill. The trailing fingers of the magnificent crystal necklace glimmered over them, emphasizing their gorgeous size and shape.

Desire flooded Agnes's mouth. She swallowed again and forced herself not to look away from the obvious challenge in Lola's eyes. Her knees shook and she widened her stance to stop herself from falling over. She couldn't do anything about her dry throat. Or her trembling hands.

Lola stepped closer, bringing with her the light scent of her rosemary perfume. "I'm ready to start whenever you are."

Inside, Agnes was dying.

Wetting her red lips, Lola touched Agnes, pressed a hand low on her stomach, and the heat of her fingers seeped into Agnes's skin, immediate and scorching.

Agnes could have stepped back. She should have. But she stood frozen by desire. The muscles in her belly tightened, and for a reckless moment, Agnes thought of letting Lola take this seduction all the way to its mutually pleasurable conclusion.

That was what Lola expected, right?

And Agnes wanted her. *Goddamn*, she wanted her.

But she wasn't so far off her own script that she would do something so outside her own moral code. Her father had slept with nearly every woman who came through The House. She'd seen how he used them and quickly moved on.

Agnes didn't want to be that.

Despite the threat of her trembling legs giving out beneath her, Agnes stepped back. She gripped the glass of whiskey she'd poured herself. It was a fine line. Leaving Lola's reach and not looking as if she were running away. "I've changed my mind. You don't have to complete this level of the interview."

"I'm just that good?" Lola's soft-looking lips curved up, and it wasn't until a vision of that mouth closing around her clitoris exploded behind Agnes's half-closed eyes that she realized just how intently she'd been staring.

She looked away and took a sacrilegiously quick swallow of fifty-year-old scotch. "Something like that."

Lola's mask slipped. "Did I do something wrong?"

The uncertainty in her voice, the vulnerability, twisted regret in Agnes's chest. It painfully echoed what Nestor had asked her when she'd kicked him out of the room for her own selfish purposes.

"No. You didn't do anything wrong." Agnes swallowed and turned to the bar with its array of drinks. How many bottles would it take to drown this feeling of stupidity? The mirror behind the bar reflected her image along with Lola standing behind her, watching. Still nude. Or near enough to it. She caught Lola's eyes in that mirror and saw the confusion there.

"Cover yourself."

After a slight hesitation, Lola stepped back into the dress and easily refastened it. The brilliant blue cloth shimmered in the natural light as she adjusted its skirts. Her necklace glowed like the stars themselves against her sable skin.

"The dress," Agnes said after a quick sip of whiskey. "It was a good choice."

Lola's chin lifted, and some of her confidence seemed to return along with that single movement. "Not the necklace?"

What was there to say about what had to be the most stunningly erotic piece of jewelry Agnes had ever seen? Not even waist beads on women she'd bedded, not body chains that had enflamed her imagination since seeing Rihanna wearing one years ago, managed to arouse her so very quickly and thoroughly.

Or maybe the necklace only affected Agnes so much because Lola was the one who wore it.

"The necklace is fine."

A smirk curled Lola's mouth. "Alright, so when should I show up to work?"

"We'll be in touch with you later on this week."

Or never. This had been a disaster from start to finish. The moment Agnes met Lola, she felt as if she were on a roller coaster, her stomach dropping with excitement, her heart thudding in anticipation. She wanted Lola close but couldn't afford to have her. Closer, that is.

Jesus.

A strange thought intervened. What if you *could* have her? This gorgeously complex and sensual creature, quirky and funny one moment, and the next...a pretty serpent waiting to strike.

No. The idea was even more ridiculous than what Agnes had just tried to do. Lola obviously had an agenda. Inviting her to share Agnes's secrets, be honest and work together to fix whatever problem she had was more naive than anything even Gretchen could come up with.

Adding Lola to her life, in whatever capacity this strange and dangerous dynamic between them would allow, would only make things worse.

Agnes gestured toward the door. "Shall we?"

She stepped back and allowed Lola to walk in front of her, keeping her eyes above Lola's waist. That didn't help. The back of her neck was a tempting slope made to be tasted and explored. With only a foot of space between them, the scent of rosemary from Lola's skin drifted to Agnes, and she licked her lips, imagining how Lola would taste. How that plump skin would feel under the barely there tease of her fingers.

But she'd resisted stronger lures than this.

For the sake of everything she'd built, for the sake of her little family, she'd resist every temptation Lola laid out in front of her. She had no choice.

CHAPTER 7

LOLA STOOD SILENTLY IN THE elevator at Agnes's side while anxiety twisted her into knots. She'd come to her sex audition ready to *come*. Or at least make someone come hard enough that they'd immediately accept her as The House's newest hire. While psyching herself up to go through with the stranger sex, Lola had even imagined the reviews that would be sent Agnes's way afterward.

She was the best I ever had.
Why did you wait so long to bring her on?
Lola is the only one I ever want from now on.

Etc, etc.

If for some unlikely reason her sexual experience was lacking, she was sure her nearly naked body showed off with the crystal necklace would at least score her some points.

The necklace, a gift from Jamika years ago, had been an incentive for Lola to get her shit together, celebration jewelry for a night she'd play princess to her perfect king or queen of a lover. But Lola never had a lover important enough to wear it for.

The honest truth was that the necklace was way too intense for her personality, which was why she'd thought it was perfect for the woman she was pretending to be. To catch a notorious madam and murderer, she needed to be shinier than she was in real life.

But Agnes had been less than impressed.

Agnes had been aloof to the point of being rude, and worst of all, she'd turned Lola away, unfucked, as if Lola hadn't even been worth her time. Disappointment had tightened Lola's throat, and she'd just wanted to rush out of there and hide out in the bathroom until the shame faded.

For a few minutes in that underfurnished penthouse, she could've sworn the queen wanted her. She recognized the signs. Heavy-lidded eyes. The proprietary way she looked over Lola's body. Her hardened nipples under that perfectly tailored burgundy dress. She'd been so sure. Then Agnes had turned away and basically perp-walked her out of the penthouse, barely saying another word.

Not that Lola had been in that much of a hurry to fuck the woman who'd had Zoe killed, but still, the brush-off stung.

"Goodbye, Lola." Agnes now gave her a nod as the elevator came to a stop on her floor. " I'll see you another time." The doors slid open and she walked out.

With the feeling of rejection curdled in her stomach like old milk, Lola stood back in the lobby-bound elevator as it began to close on the sight of Agnes's lean figure heading down the hallway toward her office. A hand darted inside the car and stopped the doors from closing just in time.

"Hey, there." A woman stepped in, breathless and smiling, and pressed the button for the lobby.

Lola stared. The woman was freakishly gorgeous, all shining hair and glowing skin, with her killer body showed off in tight jeans and a see-through blouse. Her breasts were a bouncy B-plus and perfect. She wasn't as tall as Agnes, but she looked just as polished, only with more of a sense of humor if the laugh lines at the corners of her onyx-painted lips were any indication.

"Hey." Lola stepped back to give the beautiful stranger some room. Then she remembered she was supposed to be getting friendly with everyone in The House. Investigating meant overcoming her intimidation of someone who'd been blessed with good genes.

Before she could make some obvious gesture of "let's be friends," the woman offered the tips of her fingers in a casual version of a handshake. "I'm Roxanne, but everyone calls me Rox."

"Good to meet you." Lola squeezed Rox's fingers, enthusiastic but not too tight.

Lola tried to up her smile, conscious of her over-the-top dress and necklace, the squirmy feeling of inadequacy in her belly. Even in her bright blue dress and princess-pretend necklace, she couldn't compete with how Rox looked in just jeans and a blouse. If this was the kind of woman they hired at The House, did Lola stand a chance of getting in?

Rox's inviting smile was warm, though. "I haven't seen you around here before. Are you new?" Simple curiosity lit her eyes.

"I hope so." Lola played up the innocent act and injected some perky energy into her teeth-baring smile. "Just had my interview and I'm crossing my fingers I'll be one of you guys soon."

"One of you guys?" Rox's smile faltered, her eyes blinking in confusion. *Oh shit.* Wasn't she one of…?

Laughter bubbled from Rox's glossed lips, and her sly eyes sparkled. "Oh my God, you should see your face! I'm just joking." She leaned against the back wall of the elevator, chuckling. In that pose, with her thick hair gleaming over her shoulders and the teasing glimpses of her breasts under her blouse, she looked camera-ready. "I've worked here for a while now. It'll be fun to have some fresh meat around. Maybe we'll even get to work together sometime."

Work together? Did Rox just say she wanted them to have a threesome?

The sound of the elevator's chime blended with Rox's laughter. "If you're as innocent as you look, the clients are going to *eat* you up." Before Lola could react, Rox brushed a long finger along Lola's jawline, smiling in a teasing way that could mean anything. Her touch felt both intimate and oddly cold. Was that the kind of attitude Lola needed to fit in around here?

The doors of the elevator slid open, and Rox walked out ahead of Lola, hair and boobs bouncing.

"See you around, doll face," she threw over her shoulder and slinked her way across the lobby. She walked as if she knew everyone watched her and was enjoying every second of the attention.

Lola stared after Rox so intensely the elevator doors nearly closed in her face. Damn. With competition like that, her chances of getting hired were slim to "hell no."

She needed another plan of attack.

CHAPTER 8

After throwing Lola out of the building, Agnes left the office for an early dinner with Whit and Gretchen, then a long "I told you so" session with Whit on the patio while Gretchen slept. In the quiet hush of the night, Agnes nearly confessed to Whit that she still had no idea what Lola wanted, that all she *did* have was plenty of confirmation that her sex drive was purring along just fine.

She didn't say a word, though. Instead, she kept these things secret, reliving at odd moments the tease of Lola's defiantly offered body, her unexpected vulnerability. And, at the core of it all, her own stupid and persistent desire.

Lola didn't belong at The House. She didn't belong anywhere in Agnes's world. But Agnes wasn't sure she had the strength to push her away.

The warm light of the late afternoon sun slanted across the browned-butter sofa in Agnes's office when, with her shoes off and her body stretched out on said sofa, she clicked on the e-mail Nicole, one of The House's former assets who'd made her escape to a "normal" life in Florida, had sent.

I know this girl. She's a good student at the school where I work and has plans for college when she graduates in two years. Her trust fund will activate when she turns eighteen, but until then, her aunt provides her with a decent allowance. She's a little boring, sweet, and focused on her science experiments. I don't think she did this herself. Can you help?

The link below it led to the dark web. Agnes drew in a cleansing breath to prepare herself for whatever she was about to see.

It was a virginity auction. The bidding had reached two million dollars and would end in twenty-four hours.

Photos attached to the auction listing showed a pretty girl, plump and startled-looking, a living doll with curves that had outgrown her school uniform. The eyes behind her glasses glowed with intelligence and a sort of innocence that came from being more interested in theorems and equations than the body. All the photos were candids. The girl didn't seem to have posed for any of them. It looked like she was being stalked.

Agnes's stomach twisted. If that girl didn't want this...

She found the number she needed and picked up the phone. "Are you sure she's not playing some sort of game here?" Agnes asked when Nicole answered the phone. "Maybe she needs money to fund her latest mad scientist experiment."

Breath puffed into the receiver from the other end of the line. Nicole's low voice was barely there, as if she was trying to not to wake up her new baby.

"It might be her mother," Nicole said. "She's lost custody of Monique and is living with a bastard who caters to her every whim. They could kidnap her, I think." A sound of self-directed impatience came through. "I don't know. Maybe I'm seeing this threat because of what happened to me."

But experience was a good teacher for a reason. Sometimes that experience made people see monsters where only ghosts from their pasts existed. Other times, though...

"I'll look into it." Agnes was already pulling up a list of her Florida contacts on her laptop, people she trusted to take a look at what was happening with Monique and take action if she was about to be gobbled up by a big bad wolf. "Someone will be where the girl is in less than an hour, and we'll take care of the rest."

After a few more minutes of quiet conversation, checking in on how Nicole, her new baby, and old wife were doing, Agnes ended the call. The sun had moved, deserted the couch and the stretch of her bare legs, all but fleeing the office as if it had an urgent appointment elsewhere. Agnes missed its warmth.

A shiver brought her sitting up on the couch, her legs tucked in beside her. She stared past the window, looking at nothing as unwanted memories trespassed. Too many beasts walked the world disguised as humans.

If it hadn't been for her mother, Agnes's virginity would have been sold or bartered off like so many of her father's other possessions. She had been becoming beautiful at seventeen, blooming late like one of her mother's autumn chrysanthemums, when she first noticed her father's comments.

"You're almost as beautiful as your mother was when she was your age," he'd said when she came home from boarding school one summer. "I need to do something about that flower of yours before you let someone have it for free."

Surprised and uncomfortable with her usually aloof father's comments, Agnes had gone to her mother.

"Take a lover," had been her mother's advice when Agnes had sought her out, shaking and uncertain. "Find pleasure in your body before he finds a way to make it feel like it doesn't belong to you." Her mother's deep umber eyes flared with an anger Agnes had never seen before. "Then make sure he knows the thing he wants to use doesn't exist anymore."

Her mother had come to her father willingly enough, young and naive and dazzled by his savagery dressed up in Savile Row suits. His love for her had been real yet obsessive, a trap she could never escape. But she'd always encouraged Agnes to be free.

Agnes quickly took her mother's advice.

There had been a boy at school, and a girl. Agnes didn't want to choose, so she took them both. The process had been easier than she thought it would be. And then that dangerous thing she once had, that awful virginity, was finally gone like unwanted and useless dead skin.

Her father hadn't been happy, but the comments had stopped.

Agnes shook herself and stood, slipped on her shoes. As always, when she thought about her father, she grew agitated. He was long dead. It should be simple to shrug off his hold on her life, on her emotions. But easier said than done.

Hours later, after finishing the rest of the day's work and getting reports back from Florida—Monique was being unknowingly pimped out by her mother and had been just hours from getting kidnapped—Agnes was still restless and agitated.

After reading Gretchen a bedtime story on FaceTime and reassuring Whit she'd be home later, she left the building cloaked in anonymity. Hair loose around her shoulders, no jewelry. Just the armor of her self-confidence as she slipped out into the darkness with her hands buried in the pockets of her coat worn unbuttoned over street clothes: ankle boots, jeans, and a red silk shirt.

She hadn't gone far before she felt a shadow somewhere behind her. Whit or someone she'd recruited followed. Agnes walked on. She no longer fooled herself into thinking she'd be on her own outside The House, not with these new threats to the business and Lola's mysterious presence.

"I hope you don't think you're being inconspicuous in that red blouse. Or with that face." The unexpected sound of Lola's voice paused Agnes's footsteps for a moment. Then she kept walking.

With every quiet step taking her further away from the busy main streets, the tension in her shoulders eased. The fists stuffed into her pockets loosened and became harmless fingers again.

Interesting.

It should've worried her more, being so easily found by this woman with suspect motives, but after dealing with Monique's situation, then the bombardment of memories from the past, the prospect of sparring with Lola was... a pleasure. The afternoon's work had felt heavy on Agnes's shoulders. Too heavy in a way it hadn't in a long time.

When Lola eventually emerged from the darkness, Agnes hid a smile as she noticed they wore nearly the same thing, except Lola's black coat was cropped, double-breasted, and short enough to show off the curve of her hips and backside in her tight jeans. Her hair was free, thick and kinky around her face, and she wore red Chuck Taylors instead of leather boots.

"I wasn't aiming for inconspicuous tonight," Agnes said in response to Lola's initial comment.

"Oh good. I'd hate for you to fail at anything." Lola kept step with her, hands also in her coat pockets, occasionally throwing Agnes a confident look filled with dimples and flirtation.

It started to rain, and the light evening sprinkle filtering through the city's smog felt good on Agnes's face. Her hair, though, wasn't quite so pleased with the change. She scraped it back into a tight bun at the back of her neck.

"So, where are we going?" Lola finally asked when they'd been walking in silence for a good ten minutes.

"I don't know. You're the one following me. You choose."

Even with the failure of the sex test not so far behind them, it felt good to see Lola again. She smelled like adventure, seemed lighter and somehow more authentic than before. And Agnes liked it very much.

Lola eyed her up and down more obviously now, apparently thinking much too hard about their destination. "Okay," she said finally. "I know just the place."

The place turned out to be a pizza parlor far from Agnes's usual stomping grounds. They walked for a long time with silence between them, the sound of their footsteps on the street, Lola pointing this way or that to guide Agnes.

"Here we are."

The bell over the door chimed when Lola pushed ahead, holding the heavy-looking door for Agnes to walk in ahead of her. "The pizza here is perfect."

One of the guys bussing the tables shouted out Lola's name, and she shouted a greeting back, complete with a wave and a smile.

They waited patiently in line, and Agnes took the time to look around. Family photos lined the walls, along with shots of a few celebrities. The inviting atmosphere surprised her, the photos of all kinds of people, not just Italians. An Asian film star she recognized, a group of Black women she didn't. A foursome of blond men who looked more like lovers than a platonic family.

"What would you like?" Lola asked when they got closer to the register.

Agnes had already scanned the menu. "A slice with Italian sausage and pineapple and a bottle of mineral water."

"Mineral water? For real?" Lola peered at her.

Agnes resisted the urge to squirm under Lola's disbelieving look. "Yes, it's what I want."

At the counter, Lola ordered for both of them, including a beer for herself.

They found an empty table and waited for their receipt number to be called.

"This place is interesting," Agnes said, surprising herself with the attempt at small talk.

Lola grinned quickly at her, mischievous with her round cheeks and sparkling eyes. "I think so too, and you'll love the food." The grin faded, and she folded and unfolded her receipt, glancing often to the front of the tiny restaurant where a coordinated trio moved easily between the yawning brick oven, the cash register, and a shrinking pile of pizza boxes. "You know, my sister was the first person to bring me here." Her eyes flickered down to the receipt. Fold. Unfold. "Our mom was always—always high or something, so I think she brought me here because she felt sorry for me. Maybe for herself too. The people here are really nice."

The words erupted in a wild burst, like bullets with a too-large target, spilling over the table between them, hot and dangerous. Lola's eyes caught Agnes's for a moment, and it seemed as if she was waiting for something.

Hopefully, it wasn't trite sympathy.

"Emotions are complicated things, especially when we're grieving." Agnes carefully avoided any meaningless platitudes. Lord knew she'd never wanted any when her father had died, especially since his passing hadn't been any kind of loss. "And it sounds like your sister was grieving while your mother was dealing with addiction. Sharing a safe space with you might have been one of the ways she was able to cope." She met Lola's eyes. "It sounds like she loves you and wants you to feel safe too."

Lola chewed on her lip, managing to look even younger than her twenty-something years. "Yeah…"

Emotion swirled in Lola's eyes, but she lowered her gaze before Agnes could pinpoint exactly what it was. Did she feel guilty bringing a stranger here?

Something cold touched Agnes's hand, and she nearly flinched back before realizing that, without her permission, her own hand had reached out to clasp Lola's. God, it really had been a long day.

She jerked her hand away, reaching for the shaker of red pepper flakes as if that had been the plan all along. And then she was just holding the thing like a fool.

She cleared her throat. "Where's your sister now?" Of course, she'd had Lola investigated and already knew the important details of her life.

Lola's gaze dipped again. "She's dead."

Agnes winced at the glimpse of Lola's pain and opened her mouth to give her condolences or something equally meaningless, but the busboy wandered by their table before she could say anything. He bumped against Lola's shoulder with a friendly elbow, and they exchanged a smile. Just like that, the look of twisted grief—or was it anger?—on Lola's face melted away. Agnes swallowed her useless words just as a too-cheerful smile turned her way. "This is a pretty cool place, huh?"

"Yes," Agnes said, watching Lola carefully. "It's certainly been intriguing."

Just like Lola herself.

Their pizza and drinks didn't take too much longer, and soon they were eating at the rickety little table, arms braced, with their pizzas held up for maximum eating efficiency.

A soft laugh came from Lola.

Agnes raised an eyebrow in question.

"I just can't believe you're here," Lola said, her mouth shiny with pizza grease. "With me. In this place."

"It's what you wanted, isn't it?"

"Yeah." Her smile faded a little. "I don't get what I want very often, so this is nice. I like it. Thanks for coming here with me."

"Of course. By the way, you're right. The pizza *is* delicious."

The slice of pie was greasy and loaded down with melted cheese, the pineapple sweet and fresh from the can tasted just perfect with the spicy Italian sausage, and the crust was just thick enough to remind Agnes she was eating carbs. It was heavenly. Or maybe Agnes enjoyed it so much because, except for a granola bar Clare had brought her sometime during the afternoon, she hadn't eaten all day.

A hum of pleasure left her throat as she enjoyed the moment of peace. Food in her belly. The usually frantic plans and strategies in her mind settled to a quiet hum. Her body relaxed. This moment wasn't what she'd set out to find when she left the building, but it was just what she needed.

From across the table, Lola's gaze found hers. "You're an incredible woman, you know that?"

"I'm not sure about that," Agnes said after swallowing her latest bite.

"You are. And of course, a little scary too." Lola breathed out a laugh and rolled her eyes. "I'm sure you already know that, though."

The quietly spoken words landed like a slap. Agnes swallowed the unexpected pain.

"My father was always the scary one," she said. Suddenly losing her appetite, she put the rest of her pizza down on the cheap plastic plate. "I never wanted to be that."

Lola looked stricken. She stopped eating too. "I didn't mean to—"

"It's fine," Agnes cut in. She tugged a napkin from the dispenser and wiped off her fingers. "Well, thanks for your company and the meal suggestion."

Fingers curled around her wrist. "Please. Don't go. I'm sorry."

"Don't be sorry for telling the truth." Chill settled into Agnes's voice, and the burdens that had seemed far away just minutes before dropped down heavily onto her shoulders. "I'll see you around."

Lola made a soft noise of denial and tightened her hold on Agnes's wrist.

Agnes could easily break that hold. Whit and various self-defense instructors had taught her that and more. Maybe she *was* scary.

"Can we just... Can we just finish our food, at least?" Lola pleaded. "I don't want to chase you off by being an idiot." The sparkle in those eyes had dimmed, and Agnes realized that the whole time they'd been on their little mini adventure, Lola hadn't seemed masked. In fact, her face was perfectly naked now. As if she actually wanted to spend time with Agnes, not linked to any agenda. Or maybe Lola was just getting better at hiding her tells.

But the skin under Lola's touch tingled with a long-forgotten pleasure. Agnes actually wanted to stay here and finish her greasy pineapple and sausage pizza with Lola.

"Okay," she said. "I'll stay."

A luminous smile broke through the clouds of unhappiness on Lola's face. "Awesome."

Agnes stayed with Lola until more people than there were available seats started crowding in, and Agnes felt guilty for taking up the space. After tossing double the normal tip on the table, she pushed out the door with Lola just behind her.

The smells from the street immediately washed over Agnes. Car exhaust, the distinct perfume of the gutter, the scent of baking pizza crust escaping the restaurant. The dark evening, pierced with streetlights and car lights, felt like a living thing brushing up against Agnes's skin. Cool but friendlier than before she and Lola had shared their meal. They stepped out of the path of foot traffic and smiled awkwardly at each other—odd when things had seemed so effortless before.

Probably meant it was time for them to part ways. Agnes tucked her hands into her coat pockets. "I'll leave you—"

"Well, I guess—"

They both started talking at the same time, then stopped. "Okay," Lola said through soft laughter. "You first. Although I think we're both saying the same thing."

"Yes, I think we are."

"Okay."

A man brushed past, and when his shoulder bumped Agnes, he aimed a curse her way. She ignored him.

"Thank you for the company," Agnes said, and she meant it. Lola's appearance out of nowhere was the rescue she didn't realize she needed.

"You're welcome. I had fun." Lola bit her lip, ducked her head. "See you soon."

Agnes drew in a slow breath. Lola was so very lovely. The glow from the streetlight filtered through the thick halo of her hair, spilling over her rounded cheeks and the soft-looking fullness of her mouth. A temptation. Agnes licked her own lips, imagining how Lola's would taste. Then, suddenly she didn't want to just imagine anymore.

This evening's emotional half-revelations had piqued Agnes's curiosity, and her desire, even more than Lola's practiced attempts at seduction from before. What kind of young woman was Lola? What exactly did she want? And how would it feel to lay her down on cool silk sheets and lick her curvaceous body from head to toe with nothing but honesty between them?

Heat settled in Agnes's belly.

Led by her want, she touched Lola's elbow, and that complicated brown gaze tangled with hers. Slowly, Agnes dipped her head and brushed her lips across Lola's. Lola gasped, an indrawn breath of air that Agnes ached to follow back between those full lips with her own. Electricity flickered between them, stroked delicious sensation along her spine, and she felt the grip of Lola's fingers in the lapels of her jacket. That tight hold, with the knuckles of Lola's hands pressing sweetly into her skin through the thick wool, gave a powerful hint that more than a kiss would be welcome. But Agnes pulled back, ignoring that hint and controlling her breathing.

"Take care," she said instead to a wide-eyed Lola, then headed back toward The House and the other responsibilities she'd managed to forget for a few unexpected moments.

CHAPTER 9

HAVING THE ANNUAL MEETING IN Las Vegas was a bit of a cliché, but maybe that was why the board had voted in favor of it. Agnes glanced at her watch as the elevator whisked her and her bodyguards, Michaela and Kyle, down to the twentieth-floor meeting rooms.

"Everyone is already there," Whit murmured from Agnes's earpiece. "Full court."

Agnes hummed in acknowledgment. That was what she expected.

Whit may have agreed to stay in New York to keep Gretchen safe and sticking to her usual routine, but she insisted on being in Vegas by way of all the gadgets she had at her disposal. A camera tucked in Agnes's brooch, a microphone in the slender watch on her wrist, and access to all the cameras in the hotel. She'd also sent along two of her most trusted bodyguards.

Agnes would accuse Whit of being a control freak if she didn't know Whit would take it as a compliment.

The elevator arrived at the twentieth floor with a sharp chime.

Her security team stepped out, looked around, and gestured for her to leave the elevator. Agnes liked to think she made things easier for them by not insisting she could take care of herself or any such nonsense. Pride goeth before the assassination.

Her high heels sank soundlessly into the thick carpet. A line of closed doors on both sides of the hallway guided her to a single open door not quite at the end of the hallway where four armed and dark-suited guards stood watching everything and everyone. Like Whit said, Agnes was last to arrive.

The long, oval table with its eleven chairs was full except for a single place. Each of the directors had their own security standing behind them while they occupied themselves with electronic gadgets and waited for the meeting to start. More than one pair of eyes followed Agnes as she crossed the room and took her seat.

An alarm chimed.

"Right on time as usual, *your highness*."

"I do try to be punctual." Agnes unbuttoned her jacket and ignored the sarcasm-laced honorific from Daniel, this year's chairperson. She slid her chair up to the table on its silent wheels and took out her phone.

"Where's your main guard dog?" Elena, a gray-haired woman with the face of a bulldog, asked and pointedly looked around.

"Right here, you fuck," Whit growled through the earpiece, and Agnes nearly rolled her eyes at their usual animosity.

"Why don't you try something and find out?" Agnes smiled placidly.

Daniel tapped his gavel. "Okay, now we've gotten *that* out of the way, can we begin?"

"Ready whenever you are," Agnes said while other murmurs of assent rippled around the table.

"I officially call the annual meeting of the Pacific-Atlantic Consortium of Houses to order."

They spent a few minutes on roll call, noting that all eleven directors of the most powerful houses in the US were in attendance. Although their alliance hadn't been strictly necessary, Agnes had carefully cultivated it once she'd taken over the business. The members of the Consortium collectively provided the best selection of exclusive, talented, and expensive escorts in the United States. They pooled their resources to make sure the right officials were paid off, security provided, and standards of excellence maintained. They even had a DC lobbyist. Each member house maintained its own business, but if anyone outside the Consortium came after any of the houses, then that threat would be dealt with by all.

Daniel, with the roll call completed, droned on about collective security, something Whit had already taken care of. That left Agnes's brain free to drift to Lola and their unexpected evening of pizza and confessions. Tendrils of emotional connection had wound between them at that little table, leaving Agnes vulnerable and even a little scared. Okay, a lot scared.

It had been that fear that had made her leave Lola a text message before coming to Vegas.

A gently cleared throat from behind Agnes brought her attention back to the meeting. One of her bodyguards. Cheeks warming, she stopped doodling in her notes app. God, she was one junior prom date away from looping her name with Lola's inside a heart.

A quick glance around the room assured her that no one else had noticed her lagging attention. She exhaled a quiet sigh.

"We haven't heard from the Walkers in a few weeks," Stephanie Diaz was saying. She was from the Diaz house in California, an organization that sniffed out weakness from a thousand miles away.

"They're not great communicators," a voice at the far end of the table said. Geoffrey Rake, a man who thought he was Agnes's rival.

"True, but we have to look out for potential trouble as well." Agnes slipped easily back into the ongoing conversation. "No one has been in touch with their director since the end of summer." Nearly three months ago, according to Whit's sources.

"Have we done a security check?" Diaz asked.

"Not yet." Rake sounded unconcerned. "We didn't want to jump the gun."

"Didn't want to jump the gun?" Whit's voice sounded in Agnes's ear. "They know damn well this isn't a business where you just wait and see what the wind carries your way."

They all knew that, with the exception of Tallulah who worked out of Nevada, most of their business interests were illegal. Someone or something was always waiting to trip them up. It paid to anticipate the currents of change, remain on guard, and be ready to destroy an enemy should one emerge.

"Send Tallulah to check things out." Agnes made a note on her phone to contact Tully herself.

"I agree," a woman from one of the Southern houses said.

"And *we*—" Daniel stressed the word. "—are all going to pay for this welfare check, I assume."

"As we've all agreed to, yes." The eyeroll was obvious in Diaz's voice.

"But what if they're just keeping the shutters tight and taking a little vacation?"

"Then we'll just pay the investigating team's fee, and that's it. None of us at this table are poor," Agnes said. At least not according to the financials anyone had already shared.

"Good," Daniel said. "Next order of business."

"I'd like to make a complaint," Rake spoke up again. "Or maybe just an observation."

Daniel nodded. "Go on."

"One of my assets turned up dead last month." The look on his face said it only mildly irritated him, but maybe that irritation masked something else.

"And you didn't have anything to do with that?" someone at the other end of the table asked.

"Of course not," Rake said with an impatient growl. "I'm in this to make money, not throw it off a pier with weights around its ankles."

"Is that what happened to your girl?" Diaz asked.

"Looks that way." Rake's mouth tightened. "My contact with the cops says they aren't looking too hard, since she was an escort, but I need to check this out, not just for my business but for her family."

Daniel set down the gavel to type something on his tablet. "Send me whatever info you have on the situation, and we'll see what we can find." He looked up briefly. "Let's put the security team on this one too, just in case."

Rake nodded, apparently satisfied.

Hopefully, this situation was an isolated incident, something personal instead of something that could affect them all. Agnes lightly tapped her finger on the table as her thoughts followed one after the other. All of her people were safe, but did this incident have anything to do with the businesses burning down and the attempts on her cash?

"I'm already looking into this," Whit said in Agnes's ear. "It might be nothing, but we don't want any more assets dying if this is the start of a new string of escort killings."

Already, predators found it easy to pick off working girls and rent boys. The ones who worked the streets had it worse, but the people who worked for the House still needed protection. None had died under Agnes's watch, and she intended to keep it that way.

The meeting went on for another five hours, thankfully covering most of the weekend's agenda. If Agnes could leave earlier than Sunday evening, it would be a win for everyone, including Gretchen, who she'd promised a trip up north to go ride horses.

By the time the meeting ended for the day, it was fully dark. The lights of Vegas lit up The Strip, and the air was thick with the anticipation of the night's continuing party. Business was done. Time for the strippers and cocaine.

Because she wanted to exchange a few quiet words with Whit, Agnes was one of the last to spill out of the conference room. She walked between Michaela and Kyle, who scanned the space on either side of the door before allowing her to walk through.

"One moment, ma'am." Kyle stepped in front of Agnes just in time to intercept Geoffrey Rake, who came striding out of an elevator with a pair of guards of his own. The intent look on Rake's face made clear his path wasn't a coincidence.

Agnes stiffened.

He greeted her with a nod. "Can I speak with you for a moment in private?"

The hallway was empty except for the six of them.

"This is as private as it's going to get," Agnes said, keeping her voice neutral yet firm. Experience had taught her not to trust anyone, especially when they were deliberately trying to remove her from her security.

Irritation tightened Rake's narrow lips. When he stepped close, Michaela put a hand on her gun, forcing him to come to a halt.

"A warning then." Rake lowered his voice. "You may think you're being clever, but you're not your father. If I've noticed what you're doing, other people have too." He paused, eyes boring into Agnes with a meaningful glint she couldn't decipher. "Just watch your back."

"What exactly do you think I'm doing so unsuccessfully?"

A corner of his mouth curved up, but it wasn't a smile. "I'll give you some advice, Agnes. Taking things that don't belong to you have long-term consequences. You can't keep skimming from someone else's pot and not expect the same thing to happen to you. Karma doesn't give a shit about your intentions."

As Rake spoke, fear traced an icy finger down Agnes's spine, but she kept her expression blank. "Warning noted. Thank you, Geoffrey."

"Just don't forget what I said and who said it."

"Of course."

With a nod, Rake turned and ducked into an open elevator along with his security guys. The doors closed.

Agnes slowly uncurled the fingers that had tightened into a fist at her side. His last words, more than anything else he'd said, worried her.

"He thinks something's coming," Whit said in her ear.

"Or he *knows* something's coming."

Whit hummed in agreement, computer keys already clicking on her side of the phone. "I'm putting out some feelers now. If someone's making a move, I should be able to find out."

"Let me know as soon as you do."

Agnes blew out a slow breath. There was a shelf life to what she was doing. If she'd continued her father's business as it was, only with the security upgrades and assured streams of income, she could have continued indefinitely, even passed it on to Gretchen if that had been her eventual goal. But supporting her assets, eliminating sex traffickers when she found them, shutting down the pimps and madams who made a habit of both casual and unrelenting cruelty while also staying ahead of the cops, was a balancing act nearly impossible to maintain.

For more than five years, she'd kept that balance. It was hard work, though, and every year it seemed to get harder. Keeping a handle on the threats to her life and her business was like an endless game of Whack-a-Mole. Just exhausting.

But it was worth it.

"That should be it for the day," she said to Michaela and Kyle. "Let's head upstairs."

Once on her floor, she told her bodyguards to head to their own rooms, and they reluctantly obeyed. Her only plan for the rest of the night involved whiskey and a long bath.

Walking slowly down the carpeted hallway toward her room, she eased off the jacket and draped it over her arm. Maybe she'd give Lola a call. There was nothing wrong with—

"Queen Agnes."

Adrenaline kicked into action before her brain processed what was going on. Her hand was up, firmly gripping the small handgun she kept holstered at the small of her back when Whit hissed in her ear, "I told you not to let Michaela and Kyle go until you're in your room!" Whit said a few other things, but since it was mostly curse words, Agnes felt free to ignore them. "I'm getting them back up there."

"Please! Don't shoot." A small figure emerged from behind a pillar— what idiot thought putting a pillar in the middle of a wide and supposedly secure floor was a good idea?—and took off her oversized sunglasses. "I just want to talk," she stammered. "I don't—I don't have a gun or anything like that."

Agnes didn't move her finger from the trigger. The words "don't shoot" didn't mean the person talking wasn't about to shoot first.

"Who are you, and what do you want?" In Agnes's ear, Whit issued quick and clear commands, her fingers tapping furiously on her computer keyboard. "Don't wake Gretchen," Agnes murmured to Whit as she cautiously approached the stranger.

The woman was young, slender, with pretty skin and thick hair that moved around her extraordinary face like a cloud. A bruise darkened one eye.

"Asylum," the woman said when Agnes got close enough that neither of them had to shout. Then she gave the verbal password a genuine asylum seeker would know, one given to them in the careful underground network Agnes had set up.

Every sound on Whit's end of the line stopped.

Agnes eased off the trigger just as her heartbeat began slowing from its panicked gallop. Rake's warning came back to her, and she wondered just how much of a coincidence this stranger's sudden appearance was. She didn't lower the gun.

Beyond the woman's shoulder, the hallway was clear. Agnes had asked for a floor to herself; not even security was up here with her.

"Who has your contract?" she asked.

The woman told her, and Agnes did what she always did when a woman asked her for help. She helped.

"Whit. Did you get all that?"

"Yes, I'm on it now." The slow and easy sound of Whit's breathing helped to keep Agnes calm. "Running facial recognition."

"What's your name?" Agnes asked.

"Leticia Moore," Whit and the woman said at the same time.

Although Leticia looked as if she'd had a rough time, Agnes and Whit had learned their lesson the second year when a woman had come to them saying she was trying to escape an abusive pimp. Turned out she was the pimp's sister and had faked her story, trying to find out the reason her brother was losing so many of his girls. Between facial recognition software, fingerprint and background checks, plus an extended network of allies, they now rooted out potential infiltrators before they got too far.

"Let's get you out of this hallway," Agnes said just as her two bodyguards appeared. Their guns were raised, but she didn't lower hers.

Michaela's jacket was missing, her blouse buttoned wrong, as if she'd managed to strip off some of the day's responsibilities before Whit had called her back to work. Kyle, though, was as starched and proper as when they'd started their day.

"What are your orders?" Kyle asked.

"Cover me," Agnes said. "I'm taking her to one of the empty rooms."

Grumbling through the earpiece, Whit told Agnes which room to use and snapped at the guards not to lower their weapons, no matter how cute and innocent the woman looked.

But Leticia didn't look innocent at all. With her bruised face, her body poured into a skintight designer dress, and her stilettos, she could easily have been one of the knowing women who worked in The House.

"Come." Once she opened the room with her key card, Agnes gestured for Leticia to step inside ahead of her and her security team.

The door shut behind them.

"Sit, Leticia."

As Agnes and the woman sat, Michaela closed the curtains, shutting out the darkened sky and the bright lights of the Vegas Strip.

Kyle kept his gun trained on Leticia.

"Now, tell us what you need." Agnes crossed her legs and carefully watched Leticia's face.

"I want to leave." Leticia's voice trembled. "I want to leave here so nobody can ever find me again."

Hands folded in her lap, Agnes forced a patience she didn't feel. Leaving wasn't easy. Leticia was speaking from panic. She probably hadn't thought much beyond escaping the people who'd put the fight-or-flight into her. *If this wasn't some kind of setup.*

"Where do you want to go?"

Leticia looked startled at the question, as if she hadn't anticipated being given the choice. She gnawed at her lower lip. "Anywhere." Her eyes flicked between Agnes and the two guards who now stood at the door, watching. "Isn't that what you do? Take people like me away?"

"It isn't that simple," Agnes said quietly. "I need to know what you're running from. What you want to do now that you've walked away."

"They know I ran!" Panic sharpened Leticia's voice. "If they find me, they'll kill me."

"All right."

Michaela appeared with a tray of whiskey, two glasses, and a bottle of mineral water with drops of condensation running down its green sides.

Agnes thanked her. "Would you like a drink?" Before Leticia could refuse or accept, Agnes poured a measure of sparkling water and whiskey in each glass. "Take whichever one you like."

After a quick hesitation, Leticia took the glass farther from her, then waited until Agnes had a sip before drinking. Leticia winced after a quick swallow.

"Take your time." Agnes savored the complex flavors the liquor left on her tongue.

"So far, everything about her checks out," Whit said.

That was a start.

The silence in the room couldn't have been more than a few minutes, but it felt like a small forever. Exhaustion settled like a too-heavy blanket over Agnes's shoulders, and she rolled them back, closing her eyes. She wanted a bath and a real drink and bed. Maybe even some dinner. But this was important.

"I want to leave—leave the country," Leticia finally bit out. "Go to someplace in Canada."

"Okay. We can help you do that."

When Leticia put her glass down, Kyle quickly lifted her fingerprints with a piece of plastic film and slipped out of the room.

Michaela stayed close, her gun held easily in one hand.

"What's that about?" Leticia watched Kyle go with a frown.

"A way to help keep all of us safe." Agnes drew a breath. "Now, this is what you'll need to do…"

By the time Michaela escorted Leticia, semi-disguised in yoga pants and a hooded shirt, from the room and out to a waiting car heading for a temporary safe house, it was nearly midnight. Agnes was tired but felt… good. Between making arrangements for Leticia, she'd taken a break to call Gretchen and whisper a quiet story to her over speakerphone until she fell asleep and Whit came back on the line.

With everything settled, Agnes nodded a good night to Kyle, who insisted on staying at the door to the suite until she went inside. The thought of a hot bath had her moaning with anticipated pleasure. Although, since it was so late now, she might just settle for a scalding shower, skip the drink and food, and head straight to bed. Tomorrow was another early morning. The second and last one for the weekend. Yes, that actually sounded perfect. Sliding between crisp sheets with her skin still warm from a shower. Tomorrow she'd made time for a long soak in the oversized tub.

In the bathroom, she unbuttoned her skirt and wriggled out of the silk.

Someone knocked at the suite's main door.

A sigh flowed past her lips. She'd figured Vegas would keep her busy, but this was a little ridiculous. Hastily throwing on a hotel robe, she went to see who was at the door.

"What's the point of being the boss if I can't—" Her words tumbled to a halt the same time her belly dipped.

The woman in the doorway flashed a set of dimples, eyes broadcasting a complication of feelings Agnes noticed with just one look.

"I'm not as easy to get rid of as your other one-night stands," Lola said with a savage grin. "Are you going to let me in?"

CHAPTER 10

Lola could feel a pout coming. Agnes didn't look as surprised as she'd hoped.

After all, *she* had been surprised when Maddie had called to tell her that this week was the annual meeting of some of the most powerful escort agencies in the United States. Maddie, who'd lived in Vegas before being lured to New York, said the meeting had been a huge deal for working girls and rent boys back in the day. Escorts who wanted to work for a top-notch house flocked to Vegas in hopes of catching the interest of these big dogs. Agnes would be there, she'd whispered as if giving up a big secret, and Maddie could get Lola into the hotel if Lola wanted to find a way to grab the queen's attention.

When Lola told Jamika about Maddie's tip, Jamika had practically shoved her on the plane to Vegas. Now that they were in the thick of things, Jamika badly wanted the bust.

Lola badly wanted something too. She gave Agnes her least innocent smile.

"Technically, to be a one-night stand—," Agnes said from the doorway of her opulent penthouse suite "—we'd have to spend an actual night together. Having sex, not eating pizza and discussing past trauma. At least that's according to the rumors I've heard."

She sounded so prissy it was almost cute. Lola stuffed her hands in the back pockets of her jeans and rocked back on her heels. She knew the move pushed out her boobs through her unzipped leather jacket, and she bit the corner of her mouth to stifle a smile of victory when Agnes dipped her gaze to look.

"Fine, come in." Agnes moved aside, and the slight motion fluttered the thin hotel robe around her body. Tiredness pulled down the corners of her mouth.

When the bright idea to confront Agnes in Vegas came to her, Lola had seen it all in her mind in crackling detail. Agnes being ruthlessly in control and doing her usual impression of walking sex. The two of them going back and forth about Lola's right to be in Vegas, Agnes trying—and failing—to push aside all attempts to get them into bed. Then orgasm prizes for both of them. But Lola hadn't counted on seeing Agnes like this. She looked exhausted and all too human.

It pricked the air out of Lola's victory balloon. But she couldn't afford to back down.

"Don't pretend a one-night thing wasn't what you wanted when we bumped into each other at that bar." Never mind that she'd been the one to arrange that little *bump*. "If your phone hadn't interrupted us, I'd already know what you taste like." She smiled aggressively, showing nearly all her teeth. "Nice place, by the way." Ignoring the visceral effect Agnes's scent had on her, she slipped past Agnes and farther into the room. "But I guess someone like you wouldn't be in a place that isn't nice."

You're the one in charge here, Lola lied to herself and kept her shoulders low and relaxed, shrugging off her jacket and deliberately throwing it on the couch to disturb the crisp neatness of the suite that was too big for only one person. Was Agnes expecting company?

"Please, make yourself comfortable." Agnes invited with a wry twist of her mouth.

"I will, thanks." Lola prowled the suite, poked her head into the bedroom and gave a wolf whistle of appreciation. "Definitely fit for a queen."

She didn't miss the way Agnes stiffened. *Gotcha.* With that sign of Agnes's discomfort, Lola's own body relaxed, and she felt more in control, more certain of her reason for being there.

Agnes stood near the door, her arms crossed in a classic power pose. "What brings you here, Lola?"

"I came to ask why you brushed me off."

"My message was self-explanatory."

Thank you for your interest in H Holdings. Unfortunately, you're not a good fit for us at this time.

The message had jammed a spike of pain behind her breastbone. It had come to Lola's phone the day after she and Agnes had sat across from each other at Matteo's pizza parlor and shared things Lola never expected. They'd connected. Although, to be fair, what kind of true connection could it have been when Lola had been lying to Agnes and Agnes had killed Lola's sister?

Pain twisted in Lola's belly, and she glanced away from Agnes. How could she be really attracted to Agnes when Agnes had taken Zoe from her?

Lola's own instincts, stupid as they were, had told her time and time again that Agnes didn't have anything to do with Zoe's disappearance. But that could just be her conscience trying to rationalize her desire to jump Agnes's bones.

So not the point of why she was there. She shook her head. Focus.

She was there to get into The House—or Agnes—and find the queen's weaknesses.

You're not a good fit for us at this time.

Bullshit.

Lola had set herself up to be nearly a carbon copy of Zoe. Already similar to her model-thin sister in height—though definitely not weight—she'd put on the makeup, worn the sexy clothes, and become the kind of universal hottie Zoe had impersonated on social media before she disappeared. Lola made sure she was the perfect bait. Except for not having sex with Agnes when the script had called for it, she was the perfect escort for The House.

"Nope. I won't accept that," Lola said.

Agnes raised an eyebrow. "Excuse me?"

"You want me. We both know it. I'm here. You can take me anytime you want. For the House or for yourself. It doesn't matter."

"Why are you so eager to get close to me?" Agnes asked the question as if she already knew the answer.

Lola hoped Agnes thought it was only because of her looks, her wealth, maybe even her obviously incredible body.

"Because I want you." That was part of the truth after all.

A harsh crack of laughter destroyed the resulting silence.

Lola flinched. Wearing a smile that had not even a trace of amusement in it, Agnes walked away, tightening the belt on her robe as she went. The motion of her butt under the thin silk distracted Lola for a hot minute before she got her mind back on track.

Mostly.

"I want this. You do too." Lola approached Agnes like a skittish animal, even though the last thing she thought Agnes would do was run from her. Or anyone. "Don't deny it."

Agnes turned, the Vegas skyline glowing through the floor-to-ceiling windows at her back. The sight of her like this took Lola back to that afternoon in the penthouse. When she'd prepared herself to have sex with some random person and then with Agnes, all gorgeous and overwhelming in her power suit, only to be turned away. She'd burned with shame that day, felt like she wasn't enough.

"Since I'm not in the habit of lying to myself," Agnes said, "I won't in this case. From the night we met, I wanted you." Something shimmered across her face, a silverfish of feeling that caught the light before darting back beneath calm waters. "Since then, you've turned up wanting to work for me, and that necessitated a shift in my priorities." The artificial lights of the Vegas night glimmered behind her like diamonds thrown up against an inky sky. "I won't get off at the expense of my business, my privacy, or whatever it is you want to take from me. This means saying 'no, thank you' to your offer to work for The House."

Lola froze. The lump in her throat threatened to rise up and tumble out of her mouth in an avalanche of denial. Swallowing hard, she stopped it just in time. Agnes's suspicions were normal enough. Lola just hadn't realized how strong they were. How could she push past them without being too obvious?

She had to get closer to the queen.

She had to find closure for Zoe.

Still floundering, she was on the edge of saying something desperate to get past Agnes's suspicions when Agnes brushed past her and headed to the bar.

"I need a drink for this conversation." Agnes scraped a hand through her loosely fastened hair, pushing aside hairpins and sending the thick darkness tumbling down her back. "You're obviously not going to make this easy," she said over her shoulder. "Have a seat." Her voice suddenly sounded as tired as she looked.

Guilt sank Lola's teeth into the inside of her cheek until she tasted blood. Agnes was obviously exhausted, and Lola was cornering her instead of letting her sleep.

That's exactly what you want. Catch her off guard. Get her to trust you so you can yank her off that damn throne and do what you came here for.

But the words weren't as encouraging as they should have been. Lola pressed her lips together to stop herself from apologizing. "No, thanks. I'll stand." She followed Agnes to the bar, watched her pour from an expensive-looking bottle. Two glasses. "I don't drink…whatever that is."

"It's whiskey." Agnes finished pouring, picked up the two glasses clinking with ice and liquor, and pushed one toward Lola.

Lola scrambled to grab the glass before it slipped through her nervous fingers and crashed to the marble floor. The heavy glass firmly in her grasp, Lola looked up, cheeks burning, expecting to see a smirk turned her way for acting like a nervous kid.

But Agnes's look was only coolly assessing. She paused with her own glass to her lips. "Drink up. Maybe it'll help you too."

Maybe that was the secret behind everything Agnes had in her grasp—that low and intense voice that dared anyone to disobey her. Lola had the taste of whiskey on her tongue before she could think to refuse the command.

"Fuck!" The taste was hot. Pure freaking fire. Uselessly fanning her mouth, Lola gasped as the liquor burned her throat all the way to her stomach, where it sat like a brazier. "How can you drink this stuff?"

"You sip, for one thing, not guzzle it like beer."

Lola was too busy dealing with the fire in her throat to make a proper comeback right away. She swallowed again and blew out a breath to cool her mouth. "You're trying to poison me." So much for trying to look sexy and down for anything.

"Only if I'm trying to poison myself too." Agnes pointedly took another sip from her glass, the corner of her mouth curved up in amusement.

"Fuck…" Lola said again, all her eloquence gone, even though she couldn't bring herself to regret it just yet. "You probably have apple juice in that."

"Care to test your theory?" Agnes offered her glass with another of her annoyingly raised eyebrows.

A quick shake of her head and a step back was all Lola was capable of for the moment. Her glass clicked against the bar's marble top as she forcefully abandoned it. "I'm not falling for another of your tricks."

"It's not a trick if it's the truth." Agnes headed to the couch. A low sigh left her slightly parted lips as she lowered herself into the corner of the massive thing, an arm extended along its back, her legs tucked together in a move that was both elegant and sexy. Lola's tongue fell out of her mouth a little. "But back to our discussion. I believe you were telling me what you're doing here."

Get it together, Lola.

Lola licked her lips and then, after a brief hesitation, grabbed her abandoned glass of liquor. Maybe Agnes was right and she needed this liquid courage for whatever she was about to do. She sat on the opposite end of the couch with the drink cradled in her palm. Clearing her throat, Lola said, "About what you said earlier. I don't want to take anything from you but that sexy robe you've got on."

The look on Agnes's face said she wasn't buying the bullshit, though. Lola gripped the glass and resisted the suicidal urge to knock back another swallow. Only the thought of gasping and coughing like an idiot again in front of the untouchable—if tired—queen kept the glass right where it was.

"Okay, fine. Let's say I *do* want something from you—and by *something*, I mean sex, let's be clear—what would it hurt to give in to whatever it is that's going on between us? We're both adults, and it is just sex after all."

"It's never *just* sex." Agnes shifted on the sofa to cross her long legs, making her robe gape over her smooth thighs and knees. "It's power, or it's control, or it's manipulation, or it's money." A finger tapped against her whiskey glass for emphasis. "I don't plan on giving up any of those things to you, or to anyone."

"Does that mean you're not planning on having sex anytime soon?"

Agnes pursed her lips, and Lola's eyes immediately fell to them. They were painted a deep red and glistened from the hellfire hot liquor she was drinking. "Maybe yes," she murmured. "Maybe no."

Lola swallowed.

A current passed between them, a flash of heated connection Lola felt in her belly and lower.

"You should lean more toward a 'yes,'" Lola said, all bluster and bullshit. "I'm nowhere near as powerful as you think. If anything, I'll be the one giving up control or getting manipulated every which way. Isn't that what cougars are all about?"

Agnes winced, but it seemed like a performance more than any real reaction to Lola calling her predatory or old. Gaze unwavering, she took another sip of her whiskey, and Lola found herself mirroring the action. "And the money part of this?" Agnes asked.

This time, Lola managed not to choke when the whiskey scorched her throat going down. "That's up to you, right?" She swallowed the cough rising up in the whiskey's wake, eyes watering a little. "You had the chance to make money off me, but you blew it. It's not too late, though. I'm still very available."

Silence fell heavily in the room.

The touch of Agnes's dark eyes on Lola's face, on her hands nervously toying with the whiskey glass, felt even heavier. Her expression, though, was shuttered, nothing Lola was able to read. "You're giving me a lot of words, but I still don't hear the truth," she finally said, then stood up with her now empty glass. Was she going to throw Lola out?

"Wait!" Lola jumped to her feet so fast she almost fell.

Agnes didn't stop. At the fancy bar, she grabbed the whiskey bottle and kept walking. "If you want to keep talking, come with me. If you don't, the door is right behind you."

Lola darted a gaze at her escape route. She should leave. Her heart banged around inside her chest as if it were searching for its own way out. Teasing a predator like Agnes wouldn't end anywhere good. But the dark promise in Agnes's eyes—plus the promise she'd made for Zoe—demanded that Lola follow through with what she started.

The whiskey sloshed around in the glass when she stood up and followed Agnes where she led. The *where* turned out to be a spiral staircase just out of sight of the suite's entrance. A flash of a bare foot disappearing upward teased Lola.

Lola grabbed on tight to the railing for balance, her heart thundering harder, and followed Agnes up and up, a snail's coiling path, until the stairs spit her out directly under the night sky. Standing on the rooftop terrace, clutching the barely touched glass of whiskey, Lola swallowed her fear and whatever reluctance she had.

The evening was chilled and quiet, and the madness of The Strip felt far away. Clouds moved overhead in slow motion, shadows across an even darker sky. Moonlight was only a dream there despite the full belly of the half-moon. Lola imagined she felt it against her cheek, though. A cool light.

A quick sip of the whiskey had her breathing out a fiery but steadier breath. The rooftop was fancy, as nice as any of the New York versions she'd seen in real estate magazines or in person when she and Jamika, on bored weekends, pretended to be a couple shopping for multi-million-dollar penthouses.

A border of short palm trees, their fronds green and lush, provided absolute privacy. Different types of cacti, some brightly flowering, perched in their prickly corners of the terrace while a half a dozen lounge chairs surrounded a quietly burbling hot tub attached to a small swimming pool. Soft lighting illuminated the space. It was beautiful, an oasis under the naked desert sky.

Lola didn't belong here. She clasped her hands around the whiskey glass, and the condensation from the ice wet her palms, helped to still her nerves.

She hadn't come all this way to be intimidated and sent home like the first loser in some game show. She quietly breathed in her relaxation and breathed out her nervousness. Just in time, too, since, at that moment, Agnes turned her back to the million-dollar view and confronted Lola with an unyielding gaze.

"So, you want to talk? Talk." Agnes poured herself more alcohol, then discarded the bottle on a nearby table. The movement loosened something on her robe, and it slithered a little away from the modest curves of her chest. A black lace bra peeked out.

The sight of that lace pressed so intimately close to Agnes's skin dried Lola's mouth all the way up. A fine shudder quaked her thighs, raced up her spine. The back of her neck felt hot.

God, she was weak.

But for the sake of her sister and the ones she could still save, she couldn't afford to be.

This was the woman who ran an empire on the backs of exploited men and women. What the fuck was wrong with Lola that she was so ready to roll over for Agnes? And not even because she was being manipulated but because she desperately wanted to touch every inch of that long and graceful body.

Didn't that make it easier, though, a part of her rationalized. If she enjoyed the sex, that would make the act more convincing and would get her closer to her goal of taking Agnes all the way down.

Yes. That was it.

Lola knocked back the last of the whiskey, quickly swallowing down the heat, and put aside the empty glass.

"You've made up your mind about something then?" Agnes abandoned her own glass on a nearby table and stood with her hands on her hips, her head cocked to one side. The lights glowed over her skin, the glossy fall of her hair. The silk of her robe was like water, flowing over her curves.

Lola drew another breath. She didn't come here to lose. Not this time.

In the New York penthouse, she'd been too much of a coward, waiting for the queen to take her or not. That wouldn't work here. She crossed the distance, aware of the way her jeans—her best pair—clung to her hips, how her tight T-shirt showed off her breasts and the tie at the side made her waist look even smaller. She licked her lips, trying for the right mix of seduction and certainty she assumed someone like Agnes would like.

"I've waited forever just to kiss you," she said. She was verbally feeling her way around, and the look on Agnes's face said she knew it. Lola's mask was in tatters, and she felt naked without it. Vulnerable and childish.

Agnes didn't move. "You haven't kissed me yet."

Lola's stomach dove and twisted with nerves and nausea as if she were standing at the top of a sea cliff, about to plunge down into uncertainty.

Women like Agnes were used to high heels and sex tricks—people who knew what they wanted and how to take it. Lola had been giving her that kind of vibe up until now, but maybe she was going about it all wrong. She kicked off the stupidly uncomfortable high heels.

And stepped forward. Jittery, trying to convince herself she had everything she needed: her breasts bare underneath her thin T-shirt, this dirty town, even the night sky. The lack of stars was its own seduction.

Something she could use. Darkness above and the lights of Vegas down below, glowing and nearly out of sight.

Lola took another breath. Shaking. The darkness and the light and everything in between moved through her the closer she got to where Agnes stood, waiting. Then she dared to reach out and touch.

"No." The one word was like a slap. Hard and loud, and Lola flinched from it. Her arms fell back to her sides.

"You don't get to touch me."

The sting of rejection burned through Lola's cheeks, rolling down her throat and into her chest like acid. Her arms hung uselessly at her sides. It shouldn't hurt this much. This was a game. Agnes was her prey. The woman she hoped to lure into danger so she could save others. This unwanted attraction she felt was nothing special. Nothing personal. But the choking lump in her throat told a different story.

Lola opened her mouth to throw out some bravado, but Agnes stopped it with a touch. Her finger skimmed over Lola's parted lips, warm and light as a summer breeze, and when Lola's tongue darted out, beyond her control, she tasted whiskey.

"You're entirely too naive for whatever game you're playing," Agnes said, then replaced the quieting finger with her mouth.

Lola's belly dipped. Her breath rushed out. The pulse of arousal she'd felt from that single touch of Agnes's finger against her lips, her tongue, was nothing compared to the sudden flame of lust that engulfed her, ravaging her body from lips to lips. "Oh!"

Hands gripped her arms, gentle but unyielding. Warm. Agnes's mouth pressed against hers, then moved, catching the corner of her surprise-parted lips, first one side, nearly a kiss on the cheek, and then the other.

"Is this what you wanted?" Warm breath licked her when Agnes spoke. "Is the game everything you thought it would be?" A hot tongue teased at her lips, eased them open, and instantly, Lola was lost. A pathetic little moan leaked out of her.

She met that whiskey-warm tongue with her own and shivered, reached out to grip Agnes and pull her closer, but Agnes caught her hands in mid-movement and trapped them behind her back.

"Oh!" Lola whimpered again, and her knees nearly buckled.

Wetness flooded between her legs from the incredibly hot power move that trapped her hands behind her back and, at the same time, pressed her breasts against Agnes. Her nipples ached. She writhed and panted with humiliating desperation, chasing after some friction to ease that hurt, to satisfy it.

"I want—I want to touch you." She gasped the words into Agnes's mouth, filled with desperation to feel the softness of that silken robe beneath her palms. "Please."

Why are you begging? Stop begging. But the voice at the back of her head was faint and getting fainter by the moment with each seductive stroke of Agnes's tongue against hers, every desperate motion she made against Agnes's slender body. Her thighs shifted. Her pulse galloped. Her breathing faltered. She grasped for Agnes again but still couldn't break the iron grip.

"Touching me is not an option," Agnes said, and it was only the breathlessness of her voice, proof she wasn't immune to what was happening between them, that kept Lola from wrenching away with embarrassment.

She fell back against something, one of the lounge chairs maybe, and gasped from the shock, then pleasure, when Agnes fell on top of her, slotting a thigh between Lola's. The thigh flexed. Lola whimpered again.

Already, this was good, *so* good, and all Agnes had done was kiss her. Lola had had plenty of sex in her life, but already, this experience with Agnes was putting all that past pleasure to shame. She was swollen. Slick. Desperate.

Her nails sank into the thick fabric of the lounge chair when Agnes's mouth left hers and moved south.

Control. It felt as if they were both fighting for it, and Lola knew she was losing. Regret scraped through her only briefly just before Agnes's hands, firm and unhesitating, released the button and zipper of her jeans, then pulled the pants down. She moaned at the faint puff of breath on her needful flesh. No actual touch, just the threat of pleasure hovering there. The sensation set her body alight, and she shuddered, arched up into Agnes, against the tight grip keeping her hands locked behind her back.

"You want this?" The question was another breath of torture against the wet and aching flesh Agnes had bared.

"Yes," Lola panted, unable to keep quiet. "Yes." She was going crazy with just how much she *wanted.*

A hot, hovering breath pulled the anticipation tight in her belly. Then. Agnes's tongue moved her in the faintest of touches, trailing bliss through Lola's body. Wetness like she had never felt before trickled from between her thighs. Each moan that wrenched itself from her throat was a thanksgiving, a blessing, a benediction.

It shouldn't be like this. It shouldn't.

Lola had been with lots of women, maybe dozens, in the pursuit of pleasure. But nothing had ever felt like this. So good. The universe was truly playing a joke on her. She blinked wildly up at the starless night, the breath huffing past her dry lips as she writhed and fought against the hands holding her captive and against her own need to give as she was receiving.

A sharp pain raced through her shoulder just as she felt a pop. She cried out but didn't stop, couldn't stop. The muscles of her belly tightened as she writhed, moved, thrust up helplessly against the hot mouth wrecking all of her resolutions.

Firm hands gripped her hips. Her hips? She was free? Yes, the hands that had trapped her own behind her back were gone, allowing her to touch if she wanted to. But Agnes's earlier words were a kind of shackle.

You don't get to move right now.

Lola cried out from the persistent pleasure of Agnes's tongue on her flesh and the incredible suction of her mouth. She could only dig her nails harder into the lounge chair and wail. Is this what being the madam of a hundred exclusive escorts meant? That she had the very gods of pleasure at her service and used her unfair skill at sex to turn out women and men just trying to do the right thing?

Vaguely, Lola heard her own cries of pleasure as Agnes tore her apart. The orgasm ripped a shout from her. Her body quaked, and the whole of her was electrified, as if she'd come too close to a bright, dangerous thing and been burned.

"Do you like this?" Agnes whispered.

Quivering and breathless, Lola opened her eyes to see Agnes crouched between her spread thighs, mouth wet from Lola's pleasure, her gaze as savage as that of a hunting hawk.

Lola panted. "Can't you tell?"

"I don't like to assume," Agnes murmured. Her fingers slid inside Lola, a sudden fullness, and yanked back the receding waves of pleasure, bringing them crashing over Lola again. Tears leaked from the corners of Lola's eyes, and she panted, her fingers ravaging the chair underneath her.

Oh God. It wasn't fair!

"What's not fair?" Agnes's voice was gravel. Her lush mouth slick.

She'd said that out loud? Lola squeezed her eyes shut. She had to. That one glimpse of Agnes nearly destroyed her. The robe slipping down her shoulders to bare more of the lacy black bra, the swell of her breasts and a nipple Lola's mouth watered to taste. And—God!—the slow, rolling movement of her sweat-dampened arm, a hand moving out of sight between her own legs.

Agnes was touching herself.

Was she as hot and incredibly turned-on as Lola? Would she allow Lola to just taste and not touch? Lola licked her lips, thirsty beyond belief. In all the years she'd been having sex, she'd never been one to just lie there and take whatever her lover dished out. But she apparently had a fetish for following orders.

What did Agnes just ask?

Lola pressed her lips together, trying her best to stifle her cry of pleasure, but she was too late. "You're too good at this," she gasped. "Too good."

Agnes chuckled softly and bent her head again.

Lola gathered herself together just in time and moved her hips back, putting the wetness Agnes seemed so eager to get her mouth on—again—out of reach. She waited until Agnes met her eyes, a question plain in them. *Have you changed your mind?*

Lola shook her head. "Let me do something for you."

"You *are* doing something for me. Seeing you spread out like this is very…inspiring."

"I don't want to be an inspiration. I want to give you something you can't get from anyone else." *Where did that come from?* Lola bit the inside of her cheek. *You in danger, girl.*

"You said it yourself; pleasure is pleasure. Whether I get it from you or…" Agnes shrugged, implying she could get the same from any random bitch in Vegas. How she managed to do it while still making Lola want to eat her raw was a mystery Lola was in no state to unravel.

Lola sat up fast, propped herself up on trembling arms and spoke quickly before Agnes could do anything else to make her lose her cool. "I'm not asking for your Apple ID password here. I just want to touch you and make you feel good."

Tremors still ran through her body, and she couldn't quite feel her toes. Her jeans hung off one leg, and her shirt was shoved up to her neck. She felt wrecked. Like a thing used hard for pleasure, waiting now to be thrown out.

But she wasn't a *thing,* and she had never allowed herself to be used.

Her lips felt swollen from when she'd bitten them toward the end of her last orgasm. She licked them now and bent closer to Agnes, careful to keep her hands behind her. Avid eyes followed her careful movement. Sudden anxiety fizzed in her chest, like an untimely burp waiting to burst free. *Please don't push me away.*

The possibility of rejection held her still and stopped her from moving those last few inches. If Agnes wanted to, she could cross the last little space separating them.

Apparently, she wanted.

One of them groaned at the touch of soft lips on sore lips. The rawness against Lola's teeth felt good. They exchanged breaths like the gift of life. She tasted herself on Agnes's lips and groaned again. The sinuous movement of their tongues was pleasure itself, and each stroke wreaked havoc on Lola's senses. It felt as if Agnes was caressing that hot space between her thighs. Desire rose once more with dizzying swiftness, and she moaned Agnes's name.

"I want to fuck you," she gasped against Agnes's mouth.

"Maybe later," Agnes whispered.

Lola felt the barest brush of disappointment before Agnes pushed her back down in the lounge chair and crowded her, Lola's thighs opening to accept the press of Agnes between them, the damp slide of Agnes's bare sex on Lola's hip.

"Don't move," Agnes commanded.

Her cool nose slid along Lola's throat and under her jaw. "You're incredibly desirable," Agnes gasped, her hips already moving, the slick heat of her sex catching on Lola's hip bone. "You know how much I want you." Her breath huffed into Lola's throat, hot and arousing.

Lola would have felt she was being used, yet another reason to hate Agnes, if it wasn't for the maddening strokes of Agnes's fingers on Lola's nipples, her thumbs flicking over sensitive nubs to the movement of her hips, as if she were desperate to make sure Lola found her pleasure one more time. The electric friction over her sex tore a gasp from deep inside her.

They moved together like dueling waves on a stormy seashore. Moans rising, hips moving frantically together while the cord of pleasure tightened for Lola. Tighter. Tighter still.

"Oh God!"

"You feel delicious." Damp breath tickled Lola's ear. Sharp teeth sank into an earlobe and tugged, and Lola felt it like a hot thrust between her thighs. "I want to fuck you again, just like this, with you spread out under me, taking every stroke of my fingers and begging for more."

Oh Jesus.

Lola was losing her mind.

Their moans wove together. Their bodies slotted, each to each. Sweat slid between them. The lounge chair juddered and jerked across the floor.

Then the lights of all of Vegas exploded behind Lola's tightly closed eyelids. She let loose a scream of completion, throat scraping raw. Teeth clamped hard into her neck, and the body on top of hers shuddered and shuddered and shuddered. A low, breathless curse scorched Lola's ear. And then, before she could think to fight it, the sudden and ruthless sleep that always came after intensely good sex grabbed Lola and pulled her deeply under.

CHAPTER 11

LOLA SLEPT LIKE SHE HAD all the worries of the world pressing her down into the ground. Agnes watched and couldn't look away. The trio of orgasms should have left Lola relaxed, boneless, all the worries in her face smoothed away, her body like draped silk across the lounge. But no. In sleep, her face twitched and her body lay tense, shoulders hunched as if she were waiting to be hit.

What was it about Lola? Since the last time Agnes had laid eyes on her, Lola had grown beautiful. Her makeup was much the same as last time and so were the clothes she wore, her perfume. No, there was nothing new or obvious about her looks that would serve an agenda to entrap Agnes. It was much worse than that, the worst possible thing. Agnes had grown *fond*. The word twisted in her belly like an iron pike, digging into her softest tissue, pulverizing where she was most vulnerable.

That *fucking* evening of pizza and confessions.

Sighing quietly, she twisted from under Lola's nearly bare body and stood. Vulnerably bared nipples snagged her gaze, and she sighed again. She dug her fingers painfully into her palms. She should just leave Lola lying there; if nothing else, that would show she was more immune to Lola than her heart insisted. But she couldn't do that.

Another sigh, this time of surrender, and Agnes pulled Lola's shirt down to cover her bare breasts, finished taking off the jeans that dangled off one foot, and put them next to Lola so she'd see them when she woke up. Through all this, Lola barely stirred. Agnes picked up a nearby blanket.

Lola's face stopped twitching. "Where are you going with that?" she croaked out.

"I'm sure your first guess would be the right one." Agnes draped the blanket over Lola despite her narrow-eyed stare, barely saving herself from gazing for too long at the gorgeously sprawled temptation before her. Now that Lola didn't look like the discarded casualty in some sex war, Agnes's desire flared again. Her nice-girl motives had apparently left the building.

Lola visibly shivered and clutched the blanket to herself.

Relax, I'm not going to tear it off you. Maybe. Christ, what was Agnes turning into?

Agnes refilled her glass with more whiskey and sat next to Lola on the lounge chair. Near Lola's hip, the fabric of the chair was shredded. Lola had lost control. Because of her. Agnes hid her smirk behind the whiskey glass. Taking that slow sip brought her own fingers closer to her nose, and the lingering scent of Lola's sex, as intoxicating as the whiskey, provoked a shiver of pleasure. The liquor soothed her tongue and laved her throat.

Lola shifted but surprisingly said nothing. Her desire to take something Agnes possessed was as obvious as the mouthwatering thickness of her body. Would she ever ask for it?

"What now?" Lola asked. Not quite the question Agnes was waiting for but, for now, she would go where Lola led.

"We can go inside if you'd like. It's warmer in there."

"I actually don't mind it out here. It's cold but strangely appealing." The blatant full-body look Lola gave Agnes left little doubt as to what, or *who*, she was talking about.

As if Agnes hadn't heard that before. At least the cold part. She splashed more whiskey in Lola's empty glass and passed it over before refilling her own and drinking a bit more. Normally she could hold her liquor through at least a bottle of the good stuff, but right now she could already feel it flowing like molten gold though her veins, warm and heavy. It weighed down her limbs and lightened her tongue. Although that might have been the sex.

Either way, it felt good after the tension of the day's meeting and Leticia's unexpected appearance. Sometimes being "queen" was exhausting.

"You came here like you have all the answers to my questions, but you seem to have your own troubles weighing you down," Agnes said.

A careful blankness slammed over Lola's features, and she pulled the blanket more tightly around her shoulders. "Why do you say that?"

Agnes took another sip of the whiskey and waited.

Lola was plotting. The turning of the gears behind her eyes seemed laughably obvious. True, most probably wouldn't have been able to see under that carefully constructed mask made up of dimpled cheeks and the thick fall of hair that made her seem like an angel. Those eyes, though, couldn't quite lie. There was a sparkle in that gemlike gaze when the smiles she tossed out so freely were real. Agnes had seen that sparkle only a time or two, just enough to know it existed.

Agnes tipped her head back and closed her eyes. She didn't want to play any games, but what else was she going to do tonight? Certainly not sleep. Though she was tired. The temporary relief and relaxation she'd felt from her orgasm seemed a thousand hours away. She tossed back the last of the whiskey and, with a soundless sigh, lay back on the lounge chair beside Lola's.

"You should leave," she said, although obviously Lola wouldn't. "A girl your age should be out there doing the usual things. Endless selfies and photo shoots of every meal. Hookup apps and other nice girls to take back to your place and fuck. Here is the last place you need to be."

Fabric rustled as Lola turned to her. "Right here is where I want to be, though. You may be older, but don't try to sound like my mother or some shit." Her eyes flashed drunken fire. "She died years ago. Normal for me is whatever I say it is."

The corners of Agnes's mouth lifted at Lola's curse. Apparently, the liquor was working on her too, shaking some real part of her loose. Agnes's amusement died as swiftly as it came, though. She opened her eyes and confronted the sky's darkness.

"Normal is what it is," Agnes said. "Safe. Routine. The Huxtables before we knew about rapey Bill." The stars winked down at her and it felt as if their lights suffused her body with their cool glow. "Everyone is out there living these normal lives while I've had to—" *Bury my father and everything he stood for six* hundred *feet under.* "—do this."

Lola shifted to look at her, and the warmth of her skin seeped into Agnes, banishing the coolness of stars and bringing her down back to earth. It wasn't real, but it felt good. "I doubt you've *had* to do anything you didn't want to."

Unamused laughter burned Agnes's throat raw. "You don't know what I've had to do."

"You're right," Lola said, her voice hushed. "I don't know. So, tell me."

It was tempting. So very tempting to give it all over to someone else for just a little while, all the burden she'd been carrying since she saw her father lying in a pool of his own blood.

The bitter laughter spilled out again. "I'm not that easy."

"Don't I know it," Lola murmured. "Anyway, the kind of normal you're talking about, my life definitely wasn't that." She put a hand on Agnes's thigh. "Maybe that's why I'm so comfortable here with you."

More temptation.

"Please, don't try to build some sort of false camaraderie between us just because we exchanged some bodily fluids. You're playing games, and apparently I'm a fool."

Goosebumps rippled over Agnes's skin from the coolness of the evening, and she tightened her robe more securely around her body. She should kick Lola out. To hell with all this dancing around the vague shape of Lola's deception. Lola wasn't talking. The weekend was long, and Agnes still had a lot to hammer out with the other directors before going back to New York. A long night spent on the roof while trying to guess what an opponent was thinking wasn't giving her the rest she needed.

"Let me work for you." Lola's words brought Agnes's wandering thoughts to a halt.

Moonlight fell through the thin clouds and bathed Lola in silver. Her bare thigh peeked out from beneath the blanket, and she could've been anywhere, temptation incarnate, with her soft mouth and her masked eyes that wanted to take more than they gave.

"Just because you let me fuck you doesn't mean I'll pay you back with a job." The words leapt out, intending to hurt. "I already have more beautiful and more experienced women at my House ready to drop to their knees for me anytime I say. You're not that special."

A harsh breath escaped Lola's mouth and she gaped. Surprise, hurt, and then anger chased across her face at lightning speed. "Seriously?"

Was that genuine shock? Agnes couldn't help but wonder.

Lips tight, Lola rose in a flurry of blankets, muttering under her breath as she yanked on her jeans and hunted for her shoes. Once she was properly armored, she gave Agnes a look that could've stripped paint.

Agnes swallowed against an uncomfortable feeling.

"I'll see myself out. And, by the way, *fuck you*." Lola spun and walked away, her high heels stabbing the floor with every step.

Her outrage was fake. It had to be. But then there was no explanation for the sudden sheen in Lola's eyes, although not of tears, nothing so obvious or easily simulated. Pain showed in those jewellike eyes, and for a moment, Agnes felt an answering stab in her belly, an emotion she had no business feeling.

Guilt.

CHAPTER 12

"Well, how did it go?"

"It didn't."

The apartment was quiet. An early Friday evening with, in theory, all worries left outside the door. In reality, though, all their worries, including Lola's biggest one, aka "Queen Agnes," were sitting right there with them at their small dining table.

"So, you didn't get anything when you went to Vegas?" Jamika served herself from the small dish of eggplant parmesan before sliding it over to Lola.

"I wouldn't say that exactly."

In the week since she'd come back from chasing Agnes out west, Lola and Jamika had kept missing each other. Except for a quick "hey" or "see you later" as they ran between their respective jobs, they'd barely had time to talk.

"What would you say then, because you've been in a crap mood since you got back here. If I didn't know better, I'd say you were falling for somebody. This is usually how you get. All resentful and distracted."

Since Lola didn't ever fall in love, Jamika didn't know what the hell she was talking about. Sure, she'd had crushes around every cuffing season, but they'd never meant anything.

"Um, no." She took a fresh-baked roll from the breadbasket and plopped it down on her plate.

"Okay. Now that we got your childish reaction out of the way, are you ready to tell me what happened?"

Shit. Was she? Of course. Since she never hid anything from Jamika, it wasn't even a real thought. All of her embarrassments, all the things she wished she'd been able to take back, all her bad decisions, Jamika knew. So, over the dinner they'd made together, Lola told her everything that had happened with Agnes in Vegas, even Agnes's insulting last words that Lola had taken too personally.

"Are you pissed that she didn't allow you to touch her or that you didn't get any info out of her?" Jamika asked once Lola had finished.

"The second one, obviously."

"Yeah, obviously." Jamika rolled her eyes. "What's the plan now then? She's not as easy as you thought, and I doubt she'll let you get anywhere near the business now that she's had a taste—"

"Hey! I wasn't that bad!"

But Jamika ignored her and carried on. "—you need another plan to get next to her and get the dirt on her business. My hacker contact is still trying to break through the House's firewalls, but their systems are locked down tighter than a nun's snatch." Crockery rattled as Jamika scooped up their plates and serving bowls while Lola grabbed everything else.

In the kitchen, Lola ran hot water and soap into the sink full of dishes, then snapped on bright yellow rubber gloves.

"So, for real, Delores. What's the next act of this thing, unless you want to give up?" Shoulders tense, Jamika didn't look up from moving that morning's dishes from the drying rack to the cupboard above.

Although she wanted to sigh, Lola didn't. Sometimes it seemed that Jamika was becoming more invested in this thing with the House of Agnes than Lola. It was Lola's sister who'd been killed, but with every day that passed, Jamika got more desperate. It was as if being in the same enclosed space as other detectives—who were world-weary, more experienced, and often cruel—made her want to jump deeper into their investigation of The House.

"No, Jamika Michelle, I don't want to give this up. What's wrong with you anyway?" She passed a washed plate to Jamika.

"Nothing." Jamika said far too quickly and nearly dropped the plate. "I just don't want you to wuss out because this is getting harder than you thought."

"Fuck you."

"Nope. We've already been through that. You're too much of a pillow princess for me."

Heat blazed under Lola's cheeks. Was that why Agnes hadn't taken her bait? Should she have fought more to participate in their fuck?

"Earth to Delores. Did you hear a word I just said?"

"You know I did." Lola ran back the part of the conversation that had happened while she'd checked out. "Anyway, let's leave our onetime college sexual experiment out of this and try to find some real solutions to our problem."

The sound of the sponge squishing soap across the plate as Lola scrubbed, the tapping of drying cutlery settling in the dish drainer, filled the silence.

"You could try getting at her through that receptionist person," Jamika finally said.

Lola's stomach dipped. "No way. I'm not screwing Agnes's secretary to get the information. That's the oldest trick in the book anyway. A woman smart enough to work for Agnes and not get fed to the lions isn't going to buy that one day I'm trying to get into her boss's pants and the next day I'm trying for hers."

"That's where good acting comes in."

Lola *accidentally* splashed some water at Jamika as she rinsed the last dish. "I went to Hunter College, not fucking Juilliard."

Jamika snorted. "You keep saying sex is no big deal. This chick works with escorts and all kinds of people who see sex as nothing more than an expensive handshake. It shouldn't be too hard to convince her that you're just like them and DTF whoever."

"Listen, I don't want to do that, okay?" Lola slammed the dish into the draining rack instead of passing it to Jamika to dry. Then she took a deep breath. "Fuck. Sorry, sorry. This whole thing is just getting to me."

"Yeah. It's getting to all of us. Are you sure you aren't letting this Agnes woman play you instead of the other way around?"

"You know better than that."

"I actually don't."

"God, just let it go already." This project was supposed to make things better for both of them, get them into better positions at work and bring them even closer as friends, but so far it was only punching little holes into their relationship. Maybe it really was time to just let it go. Zoe was gone. Lola couldn't do anything for her now.

She pulled off her plastic gloves. "I'm going out for a walk."

"Come on. Don't be like that. I didn't mean to chase you off."

"You're not chasing me anywhere. I'm just going to stretch my legs."

But once Lola had banged out of the apartment and down the first set of stairs, walking didn't seem enough. Her sneakered feet slapped against the stairs faster and faster as thoughts of Agnes spun in her head.

The memory of Agnes sprawled next to her on that Vegas rooftop, undoubtedly drunk but so firmly in control, burned her. It wasn't fair when Lola had been choking on her own thwarted desires. Torn between simple sexual craving and the need to worm her way into Agnes's confidence and get what she went there for. It didn't matter what Agnes had said so insultingly about paying for their sex with a job offer. It shouldn't have anyway.

But it did.

The mention of money had been a punch to the gut. A reality check. Lola wanted Agnes to invite her into The House. Not to pay Lola back for the sex but because she wanted to. However, if Agnes had fallen for the trap Lola set, then that would mean she was just like all the others. Easily led by her clit. A simpleton.

Part of Lola was glad Agnes hadn't fallen so easily. The rational part, though, was pissed. It felt as if she were fighting with herself as well as Agnes. And Jamika certainly wasn't making this thing any easier either.

Fuck.

By the time Lola shoved open the doors of the apartment building to breathe the cool night air, she was already running. In her rush to leave, she hadn't stopped to grab a coat, but she barely felt the bite of the fifty-something-degree temperature as her body warmed, then heated, then began to sweat. Her feet slapped against the pavement. Her breath came hard.

What the hell was she thinking coming out here like this? She wasn't a runner or any kind of athlete. Her idea of a strong workout was lifting a triple-scoop ice-cream cone to her mouth while shouting answers at game shows from the couch. Her body wasn't used to this. She wasn't even wearing a damn sports bra. She couldn't stop, though.

The jog took her past storefronts and double-parked cars. Past other New Yorkers out for an evening errand or walk. Some of the faces were familiar from her living three years in the neighborhood, but most were strangers probably wondering what the hell she was doing out there in her tight sweats and ripped Converse sneakers, her boobs one high-step away from smacking her in the chin.

Someone rollerbladed past her in a New York City marathon T-shirt a couple of years out of date. It was a shade of blue she remembered objecting to when Jamika had brought one home. Well, honestly, it hadn't been the color that she didn't like so much as the smaller size. If she'd put that thing on, it would've been a crop top on her. No thanks.

Lola ran, circling the neighborhood, while her own thoughts circled uselessly, spinning from Agnes to Zoe to Jamika, the exposé she was supposed to be writing, then back to Agnes again. Always Agnes. The feel of her sat like a piece of hot coal behind Lola's breastbone, alternately comforting *and* uncomfortable.

Annoyed, she huffed out a harsh breath, then, spotting a break in traffic, darted across the street toward the park. From somewhere behind her came the screech of tires and the abrupt blast of a car horn. That didn't have anything to do with her, so she kept going.

All too soon, though, she was slowing down. She'd never had the stamina that Jamika had for running, not to mention she hated it. Under the stone arch of a small footbridge, she stumbled to a halt, breath puffing in the evening air as she bent over at the waist, hands braced on her knees. God, she was so weak. Maybe that was the reason Agnes hadn't fallen into the trap she thought she'd set so well.

She straightened, stretched out her back, and stared up at the darkening sky, for a moment drawn back to another sky, another evening when soft lips had had her flat on her back and begging. Screaming. Lola squeezed her eyes shut, as if that alone could banish Agnes from her thoughts.

She'd been an idiot to think she could wield any real power where Agnes was concerned. Agnes had it all, and now Lola would have to figure out a way to turn her own powerlessness into strength.

Cool air rushed over her heated face, and her sweat started to dry under her clothes. Although it was nearly dark, plenty of people were out in the park, a few couples, parents with strollers, and even a group of kids in masks getting ahead of the game for Halloween less than two weeks away. The kids laughed and played tag, running across the grass and onto the paved path where Lola was still trying to catch her breath. She skipped back out of their way. To be that innocent and carefree again.

A flash of blue, obvious even in the growing gloom, skated just behind her and stopped. Trying for casual, Lola reached for her phone. Her suddenly sweaty hand nearly dropped it before getting a proper grip, then just as she swiped at the screen to get to Jamika's number, it vibrated with an incoming call. "I was just about to call you," she said.

"Does that mean you're not pissed at me anymore?"

"I wouldn't say that, but I can be pissed at you and still love your silly ass."

"Oh good," Jamika said, dry as dust, then she laughed. "So, what's up? Why were you about to call me?"

"I think someone's following me." All sounds stopped from the other end of the line.

"Are you someplace safe?"

"Yes, in the middle of the park with a ton of people around."

"Good, good. Get your ass home, right now. Take the most crowded way back."

"And if they follow me all the way there?"

"They get to meet my very angry face and my gun."

"Don't talk like that. It's probably nothing." She glanced around, but the blue marathon shirt was nowhere in sight. *That doesn't mean the guy is actually gone.*

Her heart tripped in her chest at the thought of him watching her now. Although she knew, in theory, this project with Jamika was dangerous, for the first time, she felt a trickle of fear. This was *real*.

She took a steadying breath, then another. Okay, so yoga breathing wasn't doing the trick. Her skin prickled, and she felt exposed from all sides. That guy could be watching her right now, planning to yank her into the bushes before she got home.

"What did you want anyway, J?" she asked.

"For you to get your ass back here, ASAP."

In the background, she could hear a steady thudding. Jamika sounded as if she was in some kind of echo chamber and running. Was she rushing down their stairs?

"Chill. It's fine." Fake it 'til you make it, right? Plus, the last thing Lola needed was for Jamika to come rushing out here to rescue her and get hurt. "You don't have to come get me or anything dramatic like that. I don't even see that guy anymore. Just me being paranoid, I bet."

"I wouldn't take that bet. Anyway, you just got a message on the burner phone. That's the reason I called."

Lola stopped walking. Her heart flew up into her throat, and even though she knew better, she looked frantically around. Marathoner was still a ghost. "What did the message say?"

"Something about you bribing a teenager for ice cream?"

A feeling of satisfaction pushed aside some of her panic. "Oh good," she said with a fierce grin. Finally, something was going her way.

CHAPTER 13

THE REST OF THE WEEKEND'S Consortium meeting went more or less as Agnes expected. More things to add to her to-do list, a few rumblings of discontent, and a renewed promise by all to keep the peace. The peace maintained between the eleven houses was better than the constant poaching of assets, threats, and occasional bloodbaths they'd all had to deal with while her father was in charge.

With this quarter's business concluded and the meeting over, she was ready to go home and just be "Nessa" again. Maybe she would end up watching one of those weird cooking shows with Gretchen and Whit while they all stuffed their faces with pizza. Hopefully, she wouldn't think about Lola the whole time.

In her suite early Sunday afternoon, Agnes folded her things and put them back in her suitcase. She realized she was humming one of the songs from that *Moana* movie Gretchen couldn't get enough of.

Her phone vibrated from the bedside table. She answered, already knowing who it was before she looked at the screen. "Whit, the car is already scheduled. Don't worry. I won't miss it."

"That's not what I'm worried about right now," Whit growled through the phone.

The hairs on the back of Agnes's neck stood up. "What's wrong?"

"Someone hacked into our servers."

She froze, limbs going ice-cold at the thought of all the information an excellent hacker could find on their servers, and immediately squashed a surge of panic. "What did they get?" Agnes stalked away from the bed and grabbed the rest of her things, shoving them into the suitcase without nearly as much care as before. Was this the mystery threat Geoffrey Rake had hinted at?

"Not much," Whit said. "We hope. Our firewalls killed most of the incursion before they could get too far, but I knew you'd want to know."

"Damn right." Agnes sent her security team a quick text letting them know she was ready to leave, and they replied back in seconds. "Shut everything down tight. Change all the codes, triple the security, whatever it takes."

"Already on it."

"Good." With her suitcase zipped shut and her laptop bag already locked and ready on the bed, she glanced around to make sure she wasn't leaving anything behind. Her security team was supposed to be outside her room soon. "I'm leaving the hotel now."

"There's nothing you can do that I haven't already done."

Whit spoke the truth. But this breach was more than just an attack on their computer systems. Their very security was compromised. Someone wasn't doing their job, or maybe someone else was doing theirs a little too well. A digital attack could mean another kind of attack was on the way, and Agnes wanted to be home if or when that happened.

"Please let the pilot know we're leaving earlier than planned." Ever since she'd taken over the reins of The House, Agnes had been in a state of waiting. Waiting for someone to challenge her for what she'd inherited. Maybe that day was finally coming.

Whit grunted in her ear, but that was all the agreement Agnes needed. Someone was coming for her, and she needed to find out who it was before they got to her.

The flight back to New York took forever. And although she logged onto The House's system to double-check everything for herself, Agnes still itched to be home and set eyes on what really mattered.

"Nessa!" She'd barely kicked off her shoes after she got off the elevator before Gretchen flew down the hallway with her arms spread out. "You're back early!" She squealed in Agnes's ear and held on tight.

"Only a little bit, sweet." Agnes swung Gretchen up into her arms and hugged her tight, inhaling the scent of fresh-baked bread that clung to her.

Over Gretchen's shoulder, Whit appeared. She wore an apron over her usual monochromatic outfit and slowly wiped her hands on a dish towel as she skimmed critical eyes over Agnes. She didn't look too upset, so that meant Agnes would have some time to hang out with Gretchen before she and Whit got down to business.

"What kind of bread did you two bake today?" Agnes hitched Gretchen up on her hip—

God, she was getting heavy!—and walked past Whit, gently bumping her shoulder.

Whit grunted softly and gave her a version of a smile.

"A focaccia—" Gretchen struggled only a little with the word. "—with a flower garden made from vegetables baked into the top."

"Very ambitious."

"Go big or go home. That's what Whit said."

"Imagine that."

"Come see!"

Even though Agnes was the one carrying her, Gretchen led her toward the kitchen, finger imperiously pointed forward, her face lit up in a smile. A line of white flour dusted her forehead. Agnes wiped it away and brushed a kiss on her temple. "So, tell me what you two have been up to since I've been gone."

With an excited laugh, Gretchen jumped down from Agnes's arms to turn on the oven light. "Look!"

"It was a difficult project." Whit leaned back against the counter looking as calm as ever. "More time than we thought but, in the end, our goals were secured."

"Why are you talking like that, Whit? The bread is amazing! Better than on the television show. And we have three..." Gretchen chattered on with excitement about what she and Whit had worked on during the afternoon. "It's the greatest," she finished. "Right, Whit?"

"Right, love. Everything turned out perfectly."

"That's a relief to know," Agnes agreed. "I'm glad my replacement was adequate." She teased Gretchen with a light tug of one Afro puff.

The puffs bounced around Gretchen's head as she shook her head, then flung her arms around Agnes's knees. "Nobody could ever replace you."

"That's good to know, darling. I'd hate to be so easily tossed aside."

"Never!"

"So, what are we going to do with all this beautiful bread once it bakes?" Agnes looked at Whit with a raised eyebrow.

Gretchen bit her lip and looked up at Agnes, then Whit. "I want to take one to school tomorrow to share with my class. Can I?"

"Of course, love. But what about the other twenty?"

Whit rolled her eyes while Gretchen giggled and hooked her arms tighter around Agnes's knees, bracing all her weight there and flinging back her head. "Silly. It's only three more. We can just have dinner early since you're back."

"Just bread."

"And butter and cheese. There's already vegetables on them."

"We have some chicken already baked from this afternoon," Whit said.

"Boring." Gretchen stuck out her tongue and Agnes laughed, leaning down to give her sweet girl a noisy kiss on the cheek. It was so very good to be home.

They ate dinner together in the dining room, played a board game, then watched about an hour of TV.

Once Gretchen was tucked in bed, Agnes was able to talk openly with Whit about what had happened while she was gone.

"It's nothing more than what I told you. It looks like we stopped them from getting too deep into our systems, then destroyed the source of the incursion," Whit said from the other seat in front of the fireplace, where Agnes had started a fire even though it wasn't that cold. She sipped from her glass of sparkling water while Agnes swirled the whiskey in her glass, watching the liquid whirlpool in the crystal.

"But you're not one-hundred-percent certain?" Agnes asked even though she knew the answer.

"About this? No. But Ty did his job. Security is tighter now, and he's been running scans all afternoon to find out what they took."

In that moment, Agnes would've killed for more certainty. But Whit was right. Nothing was certain. And nothing could be taken for granted. "Double the security on Gretchen at school, and I don't want you going anywhere alone."

A frown creased Whit's forehead. "I'm not a child, Agnes. I can take care of myself."

"Still, it would make me feel better. Something is coming, and I want us all to be prepared—and alive—when it gets here." Agnes stretched her bare legs toward the fire and pretended not to see Whit roll her eyes.

"Speaking of threats, how did it go in Vegas?"

Agnes's pulse tripped in her throat. It was the worst idea she'd ever had, to keep something secret from Whit, but she hadn't said a word about Lola showing up at her hotel. Now she fought like hell to speak normally. "You were listening in on most of it. There's nothing I could tell you that you don't already know."

"I'm not talking about the meetings, and you know it. Did you fuck that girl?"

The blaze crackled in the fireplace, logs popping and showering sparks behind the safety of the grate. Agnes could lie, but what would be the point? Whit already knew *something*.

Agnes took a slow sip of her whiskey and kept her eyes on the flames. "I did."

When the ensuing silence grew to be too much, she looked up from the flames to Whit's face. Whit didn't look surprised.

"So, now what?" she asked.

"I honestly don't know. She's one of the dangers that's cropped up recently or at least one of the new variables that can't be a coincidence. We've already talked about this. I have it under control."

"If this is what you having things under control looks like, now I'm really worried. You let her into your bed. You know she's using you."

"Who's to say I'm not the one using her?"

Whit held up her hand. "This is not what strategy looks like, Agnes." Her sigh joined the sound of the crackling fire. "Since you've already had her, you can't go back and change what that means for you."

Agnes bristled. "It doesn't mean anything."

"You know I've never allowed you to lie to yourself, and I'm not going to now. Whenever you get your itch scratched at that club, you never come back thinking about those women. You get in, get out, and forget about them. This woman had you in the palm of her hand since day one."

Agnes flushed hot and squirmed a little. One day, she'd learn not to underestimate Whit and her power to find out just about everything Agnes did in her waking hours. "What, are you following me now?"

"You know I am. That's part of my job. What kind of protector would I be, letting you disappear from my sight and into an enemy's line of fire?"

"That doesn't mean spying on me when I'm not in The House."

"Actually, that's exactly what it means."

Agnes should probably be angry. But Whit was right. She wouldn't be doing the job Agnes agreed to if Whit just let everyone in her care wander all over the place without knowing exactly where they were and with whom. This was the life Agnes had chosen after all.

The whiskey boiled in her stomach, and she set the crystal tumbler on the side table with a gentle click. "Sometimes, I think about giving this all back—and just, just walking away."

"For one thing, there's no one to give this time bomb back to," Whit said.

Everyone was dead or gone. Agnes had been on her own from the moment she chose to go against her father. That long-ago decision could not be unmade. The steps afterward could never be retraced. "Still, a girl can dream," she said.

"But a queen can only live in this reality and plan for the future."

Agnes sighed and swallowed the burning truth. She didn't always hate it when Whit was right, but this was definitely one of the times she did.

CHAPTER 14

I DON'T CHASE.

Agnes clicked through the list of The House's clients on her laptop, distracted. Lola, like a particularly stubborn thorn, had lodged herself in Agnes's brain, and Agnes couldn't get rid of her. But, damn, she tried.

Since she'd taken over The House, Agnes had been careful to keep her life there separate from her home life, her life with Gretchen. Work never made it across the threshold of her home, not even in the home office she kept under lock and key. The cyberattack had changed that.

In the home office overlooking the river, Agnes went through the list of her best clients, the ones she trusted to care for someone vulnerable, the ones who, she knew, were looking for more than just sex. She hummed along to the Janelle Monáe song coming from the Bluetooth speaker.

I don't chase.

The words popped into her mind again. For a luxurious moment, she let them linger and reach their inevitable destination.

I don't chase.

But damn, I want to run Lola down and drag her back here to...to do something more than what we'd indulged ourselves with in Las Vegas.

Lola was dangerous for Agnes to have in her life. She shouldn't have her anywhere near Gretchen or her business. But she wanted her so damn much, needed to see her spread out under her again, begging to be kissed, to be fucked, for someone to rip away her mask and see the real her.

As if she'd let you.

Agnes hissed out a curse and once again shoved away the rebellious thoughts. She scanned the client list again, searching for a likely candidate to play Richard Gere's *Pretty Woman* character to one of the women in The House who wanted to leave the business. Having a knight or lady in shining armor coming to her rescue would make the transition much easier for—

Her office door banged open.

"Nessa, we're back!" Gretchen dashed in with a big grin. Dirt smeared down one side of her jeans.

In reflex, Agnes darkened the computer's screen. "Gretchen! What have I told you about interrupting me when I'm working?"

"But it's Saturday." Gretchen drew out the word, jumping up and down in front of Agnes's desk, her single Afro puff bobbing on top of her head. Her sneakers slapped against the marble in a rhythm that was about to drive Agnes mad.

Agnes pushed out a harsh breath. "Gretchen!" she snapped. "I'm working. It doesn't matter what day it is."

Gretchen's face fell. She stopped jumping. "But I—"

"But nothing, Gretchen. Please give me some peace and quiet to finish my work, and we can talk later."

Tears filled Gretchen's expressive brown eyes, and her chin wobbled. She backed away from the desk. "What if I don't want to talk to *you* later!" Sobbing, she rushed out, sneakers slamming harder against the tile floors, and that sound was somehow worse than when she'd been jumping up and down in her excitement.

Fuck. But Agnes couldn't take it back without seeming like an inconsistent parent.

"You didn't need to talk to her like that, you know." Whit appeared in the doorway.

The leather of the chair sighed as Agnes leaned back in exasperation. "Not you too. I need to get some work done today."

"Actually, you don't. Don't take out your frustrations on Gretchen or on me. Deal with your shit." The sharp click of the door closing drove Whit's point home.

Agnes cursed again. A swipe of her hand brought up the screen she'd been looking at before Gretchen had barged in. Over the past few days, worry about the cyberattack had pushed Agnes to accelerate the timetables of a few ongoing projects. Rushing only led to mistakes, but she couldn't pretend there wasn't more to her irritable mood.

She couldn't get Lola out of her mind.

The last time they'd seen each other, Agnes had been cruel. She acted this way on a regular basis, but for some reason, this time, guilt gnawed at her. Yes, Lola could be playing games, but there were other more productive ways to handle that kind of thing. Being a bitch wasn't one of them. And speaking of which... Agnes's gaze drifted to the closed door of her office. She pushed back from her desk and headed into the hallway.

The sound of harsh sobs led her to Whit's overlook, which Whit called her office and command center, at the very top floor of the penthouse. Unlike Agnes, Whit never closed her office door, no matter what she was doing. Not to Agnes and certainly never to Gretchen. Agnes hoped Whit wouldn't break that tradition today, although, with the way she'd been acting over the past few days, she couldn't say she didn't deserve it.

She sighed with relief when she saw that Whit's door was indeed still open. After taking a deep breath, she walked in.

At the sight of Gretchen sprawled in Whit's lap, her cries muffled in Whit's blouse, Agnes's heart fell out of her chest and smashed to pieces on the floor.

Whit, proper in her usual librarian's outfit, curled on the sofa around a weeping Gretchen, looked up with murder in her eyes. She pulled a piece of paper from her pocket, balled it up, and threw it at Agnes's feet. "Go, before Gretchen and I put you out of our misery. Very *painfully*."

A hiccup shook Gretchen's slight body, and she curled up tighter in the shelter of Whit's lap. She kept her face turned away.

Hesitantly, Agnes placed a hand on Gretchen's back. "I'm sorry, darling. I was wrong to shout at you." Gretchen's only response was to cling to Whit even tighter. Agnes felt sick. "Can you please forgive me?"

A reddened eye emerged from behind the starched ruffle of Whit's blouse. "Why did you do it? Did I do something wrong?" The words were a stake right through Agnes's heart.

"You didn't, love. I was just... Something else upset me, and I took it out on you. But I'm done with that now."

A sniffle. "Are you sure?"

"Yes." She met Whit's eyes over Gretchen's head. "I'm sure."

"Good!" With a wide grin, Gretchen flew into Agnes's arms.

Thank God Gretchen couldn't hold a grudge. Arms trembling, Agnes held on to the small and precious creature in her arms. "Let me make it up to you, okay?"

"With ice cream?"

Agnes winced. She should have known that one was coming. But… "Yes, with ice cream."

"Yay!" Gretchen jumped up, the top of her head gently bumping into Agnes's chin as she flung herself to her feet and ran for the door. "I'm going to put on my ice-cream clothes!"

As Gretchen's sneakered feet pounded down the hall, Agnes drew in a long breath and slowly let it out. The relief she felt was dizzying. Ever since she'd taken on the responsibility of caring for Gretchen, she'd lived in constant fear that she'd do something to damage Gretchen for good. Nearly five years later, that fear still hadn't completely gone away.

She was grateful every day to have Whit by her side to help her. The regret she felt for her asshole behavior demanded she make an apology. Instead, she picked up the paper Whit had thrown at her without looking to see what was on it and slipped it into her pocket. "It's not very nice to threaten your friend," she said to Whit.

"You haven't been acting very much like a friend recently."

Agnes winced. "I know, and I'm sorry."

"I know you're sorry." The corner of Whit's mouth curved up. She switched to speaking French. "It'll take more than an ice cream bribe for me to let your asshole behavior go."

"What exactly will it take?" Agnes asked although she had a sneaking suspicion what that would be.

"The manager at Halcyon is waiting for your call." Whit dipped her head, indicating the paper in Agnes's pocket. "The place is secure. Invite any of the women there up to a private room. Screw this shitty mood out of your system."

Agnes hadn't been to Halcyon in weeks; she hadn't even felt the urge to go. Thinking of her private club only reminded her of the last time she'd been there. When Lola had walked into her life.

Agnes felt for the mound of paper ruining the line of her slacks. She had no desire to be anywhere near the club. Lola, though, was a different matter altogether. Maybe if she showed up at Halcyon, she'd run into the troublesome woman again…

CHAPTER 15

AGNES TOOK WHIT AND GRETCHEN to their favorite place, a gourmet ice-cream shop that also carried odd flavors of sparkling water. The shop flourished next to a small neighborhood park in Brooklyn that Agnes had accidentally discovered on one of her restless nights. They each ordered their usual and strolled toward the playground nearby while four bodyguards trailed behind them in a way that was not in the least bit subtle.

Despite the day's chill, a trio of kids darted around the playground. Their high voices, shrieking in simple happiness, already made the day seem lighter.

"This is my favorite." Gretchen held up her crème brûlée and almond ice cream already melting in its cone.

"I know it is, love." Agnes opened her bottle of guava-mint sparkling water.

"Just in case you pass by here on your way home one day." Gretchen dimpled up at Agnes, even though she knew well enough the shop was nowhere near where they lived.

"I'll take that under advisement."

Whit snorted a laugh. They both watched as Gretchen skipped ahead to peer up at a new sign that had appeared since the last time they were in the park. Although new to reading, she was learning at an accelerated rate and was still at that phase when she thought all words were magical.

"She'll make a good successor one day." Whit's mango and hot pepper ice pop was nearly half gone. "One look from her alone could get people to do whatever she wants."

A bodyguard was right on Gretchen's trail, quickly passing by Agnes and Whit to keep Gretchen both within sight and grabbing range.

Agnes swallowed a mouthful of the sparkling water that didn't taste nearly as questionable as expected. "I don't want to burden her with that." Even with the positive outcomes she was able to bring about, running The House was a hard business, sometimes a dirty one, where she had to see things no one should. It could be soul-breaking, and the thought of Gretchen having to deal with it, even later as an adult, turned her stomach. When it was time, though, she did intend to give Gretchen the choice instead of making it for her.

"Fair enough," Whit murmured. "Just don't think you have to bear the burden alone."

"I know I don't. There's no way I could've done all this without you, Clare, and the others." A cool breeze whipped through the park and slapped the hem of Agnes's unbuttoned coat against her legs.

Some days, The House felt too much to handle, even with the help she had. On those days, she wished she had a farm, someplace quiet with horses, and nothing but the physical labor that came from working outdoors to worry about. Her aching body at the end of the day, the callouses on her hands, would help shut off her endlessly buzzing mind and give her something simple to do.

This work was important, though. She couldn't allow her laziness to let it fall apart.

Gretchen ran up to them, her thick hair bouncing in the brisk breeze. "Can I go play?"

"Of course. You have to finish your ice cream first, though."

"Oh." Her shoulders drooped. "Okay." Then she looked at Whit, who was just finishing the last of her popsicle.

Agnes knew what was coming before Gretchen even opened her mouth again.

"No. Whit can't finish it for you. This is the treat you asked for, remember?"

"Nessa…" Head tossed back to reveal the most pitiful face ever pulled by a five-year-old, she dragged out the sound of Agnes's name. "Pleeeeeeeease?"

Agnes's resolve didn't last long. "All right, go ahead." She reached out for the half-finished ice-cream cone and hid a smile when Gretchen squealed with happiness before leaving Agnes with the cone and running off to play.

Soft laughter from Whit floated to Agnes on the breeze from a few feet away as Whit paused to check the area around them yet again. "Don't you ever tell me that I spoil her."

Agnes just tucked her bottle of sparkling water into her coat pocket without saying a word. They both knew Gretchen had her—and all of them—wrapped around her little finger.

The ice cream was as sweetly delicious as Agnes remembered. The sweet cream melted on her tongue with bits of caramelized sugar and vanilla bean, leaving behind pieces of almond she slowly sucked between her tongue and palate before chewing them. This was one of her favorites too.

"Want some?" She offered the ice cream to Whit in lieu of any comment on the obvious.

"Sure." Whit took the cone with obvious pleasure, immediately taking an unnecessarily large swipe of the melting cream with her tongue. "It's not fair for you to enjoy this all by yourself when she was about to give it to me anyway."

"You should have spoken up sooner," Agnes teased back.

"Well, *I* spoke up just now, which is why I have this taste of heaven in my hand."

Fall leaves crunched under their feet as they followed the path to the playground, Agnes with her hands clasped behind her and Whit eating the ice cream as if she was never giving it back. The breeze whipped fallen leaves in the air and brought with it the smell of autumn.

Agnes should have done this sooner, taken Gretchen out and enjoyed the day instead of working in a quiet panic to make sure the hacker's attack didn't leave any damage she couldn't repair. Family was important. If there was one thing the past few years had taught her, it was that. Hold on tight and love the people who matter. In a blink, they could disappear.

A tightness constricted Agnes's chest.

"You know she's going to want to stay out here for hours." Still eating the ice cream, Whit leaned back against a nearby tree, her eyes focused on Gretchen and the neighborhood children.

Agnes was about to comment when Whit jerked upright and whipped around to look behind her, hand moving toward the gun in her shoulder holster. Automatically, Agnes turned too, just in time to see two of the rear security guards come tramping from the cover of nearby trees with a figure struggling between them.

Anger rushed hot and fast through Agnes, gathering like a fireball in her chest. Who the hell...? A quick look reassured her Gretchen was still playing with her friends.

"We found her spying on you," one of the guards said. "She said she knows you." He shoved the hooded figure toward Agnes but didn't let go.

"Hey, don't be so rough!" The high, feminine voice gave away who it was before Agnes focused properly on Lola's face, partially covered by a burgundy hoodie.

Gretchen. Was that who Lola had been after all along? Reason-destroying fear obliterated everything until Agnes couldn't see anything but Lola. Her pulse knocked hard in her throat.

"Funny running into you," Lola said, looking much too confident for someone being held tight by two men twice her size. "The ice cream over here is really good. Have you guys tried it?"

At Lola's flippant words, adrenaline pulsed through Agnes, destroying most of her fear and leaving killing rage behind. Her fingers twitched toward her hidden knife.

CHAPTER 16

"Is stalking me a bad habit I need to break you of?" Agnes stood in the middle of her guard dogs, looking calm enough, but Lola noticed the ticking muscle in her jaw that broadcasted how pissed off she was.

No, she wasn't happy at all. Not like the night they'd had pizza and Lola had spilled her guts about Zoe.

Lola's eyes flickered around the little gathering of tough-as-fuck guards. One of them, who'd been leaning against a tree, had a pistol in her hand. A blob of ice cream in a crushed cone melted on the ground near her feet. Jesus. The woman was dressed in a skirt and some kind of frilly blouse Lola swore she saw in Old Navy last week. But her look was ruthless. She held the gun just out of casual sight under a loose peacoat but gripped in a way that looked frighteningly competent.

Lola hadn't meant to sneak up on them, at least not to come this far. After getting the text tipping her off that Agnes was here, she had to see the woman again. Her dreams had been haunted for too many nights by what had happened between them in Vegas, not just the incredible sex but the shitty things Agnes had said to her at the end. Yes, Lola was hurt, but the more she thought about it, the more she realized those words had been a sign—an unhealthy one, but still—that Agnes actually cared for her and was scared. Or pissed off.

"I wasn't stalking you," Lola said quickly when one of the guards, a beefy guy with a massive hipster beard, roughly shook her shoulder for not answering Agnes's question fast enough.

"Then why are you here?" Agnes took a step toward her, eyes dark and flat. "I didn't tell you where to find me." There was anger in her voice now but also something else. Fear?

"Of course, you didn't," Lola said, feeling the unfamiliar shame of letting her curiosity get this far. Although, damn it, this was part of her plan. "You let it slip once that you liked this place."

Agnes's eyebrow rose, and the tall woman with the gun looked at Agnes without moving her head, disbelief on her face.

"I—didn't." Uncertainty leaked through Agnes's voice.

"You told me once that you liked a place that had weird flavors of mineral water," Lola said.

"You must be a regular Sherlock Holmes." The Amazon spoke up. "That clue led you to this place? At this exact time?"

This wasn't going well. At all. They could tell Lola was lying.

"Sort of." Despite the punishing grip on both her arms, she was trying her best to look relaxed. Her fear was definitely there—her heart pounded loudly enough to drown out most of her logical thinking—but she didn't want to show it. "I—" Lola silently groaned. What could she say that wouldn't sound as if she really were a complete stalker? She licked her dry lips. So much for not showing fear.

Lola watched everyone in the clearing, trying to keep track of the Amazon's gun, Agnes's position, and also prevent the two strongmen from accidentally breaking her arms that they were *definitely* holding too tightly. So, she noticed when the Amazon's gun twitched against her thigh.

"We need to get rid of her," the woman said.

Lola held up her hands, or at least tried to, before the men, working in tandem like Schwarzenegger's *Terminator* robots, yanked her arms back to her sides. Fear snapped her spine tight. "Hold on a second!"

"Whit…" Agnes took a quick step forward, which Lola was grateful for, but it sure as hell wouldn't be enough if the tall woman decided to shoot her then and there.

Lola swallowed the fear clogging her throat. It seemed pathetic now, how she'd come all the way out here all because—no matter how much she tried to tell herself otherwise—she wanted to see Agnes, relaxed and beautifully human again, outside of The House. She wanted to see her real smiles, maybe even hear her laugh. And that was why she'd stupidly bribed one of the students working at the ice-cream shop to text her the next time Agnes showed up.

Heart racing, she confessed everything to the Amazon while Agnes looked on, her smooth face expressionless. "And that's the complete truth," she finished. "I just wanted to see the queen again, away from her castle."

"Who exactly is this bribable ice-cream scooper?" The Amazon asked the question in a way that did not bode well for the bubbly teenager who'd happily taken Lola's fifty-dollar bill. "If you don't—"

The crackling of leaves distracted Lola from the men threatening to yank her arms off. A child ran up to them while two other strongman types rushed after her. The men looked a little panicked, but the child was fearless.

"Who's the queen, Nessa?" the little girl asked, breathless and smiling as she danced up to Agnes with her thick puff of hair swaying. She looked about six. With her long-lashed eyes, friendly smile, and cleft chin, she was terminally adorable. The girl had dried leaves and little twigs stuck to her clothes and hair as if she'd been rolling around on the ground making a fall version of snow angels. Leaf angels?

Was she Agnes's kid? They looked nothing alike.

Before "Nessa" could answer the question, the Amazon swooped the girl up into her arms and spun away in a whirl of her dark cloak, heading at a fast clip toward the playground where a couple of children shrieked joyfully at each other, ignoring all the grown-up drama. Two of the security men quickly followed them but not the ones with death grips on Lola's arms.

Another flicker of fear showed in Agnes's eyes before she could hide it.

Lola watched the girl go, or at least the small part of her that she could see past the Amazon's protective embrace and hurrying footsteps. "Who's that?"

"None of your business," Agnes said, her face tight. She looked one breath away from yanking Lola from the bodyguards and tearing her apart herself. "You really shouldn't be here."

Lola silently agreed. The worst part of this whole thing was the fear lurking in Agnes's eyes for the child. Lola would give anything to erase that.

God, she was crap at this.

"I promise I'm not here to spy for anybody," Lola blurted out. The child was obviously special to Agnes, but Lola would never think about using her as a weapon in their war. "I'm only here for myself."

Some invisible signal must have come from Agnes because the goons released Lola's arms at the same time and, after giving Lola matching threatening looks, stepped away. She couldn't help but notice that they stayed within easy shooting distance. Lucky her.

Relieved to have free movement of her arms again, she rolled her shoulders back. "You know, I'm serious. I do want to see you again." She scratched the side of her neck, hyperaware of the heat rising in her cheeks, torn between what she should be doing—*not* trying to date a maybe killer—and what she desperately wanted to do—definitely date a maybe killer. "You want to see me too. I know it. It's in your eyes, no matter what you actually say."

Agnes's expressive eyes flashed, and Lola almost smiled. What she'd said wasn't quite true. Agnes had a poker face like nobody she'd ever seen, but maybe, with that small lie, Lola could keep her a little off guard. Give her a taste of what she did to Lola every time they were in the same room. Or street.

As if she couldn't help herself, Agnes looked over her shoulder to where the Amazon had disappeared with the child. The thick black coat blew around Agnes's rigid body as she turned her back to Lola, something she should never do to an enemy. Obviously, her head wasn't completely in the game.

"What are my eyes saying to you now?" Agnes was suddenly right there, her eyes a universe of darkness, and a scent of sweet cream and anger was right under Lola's nose.

A root tangled with Lola's feet as she jerked backward with a gasp and nearly fell. Her pulse thudded in her throat, and the danger she'd half-expected to feel in Agnes's presence since she'd started this thing smothered her in its suffocating cloak. Terror skittered up her spine. She licked her lips again. "That you're not very happy with me right now?" Her voice shook, and she didn't even try to hide it.

"That's good. I'm glad you have enough self-preservation to realize at least that much." Agnes's breath, sweet and hot, brushed against Lola's lips as she spoke. "I should push you far, far away from me. From us." Agnes's eyes were unblinking. A muscle leapt in her jaw, a minuscule reaction that told Lola she was torn about something. And still scared.

Fuck.

"For what it's worth, I'm sorry," Lola said quickly before her nervousness could make her back away from Agnes. Or say more stupid things. "I don't want to make it seem like—" She bit off the words, shaking her head. "I won't tell anyone. About the little girl, I mean. Obviously, you want to protect her, and I don't want you to think I'm someone who'd put a kid in danger just for a—whatever. Okay?" Her word vomit was miles away from coherent, but she hoped it got the job done.

"Okay," Agnes said after a loaded silence. Some of her fear faded.

A business card appeared, and Agnes pushed it into Lola's hand. The card slid against her thumb and sliced into her skin. She hissed as scarlet bubbled up. It burned, but she didn't let the card go. This felt like another test. Another challenge.

"I'm giving you what you want," Agnes said softly. Intently. "You work for me now." She paused, still holding onto the opposite end of the business card. "Betray me, and you won't like what you next see in my eyes."

Lola swallowed and barely stopped herself from taking a cowardly step back. She took careful sips of air though her parted lips. "You don't have to threaten me, you know."

"I'm not threatening you, Delores Aida Osbourne. I'm making you a promise."

CHAPTER 17

"SHE WAS ASKING FOR TROUBLE showing up at the park like that."
Whit scowled into her hot apple cider before taking a long drink.

Agnes grimaced at the understatement. One wrong move and the
security men would've taken Lola down, breaking bones in the process.
They were all on edge due to the aggression coming at The House from
hidden corners.

"I wonder what she was really hoping to find by tracking me down." It
couldn't be as simple as wanting another pizza date. Could it?

The smell of Whit's drink was spicy and sweet, mixing with the
crispness of the evening. She and Agnes sat in the tree-enclosed balcony
just outside Agnes's home office. The evening breeze was a shade too cool
for the oversized hooded sweater, long skirt, and fuzzy socks Agnes wore,
but she didn't want to go inside.

They'd all had the chance to shower and change since getting back
from the park. Agnes had insisted on it, not wanting to talk about what
had happened with Lola while she was still angry, still scared. But she could
only push the conversation away for so long.

Gretchen was in her room remotely playing video games with some
friends from school, her absence giving the adults the privacy they needed.
The tablet at Whit's side monitored the video game's screen as well as the
cameras in the rest of the apartment.

Whit's hand curled tight around her cup of cider. "Maybe she found
exactly what she was looking for."

Gretchen. Agnes's weakness. And also Whit's.

Like Agnes, Whit would give her life to protect Gretchen. They'd both watched her grow from a frightened infant into this sweet, intelligent child who knew she was loved.

Gretchen deserved to be sheltered, treasured, but also given room to grow. Long ago, Agnes swore to herself she'd never allow Gretchen to be treated like a commodity and to be used the way Agnes's father had used her. First, by teasing his "associates" with the possibility of buying her virginity. Then later, at House events, parading her in front of them as his untouchable showpiece, practically daring anyone to kidnap her. One of his frenemies had eventually accepted his dare and died with her father grinning at him from over the barrel of a smoking gun.

If Agnes were a better person, she would've allowed Gretchen to get adopted by a nice, normal family. But she wasn't always nice. She was her father's daughter after all.

"Lola isn't going to use Gretchen against us," Agnes said softly.

Her instinctive panic and rage had blinded her at first, but she was thinking more clearly now. Lola played games, but she wasn't cruel. From everything Agnes had seen so far, Lola was the type to put herself in danger, not someone else. Certainly not a child.

Whit speared her with a single glance, looking so much like a stern teacher in her black sweaterdress and pale green scarf. "How can you be so sure?"

"I just am."

Lola's almost aggressive apology had felt real. After the initial burst of bravado, regret had curled her in on herself, and she'd stood before Agnes like a penitent, ready to take whatever punishment was handed out. She'd seemed surprised when Agnes had told her she was hired.

Maybe Agnes shouldn't have gone through with hiring Lola. But self-protection demanded she keep Lola close. Something in the shadows was moving against them. It felt big and dangerous. Especially coming so close to the yearly masquerade ball. If Lola was part of this threat, Agnes wanted her near. To watch, to question, and if necessary, to trap and use as collateral.

Sighing out her frustration, Agnes abandoned the sofa to look out over the balcony at the beginnings of night unfurling in the city. Lights slowly flickered on in the building below, ribboning lamplit streets flowing toward the horizon. The city was so beautiful. Sometimes she actually forgot. Until moments like this, peaceful and quiet, away from the burden her father had left her.

Speaking of which…

Agnes turned her back to the night. "Do we have any numbers for asylum seekers on the night of the masquerade ball?" She asked the question in French, just in case Gretchen was nearby.

A muscle ticked in Whit's cheek. Obviously, she didn't want to let go of the Lola discussion, but Agnes refused to continue it any further. After a brief staring contest between them, Whit checked her tablet, flipping between screens until she found what she was looking for. "So far, twenty-six," she answered in the same language.

"A big jump from last time." As the years went by, more escorts approached The House about working there, attracted by the more asset-friendly contract terms, health benefits, and tight security. The House was expanding fast. Maybe too fast. "And how many want to change houses versus disappear?"

"All except for five," Whit said.

"And they all check out?"

The look of scorn Whit gave her was well-deserved. She held up her hands in apology. "Stupid question."

"Yes, it was." Respect was dead in this house.

Agnes huffed out a laugh. She drifted back to the couch and, with only inches separating them, lightly squeezed Whit's hand. Their eyes met. *We're okay?*

A nod. *We're okay.*

"You know," Whit said after a long while. "Pretty soon people are going to put it together that, days after the masquerade ball, they lose assets."

"Do you think this is what Rake was talking about in Vegas?"

"Possibly. He may also think you're stealing assets instead of…" Whit trailed off, frowning. They'd never called what they were doing by any particular name. It wasn't "rescuing," because many of the women and men who worked for The House made a choice to be in this business.

"Helping to ensure their better well-being?" Agnes supplied, to which Whit shrugged in response.

"This isn't a stable business. Your little buddies know that. Unless they have a literally captive workforce, the attrition rate is pretty high. And as for the ones who are losing assets they treat like garbage…"

"They don't want anyone to know they've lost their so-called property and consider their organization weak." Agnes finished the thought.

With a few variations on that week's incoming threats, this was a conversation they'd had countless times over the past few years.

"So, we should be fine," Whit said, although she was the one who'd brought up the doubts this time. "All we can do is be prepared and head into the masquerade with as few distractions as possible."

The sound of light footsteps from inside turned Agnes's head toward the office.

"Are you guys talking secret stuff again?" Wearing unicorn pajamas, Gretchen stood in the doorway leading from the office and, even from the slight distance, smelled of the lavender-scented baby lotion she liked, even though she always told anyone who would listen how much she was *not* a baby.

"Why would you say that, sweet pea?" Agnes held out her arms, and Gretchen immediately flew into them with a happy laugh. Damn, she was getting heavier every day. Her little elbows and bony knees dug into all of Agnes's soft spots before Gretchen settled down in her lap.

"Because when you guys don't want me to understand something, you talk in that funny way."

Smart girl. Agnes smoothed back the edges of Gretchen's hair and exchanged a look with Whit.

"We're just chatting in French," Whit said. "You'd only be bored if you understood what we're talking about."

"No, I wouldn't." Pouting, Gretchen twisted to look up at Agnes, her face set in a determined look Agnes was unfortunately very familiar with. "Teach me French then. I want to understand everything."

Oh Lord.

Agnes met Whit's gaze and subtly tilted her head. They'd have to continue this conversation another time. Whit nodded, obviously fighting a smile.

"All right then," she said to Gretchen. "This is your first lesson…"

CHAPTER 18

AGNES KNEW LOLA'S REAL NAME.

All of it. Even the middle name she never put on any of her official IDs. Although, if her Marathon Stalker was any clue, Agnes and her people knew even more than that. Lola's apartment was off the radar. Just by coincidence, Jamika was the only one officially on the lease. She was the one with better credit. But Lola's stalker in the blue shirt knew her neighborhood. Who else could it be but someone from The House?

That, more than Agnes's reputation as the ruthless head of a very illegal business enterprise, scared Lola shitless. Never mind that she was starting to catch feelings for Agnes. Okay, maybe not *starting*, exactly. If feelings for Agnes were the flu, Lola would already be flat on her back in an ICU with IV fluids and a priest saying last rites.

"You sure you're ready for this?" Jamika asked.

Sprawled in Lola's rocking chair and wearing booty shorts and a crop top with "butches bottom too" scrawled across the chest, Jamika was calmer today. But she still gave off those vibes of restlessness and tension from before. She'd barely met Lola's eyes the whole day.

Lola had already asked Jamika what was going on, and after getting another round of "everything is fine," she was letting it go. For now.

"I better be ready," Lola said.

Three nail-biting days after her confrontation with Agnes at the park in Brooklyn, Lola had finally gotten word of her first assignment for The House. She'd half-expected to get another message saying she "wasn't the right fit" after all. What she'd received instead were orders to pick up an outfit from a boutique and word of more detailed instructions to come.

She turned, examining herself in the full-length mirror. Her dress was tight-fitting and knee-length, a purple so deep it was nearly black. Its high neckline dipped just below her collarbones and somehow made her throat look slender and vulnerable, like she was waiting for teeth to clamp down on her neck and claim her.

She felt nearly naked. A gift ready for someone to open with little effort.

This was what she wanted, so why did sickness churn in her stomach at the thought of a stranger's hands on her? Lola bit her lip and turned away from her reflection.

Although she wasn't nervous *per se*, Lola shivered and brushed her hands up and down her bare arms.

"Take this." Jamika tossed Lola the cropped white fur coat that had been included in the garment bag, not saying a word about Lola's obvious jitters.

When Lola put it on, the fur brushed the underside of her jaw and smelled faintly of the uptown boutique where she'd picked it up. She drew in a deep breath and pressed a hand to her stomach.

Now, she was officially an employee of The House of Agnes. A business card with an uptown address and a new cell phone had been delivered to her PO box along with instructions on how she should conduct herself tonight. With professionalism. Nothing overtly criminal in the typewritten note, no "I just got hired as a hooker by this famous madam, so come and arrest her please" type of incriminating evidence. If it had been that easy, she would already have done it.

Maybe.

For now, she had one of Jamika's listening devices in her tiny purse, the address of her first assignment memorized, and a bushel of butterflies fluttering in her stomach. After a steadying breath, she straightened. "I should leave now. I don't want to be late."

"Okay." A flash of her eyes, then Jamika dipped her head, hair falling around her face to hide what Lola swore was a look of uncertainty. "Be careful, and call me if anything goes wrong."

"I will. Both of those things."

Less than an hour later, Lola found herself in a limousine pulling up to a large building, graceful and majestic in its old age, at the end of a long driveway. Hers was far from the only limo there, and as she got out of the long black car, fighting nerves and psyching herself up to avoid freaking out, another car pulled up behind hers, a Town Car. A couple emerged, both of them masked.

Oh.

Lola dipped her head to speak to the driver. "I didn't know this was a masked event." Then she could've slapped herself. The driver wouldn't know what was going on here anymore than she would.

"The mistress told me to give you this when you arrived," the driver said, surprising her. He picked up a glittering silver mask from an open box on the seat next to him. It was expensively made and in the image of some sort of cat. "Put it on before you go inside."

Okay, so maybe the guy did know more than she did.

With a murmured "thanks" she took the mask and slipped it on. Made from a silver laser-cut metal, it was cool in her hands yet soft against her skin. The mask's firm contours fit perfectly over her face, its bright lines glowing against her dark skin like lace, accentuating her features instead of hiding them. Her face, reflected in the limo's window, looked exotic and savage.

"You're also to leave your purse and all other belongings in the car," the driver said.

What? Panic grabbed ahold of her stomach, and Lola thought she was going to be sick again. "No, I can't do that. I have things in there." She let her voice drop to insinuate what most men were deathly afraid of. "Personal lady things."

He wasn't moved. "Everything you need is inside. If you're not able to comply, you cannot go in." The man stared ahead as he said the words that sounded memorized from a script. It didn't seem like it mattered to him whether Lola ended up inside the mansion or back in the car on her way home.

Shit.

"All right then," she said, channeling a bit of Queen Agnes's signature arrogance, as if none of this mattered. Inside, she was screaming her head off. "Thank you very much."

When she got out and stepped aside so he could drive off and not roll over her toes in the process, she watched her only link to Jamika, her phone, plus the bugs in her purse, drive away.

Fuckety fuck fuck.

Heels sounded against pavement, and she turned to see a woman walking in, handsome in a tailored three-piece suit, her thick hair streaming over her shoulders and down her back. She was obviously intent on passing Lola, but as she drew closer, she paused, gave Lola's body a long and thorough look as if she were shopping for her next life-sized treat. The greed in her eyes was obvious even with the half-faced Mardi Gras style mask she wore.

Heat lit Lola up from head to toe. She'd been to plenty of clubs, had been sized up as a potential sex partner for the night by plenty of people, but she'd never been completely eye-fucked and claimed like this.

Right. It was *that* kind of party.

It felt like it took forever, but finally the woman passed her by and headed up the driveway with her uber-confident stride.

The lights from the mansion swept over the wide verandah, highlighting the towering Greek columns, the pruned shrubbery, and the trickle of beautiful people. On each side of the massive double doors, an attendant stood in a tuxedo, wearing a generic black mask like the kind Antonio Banderas wore in that *Zorro* movie. They seemed to be checking invitations and names off a guest list.

Lola gave them her name, and after they each confirmed whatever information they had on their tablets, they let her through.

Oh… Passing through the doorway of the mansion was like stepping into another world. One moment, she was on the outside, one foot paused to enter, watching the beautifully dressed people file in and out, and the next, she was in a rich person's fairyland.

It wasn't at all the cheap orgy scene she had expected. No dirty old men sat with their legs sprawled in thronelike chairs while naked women bounced in their laps. The smell of sex didn't suffocate her every breath.

Instead, it was all very elegant. Marble floors and crystal chandeliers, waiters passing by with drinks on their trays. A wide hallway leading into a ballroom, and a sumptuous double staircase. Low, sensuous music throbbed in the air, saturating the space in a very particular kind of atmosphere. One of tasteful sensuality with a touch of decadence. And people. They were everywhere. All of them in masks, all beautifully dressed.

Excitement buzzed over Lola's skin as she slid into the fray, bumping shoulders with people who smelled of expensive perfume and hundred-year-old scotch. She murmured soft "pardon mes" as she moved around the lower floor, trying to take it all in. But, try as she might, she couldn't tell the House assets like her from the clients who would be able to buy whatever they wanted for the night. Or the next few hours.

"You look lovely."

Lola turned. It was the woman from the driveway. Although it had only been a few minutes since Lola had seen her, she already had company. Two women who wore catlike masks similar to Lola's held onto the woman's elbows. These women were gorgeous, with their painted mouths and sexy bodies. Both looked House-bred, sensuous and obliging, ready to do anything the woman in the suit wanted.

"Thank you," Lola said to the woman. The suit. "You don't look too bad yourself."

A low laugh floated from the woman's lip-glossed mouth, and the two women with her smiled as they looked Lola over and sipped from their nearly empty glasses of sparkling wine. Well, knowing Agnes's wealth and taste, it was more than likely actual champagne from that French town.

"Not bad?" one of the girls said with an inviting laugh. "She looks killer. Don't you think so, Evie?"

Evie was apparently the woman on the other elbow. "Killer," she agreed with a Cali girl accent.

"You should party with us, little lynx," the suited woman said, coming closer and towing the others with her.

Lynx?

The first girl must have read Lola's mind. She lightly tapped the edge of her champagne flute against the side of her own mask. "Your mask."

Lola touched her mask, the smooth metal over her cheeks, the high and pointed ears.

Interesting. Tonight then, whatever the species of cat, she was supposed to be Agnes's pet. Was the mighty queen already here?

"I'm actually meeting somebody," Lola said in response to the invitation.

"Aren't we all?" Evie giggled.

"This particular person told me to find them as soon as I got here," Lola said, although aside from being directed to the mansion, she didn't know who she was supposed to see or, to be more precise, who she was supposed to fuck.

An unforgiving shudder ran through her at the thought of finally having to do what she had been trying to convince Jamika was no big deal. She shifted her stiffening shoulders under the soft material of her dress and drew a long and silent breath. *Keep it together, Delores.*

"If they're so eager to have you, they should be the one looking for you," not-Evie said.

Agnes look for her? Lola choked back a laugh.

As if she had conjured her up from thin air, Lola caught sight of a familiar profile, unmasked and unsmiling, on the other side of the ballroom. Her heart rate kicked up.

"Excuse me," she said and damned herself for sounding breathless and downright eager as she pushed through the crowd.

Agnes stood with another unmasked woman, the two of them with hands clasped behind their backs as they faced the dance floor packed with couples and threesomes and more-somes moving to the music. As she slid close, Lola caught a word or two of what Agnes and her companion said to each other. They weren't speaking English or even the Spanish she'd learned on her neighborhood streets. *Figures.*

"Good evening, Queen Agnes," Lola said, stopping at what she hoped was a respectful distance. This was a delicate game, and she had to get everything right. At least in public.

The woman with Agnes turned, smiling as she looked down at Lola from what had to be at least six feet. "Ah, I believe there's someone who wants your attention, my dear." Her eyes were warm and amused, nothing like the cool gaze Agnes leveled at Lola.

"So there is," Agnes murmured. Her eyes skimmed over Lola, and Lola shivered in reaction, then mentally called herself a lust-struck idiot two seconds later. "The mask looks good on you." Though Agnes spoke softly, Lola heard every word over the insistent beat of the music. Agnes's intent eyes were like a caress over every part of Lola's face, heating her skin, speeding her pulse. "It fits you. Perfectly."

Agnes's friend made a low noise. A hum of amusement. "We'll catch up later on, darling. After tonight's appointment, give me a call and we'll do dinner or something a bit more intimate." What was more intimate than dinner? A mutual tossed salad? Lola did her best to keep the scowl from her face as the woman leaned down to brush her cheeks against Agnes's, one after the other.

"I'll have someone send the information you need for tonight," Agnes said before the elegant, smiling creature walked away in her thigh-high hooker boots.

"I didn't mean to chase off your company."

"Don't worry. She hasn't gone far." As a waiter passed by, Agnes snagged a couple of glasses of champagne from his tray and passed one to Lola.

"Should I be drinking on the job?" Lola asked, raising the glass to her lips. The champagne was crisp and fresh on her tongue, not what she preferred, but it helped to wash the taste of unease from her tongue. She hated feeling out of her element.

"I wouldn't advise you to have more than one, unless you're the type to get tipsy from just the smell of liquor." Agnes's lower lip glistened with a drop of the champagne, but it did nothing to spoil the picture Agnes made, tall and elegant and untouchable in a fitted white suit, her hair pulled back in a French twist. Her lipstick was the same warm shade as her skin.

They'd shared multiple glasses of Agnes's ridiculously expensive whiskey in Vegas, so Agnes knew Lola could hold her liquor. Wait…was she flirting? No, not after what had happened between them the last time they saw each other. Nobody flirted with someone they'd just threatened.

And boy, did Lola feel threatened. That *promise* Agnes made, right there under the sun with the laughter of the mysterious child still ringing in the air, never left Lola. The child was important. Agnes had been all but playing nice that afternoon until Lola had seen the little girl. Just who was she?

"I think I'll be able to handle this one glass and then some," Lola said, circling back to her original thought.

"I'm counting on it."

Or was she counting on the fact that Lola would fail and trip herself up?

For Zoe's sake, and all the women The House was taking advantage of, Lola couldn't afford to fuck up.

"Speaking of which, what do you want me to do now that I'm here? Your instructions were a little vague." She turned her gaze to the dancers moving around the ballroom and hoped Agnes couldn't see how nervous she was. Hell, she'd mostly hidden the nerves from herself until about ten seconds ago.

The music grew louder, its bass line pounding a little deeper, the breathy voice of the singer rising and forcing Lola to inch closer to hear whatever Agnes had to say. Her breath hitched in her throat. Just another inch and they would touch.

"I have—" Agnes stopped. She looked at her wristwatch, one of those digital kinds hooked to a smart phone. It must have vibrated with some sort of alert. From where Lola stood, she could see it was a notification of a text message. One word leapt out at her.

Nessa. That was the name that little girl had called Agnes.

When Agnes dropped her wrist back down to her side, she met Lola's gaze.

The music swirled around them, seductive and deep, pulling an unconscious rhythm from Lola's hips.

"Lynx!" Not-Evie bumped Lola from behind. "Come dance with us." With Evie and Suit in tow, she tugged at Lola on the way to the dance floor, but Lola broke away from her light hold with a smile.

"Maybe later," she said, and once the women drifted off to the dance floor, she turned her attention back to Agnes.

"I see you've been making friends," Agnes said. "Good." She was cool to the touch as she slipped something into Lola's hand. A key card. "Your client is on the third floor, the Peacock Room." She paused, her lips parted and her tongue appearing briefly as if she was going to say something else. Lola drew in a breath and waited. But Agnes just shook her head. "I'll see you in the morning."

Then she was gone, a sylph vanished into the crowd, leaving behind only the echoing silence of her unsaid words.

CHAPTER 19

THE AUTUMN MASQUERADE BALL WAS whatever anyone wanted it to be. For most, it was an avenue to sex, the chance to touch and be touched by an object of desire, a source of pleasure, usually far out of reach. For some, it was a chance to escape a life they never wanted.

For Agnes, it was work.

She stood on the second floor of her father's pretentious Westchester County mansion, wearing her boring suit, with all her emotions carefully tucked away. At least they had been tucked away, until she'd glimpsed Lola walking in a moment ago.

The breath rushed from Agnes's lungs, and she felt light-headed.

It was more than the purple designer dress Lola was wearing. Definitely more than the makeup or the way she swung her hips like a dinner bell. By now, Agnes could admit that from the first time she saw Lola in the club, she'd been tempted. Thick women had always been her weakness, and every time her eyes touched Lola, she wanted her even more. That taste in Vegas had only fed her hunger.

Below her, Lola moved among the other beautiful people, ready to take on a job she didn't really want. The more Agnes thought about it, the clearer that became. Getting into The House was part of her strategy, not her endgame.

So, what now?

Maybe all Agnes could do was watch and wait.

She rested a hand on the balustrade a level above the main room, watching the guests, a mixture of clients and assets, enjoying themselves. Her mind hummed with calm. Lola was here, but Agnes also had to work.

For the sixth year in a row, the Autumn Masquerade Ball was happening. It was the culmination of the year's planning and preparation and one of the first projects Agnes had set up once her father was gone. On the surface, it was just one big party, featuring some of the most sought-after, and most expensive, escorts in the world. But to those who needed it, the masquerade was an invitation, issued deep underground, to assets from every sex-work organization in the Americas and Europe. If they wanted to escape to something better, to something else, even if that meant a real life outside of the business, The House of Agnes was a way out.

Not that anyone knew it was The House that offered the escape. On the surface, the ball was a joint effort of The Consortium. A massive party and the opportunity to showcase some of the most exclusive assets in the world to the richest clients in the world. Each year, a different house took turns hosting the event, although it had been agreed for the past few years to keep it at the Upstate mansion for convenience's sake.

Agnes didn't mind.

Behind her at the railing, the air rippled as people moved past, some calling out in greeting, others glancing her way and moving on. Her stiff back and cold face, she knew, didn't invite anyone to stop and chat. It was how she preferred it. Being removed. Keeping apart.

But downstairs, Lola's presence tempted her to engage. Even with the distance between them, Lola glowed like bioluminescence among dark ocean waves, effortlessly drawing Agnes's attention.

There was work to be done, though. Hard work. For this, Agnes had to be bloodless.

But her body wasn't listening.

Unlike the previous years of the Autumn Masquerade Ball, Agnes felt weakened by the promise of pleasure. The assets in the mansion were all richly dressed, each gorgeous in their own way.

Usually, she wasn't moved. Some of the most beautiful women in the world had gotten to their knees, begging to please her, and she'd said no. But tonight...

Her eyes drifted back to Lola. Lola glided through the crowd, obviously puzzling at the faces underneath the masks, probably wondering who she was being paid to sleep with tonight.

God, she was gorgeous. The silver filigreed mask made her even more so, showing off the ripe red of her mouth, her high cheekbones, her expressive eyes.

Since that night in the club, Agnes's hunger for Lola had only grown sharper. Lola was a liar. She played games. But Agnes wanted to fuck her so badly that it made her teeth ache. And other places. Beneath her tailored silk suit, her skin was abuzz, lit up with desire for the little snake she'd invited into her lair.

It was dangerous, it was stupid, but she was longing for the little beast to bite. Just to find out why she was there.

A flash of gold caught her eye, and she saw Rox, nearly nude with only crystals covering her nipples and the V of her sex. In high heels, her hair loose and hanging down her back, she stalked a level above where Agnes stood, a hand trailing along the bannister as if she owned the place. She was putting on a show, and many were watching.

Two of Rox's steady clients were here tonight, and both wanted her company. Apparently, she'd suggested a threesome, and both men had agreed.

Agnes felt a smile tease her lips. Did the men know what they were getting into? They would find out soon enough.

"Are you thinking about that girl again?" A whisper of a voice came at her back, and she only managed not to stiffen by force of will.

"If by 'that girl' you mean Rox, then yes."

Whit stepped in front of her, immaculate in head-to-toe black, a pantsuit and jacket, her face bare. "Deflection doesn't work on me, your Highness. You forget, I know you more than most, and I know you're not ready to let that girl go."

Warmth rushed into Agnes's cheeks, and for once, she didn't know what to say. It was just a relief that Whit wasn't talking about killing Lola anymore.

Whit laughed. "Don't worry. I won't tell anyone you've been writing love poems at your desk instead of doing any real work."

"Thanks." Agnes made sure the sarcasm was naked in her voice. Then she turned from her contemplation of the room. "Don't you have something to do?"

"I could ask you the same question." They exchanged a smile. Then Whit was all business again. "So far, we have six more requesting asylum."

And the night was just getting started.

"We can handle that." Agnes looked down over the crowd again, tracking Lola's progress.

Since the warning from Rake in Vegas, Agnes worried. Add to that the hacking of The House's servers, she'd thought about suggesting to the board that the masquerade ball be cancelled. But that would've brought more attention to her, not less.

Just then, Whit made a noise that sounded suspiciously like a laugh, forcing Agnes's attention from Lola a floor below.

"Jesus, your Romeo act is getting painful to watch. Just don't forget the real reason you're here tonight." Whit walked away without giving Agnes the satisfaction of telling her she was wrong. As if there was any point in lying to the woman who'd grown to be her best friend over the past ten years.

Romeo act, though? Ridiculous.

Still, Agnes headed down the stairs, footsteps measured and unhurried toward where Lola stood talking with a group of women. Music pulsed from the dance floor, sensual and seductive, the decadent atmosphere she had become mostly immune to raising the fine hairs along her arms. She was vaguely aware of people making room for her as she moved, as if she walked in her own bubble of protection. No one touched her. Some eyes dropped with respect. Others met hers boldly, flirtatiously, but no one dared to come close.

"Oú est cette douce morceau que tu m'as promis?" *Where is that sweet morsel you promised me?*

At the sound of the low voice, Agnes turned. "Delphine," she said to the woman who'd stopped her. "I didn't think you'd get here until much later."

The Frenchwoman, who insisted on speaking French when they conducted business but preferred English when they met socially, glided closer in all black—a translucent silk blouse and miniskirt that ended an inch above her thigh-high boots. A diamond choker emphasized the elegant slenderness of her throat.

"That was my plan," Delphine said. "Then I became too eager to stay home. I want to see if I can spot this treat you have in mind for me before she ends up in my bed."

"Seeing her before won't affect your enjoyment either way," Agnes said. "Perhaps, perhaps not."

Tonight, Delphine wasn't wearing a mask. She rarely did at the masquerade, preferring to show off the staggeringly gorgeous features she'd inherited from her fashion model father. She was a little older than Agnes, generous with her considerable fortune, and a sweetheart who preferred to have strictly controlled encounters instead of bothering with women out in the real world. She was one of The House's best clients. She was also the woman Agnes had picked to be with Lola. The morsel.

Delphine's tastes were varied but nothing too kinky that would frighten Lola, and from what the others who'd been with her had shared, she was a generous and practiced lover. No matter what Lola's game was, she deserved a good first-time experience, and Delphine would give that to her. The electronic key to the Peacock Room burned in Agnes's hip pocket.

Diamonds flashed as Delphine turned her wrist to look at her watch. "Only another hour until I meet her. Are you sure you won't give me a little hint?"

Agnes opened her mouth to say something about Lola, but the words didn't come. She tried something different. "I'll give you more than a hint —" Delphine's mouth curved up in triumph. "—in an hour." And it shouldn't have pleased her so much to see Delphine, who everyone normally catered to, lose that air of satisfaction she usually wore. "It'll be worth the wait, I promise."

Full lips pursed, then smiled again. "You have never disappointed me before, my dear. I do not expect you will this time."

The card pressed warmly against Agnes's hip, as if it were trying to remind her it was there. That wasn't something she was about to forget. While she smiled at Delphine and reassured her of her satisfaction by the end of tonight's party, Agnes reached a decision, quickly rearranging the plans she had for the night.

A familiar scent reached her nose just before she heard the woman she'd been thinking about all night. "Good evening, Queen Agnes."

Her heart knocked once, powerfully, in her chest, and warmth spread through her like sunlight across a snow-covered field. If she hadn't realized it before, Agnes knew it now. Where Lola was concerned, she was well and truly fucked.

CHAPTER 20

THE PEACOCK ROOM WAS ONLY easy for Lola to find because someone had told her where it was. Otherwise, she would've been wandering around the massive house half the night. On the third floor, the music was softer, a barely there background in the wide hallways decorated with large paintings of foreign landscapes and fruit.

Lola stood outside the door to the Peacock Room—notable because of the peacock feather etched just above the door's handle—and willed her runaway heartbeat to calm the fuck down.

Once she was sure she had herself under better control, she knocked. Then knocked again when no answer came. Screw it. She had a key card for a reason. Lola swiped it over the strangely modern electronic panel embedded in the door and let herself in.

The first thing she noticed was that the room was empty. The second thing was that it was beautiful, sumptuous, a place made to lose inhibitions in. Someone had been in there before, had made it ready. That made sense. After all, what self-respecting escort agency would bring a high-paying client to a room that smelled of cobwebs and mildewed money? Especially if it was a way to screw someone who was supposed to be worth every penny and then some. Everything she'd heard about the "assets" who ended up at the House of Agnes said they were incredible. Perfect. Worth every hundred-dollar bill.

No pressure.

Lola stood in the doorway, seeing nothing but the large bed with its slatted wooden headboard—perfect for securing handcuffs—and the soft-looking royal blue sheets, gold pillows, and turquoise comforter.

A mirror on the ceiling, and another that took up an entire wall, reflected back the empty bed. There was nowhere to hide. If someone walked in right now, they would see her and only her.

She closed the door.

Even though they were paying for it, these people who came to The House were pretty standard, right? Like anyone who enjoyed sex, they wanted to feel good. They wanted pleasure. That, Lola understood.

She could give pleasure, but the type depended so much on what the person wanted. Hard pleasures or soft. Kinky or vanilla. Experienced or a pretend virgin. After a more thorough check of the room—drawers of the bedside table, closets, the attached bathroom—Lola went back to stand near the headboard, trying to imagine how this night would go.

She was still contemplating the beautifully laid out bed and considering her options for her mystery client when the door handle clicked. A trickle of nervousness had her smoothing down the front of her dress as she turned to face the door as it opened.

A woman walked in. Naked. Masked.

Lola barely registered the click of the door closing, locking. Her throat dried as she stared. And kept on staring. The woman was naked. Masked.

She crossed the room. Proud. Her body was willowy, lightly muscled, and with a high handful of breasts, dark-tipped and trembling slightly as she came to a graceful standstill on high heels the same passionate red as her lips.

The mask she wore was made of crystals. Every part of it glittered, throwing arcs of light around the room, making it impossible to focus on the details of her face. Even her mouth, a deep shade of red, glimmered with a high-sheen lipstick. The mask was of a gazelle. Or some kind of deer. A prey for cats at the very least. Lola had seen enough *National Geographic* shows to know that much.

She swallowed hard. "Hi."

Jesus. How mature was that? This woman was paying for an experienced escort, not a fumbling high schooler.

"Buenas noches, cariño," the woman said in return. *Good night, darling.*

Oh… Lola's stomach flexed with unexpected desire.

The woman's voice was a throaty purr, perfectly matching the feline way she strode into the room and toward Lola despite her gazelle mask.

She was distractingly naked, but once she spoke, Lola could only stare at her lips, at the bright red curve that dripped sensuality and stroked instant arousal between Lola's thighs.

She shivered. Was she just a slut for anyone? A few minutes ago, she'd been ready to fall to her knees for Agnes.

But this is what you're getting paid to do, an internal voice rationalized. *You might as well enjoy it.*

Her hands trembled, and her stomach did its little dance again.

The woman didn't look nervous, though. She just waited. Silent and tempting as a ruby-ripe pomegranate hanging on a low branch. She was ballsy, Lola would give her that, already nude and waiting for a stranger to accept or deny her. That was the way Lola sometimes felt in front of Agnes, vulnerable and completely at her mercy even though Lola was the one chasing her, hoping to capture a queen and get answers to questions Zoe had left at her door.

Then.

Like smoke before a strong and cleansing breeze, all of Lola's nervousness drifted away. She would do this. Gain Agnes's trust. Please this woman. Prove to herself that everything she'd said to Jamika about sex with strangers who paid for it was no big deal.

Lola took off her mask.

"You're lovely," the woman said, still speaking Spanish.

Lola replied in the same language. "So are you."

"You don't have to say that because I'm paying you to be here." The woman smiled, a red curve just under the opening of her mask, and took a step. She walked around the room, around Lola, with graceful and confident strides. The sound of her high heels against the prettily colored rug was soft yet firm, its own sensual interplay, and her curvaceous hips swayed tantalizingly from side to side.

She stopped in front of the wall-sized mirror. From there, Lola saw her from nearly every angle, her flawless figure from throat to feet, sexy enough to curl Lola's toes and wet her tongue with the desire to lick her up, then down.

The reflection of her backside was equally inspiring, like a photo from an art magazine. Her long thighs looked strong, as if they could smother

Lola and then bring her back to life. And those calves, muscled and tight, flexing beautifully from her sensual stance in those high heels.

Lola's breath tripped and stumbled on its way out. She was definitely in lust. Without anyone asking, she would have fucked this woman for free. Then an image of Agnes rose up in her mind, cold and fiercely judgmental. Irresistible. Okay, maybe not for free. Not if she had the chance to choose between Agnes and a stranger.

That only makes you a fool, an internal voice said.

Lola swallowed and mentally steadied herself, pushing away all irrelevant thoughts of Agnes. She closed the space between herself and the woman. "You're so tall," she murmured, making sure to inject a note of teasing in her voice while eyeing the woman's six-foot-plus height. "Come on down here with me. Those heels have to be hell to walk in. You didn't have to wear them to impress me. You're already sexy just as you are."

"Who says I'm trying to impress you?" The woman's voice was ripe with a tease of her own as she kicked off her red stilettos. "I might just want to be sexy for myself."

Lola hummed in genuine pleasure when the woman's delicious everything was in closer reach. "That's much better." She pressed a kiss to the middle of the woman's back, her shoulder, her throat. "Whatever the reason for your sexy looks, I fucking love it." Lola took the woman's hand and guided it under her dress. "See?"

A jolt of pleasure made her moan at the woman's seeking movements, long digits stroking in Lola's wetness and pressing against her clit. She shivered. Then clung to the woman's finely muscled arms when the moments deepened and a low grunt, deliciously aggressive, left the woman's throat.

"All this is for me?" Amazement and desire deepened the passionate words. Experienced fingers circled and toyed with Lola's sex.

"All for you," Lola gasped out.

This stranger was so good, so fucking sexy. If Lola didn't keep herself on task, she would definitely get swept up in the pleasure and forget she was the one who was supposed to be providing it.

She drew back. Grabbed the hand threatening to make her lose her mind.

With her breath coming quickly, too quickly, she twined their fingers together, and a wave of heat rolled through her at the feel of her slickness between their linked fingers. She kissed the woman's palm, her wrist, then sucked her fingers, limned with the wet essence of Lola's own lust, into her mouth, one by one, cleaning them off, savoring the taste of herself.

By the time Lola was done, the woman was panting, her pretty breasts quivering from the urgency of her breaths. Her nipples were like juicy blackberries, firm and inviting to Lola's tongue. She didn't resist them either.

The taste of this woman was perfect, like hot tea on a cold day. Slightly salty skin. A hint of a spicy perfume.

"Ah…" A stream of incoherent sounds left the woman's throat, and she quivered against Lola, a hand light at the back of her head, not forcing, just guiding her from one delicious breast to the other. Lola eagerly accepted that guidance, licking the tight nipples, sucking them, enjoying the feel of the woman unraveling under her mouth. Her own body tingled, burned in response.

"Come to bed," she whispered into the softness of the woman's throat. "I can't properly enjoy you with both of us standing like this. You're tall, and I'm…not."

She guided her lover of the moment to the bed and gently pushed her backward, and the woman went, unresisting, sprawling her long body across the sheets. "I'm going to enjoy you," Lola murmured, already imagining it, the pleasure and heat she'd find between the stranger's thighs. "Then I'm going to fuck you."

A pink tongue appeared, licking at vermilion lips. Flares of light from the crystal mask flashed across the beautiful skin, the bedspread, and the antique wooden headboard Lola wanted her to hold on to as she fucked her deep and good.

White teeth and the intimate insides of her mouth appeared when the woman moaned, an agreement of sorts that Lola planned to get more into later.

The woman opened her legs, inviting Lola between them, and Lola eased back, slid off her dress and shoes, and let them fall wherever.

"Your skin is gorgeous," the woman said once Lola resettled between her thighs.

Her hands warmed Lola's back, her shoulders, her breasts and nipples, and Lola shuddered from the pleasure. Desire slicked her thighs, sticky and hot, and she shifted under the woman's touch, squeezing her thighs together and fighting back a low groan.

"I want to hear you, *cariño*. Show me you enjoy the way I touch you."

Lola bit her lip. "Oh yeah?"

"Absolutely."

Her sex tingled, dripped. Her nipples were hard and begged to be sucked. To ease the ache, she brushed her chest against the woman's. She groaned. Then they both did. "You feel incredible." Lola kissed under the woman's jaw, gasping into the soft skin from the possessive clutch of hands on her ass.

The woman shivered quietly beneath her and, for a moment, Lola had a strange double-awareness, that it was Agnes who moved under her, who submitted so well to her touch. Then Lola shook herself out of the delusion. It wasn't fair to the woman to compare her to Agnes, especially since she was paying a fortune for Lola's undivided attention.

Stiff nipples prodded against Lola's, a delicious friction, and pulled her firmly back into the moment. Hips moved beneath her, grinding up, the thigh between hers giving her something to slide against, and damn it was good. A shivering moan slid past her lips. Alight with pleasure, Lola moved her hips too, following the rhythm of the blood beating fiercely in her veins. The slick of her sex felt incredible against the woman's thigh, and she clenched her internal muscles hard, close to being overwhelmed by the wet press of the woman's center on Lola's thigh, the slick sounds they made together, and the puff of the warm breath against her ear.

"*Sí, cariño.*" Another gasp, a divine rasp of pubic hairs against her thigh. "*Muy rico...*"

This was too good.

Pushing aside her intense arousal, Lola pressed one last kiss into the woman's throat before moving down, deliberate with her intent, eyes up to catch the lust-clouded haze of the other woman. At least she thought that was what she saw beneath the luster of crystals and the disorienting light reflecting off the mask. If nothing else, the woman would see the eagerness in her eyes and be as turned-on as Lola was. The scent of her was mouthwatering. Musk and sex and a hot promise of pleasure.

Wet flooded her tongue. God, it felt like she'd been hungry for years.

Groaning low, Lola inhaled the delicious scent, ghosted a breath over the hot, dripping flesh, and dove in, lapping with the broadened flat of her tongue. The woman let out a choked-off cry.

Lola's belly fluttered at the sound, her arousal deepening, the hunger to devour growing more intense with each desperate, breathless sound the woman made. With a thigh over her shoulder and the other pressed nearly flat against the bed, she feasted.

A hand touched her hair, a light, barely there presence, a tease of touch. She mustn't be doing it right then. Lola upped her game, sliding her tongue through the slickness and tapping it against the hard nub of pleasure with each pass. The gasps grew louder. The hand tightened in her hair. Hips furiously fucked her mouth.

That was more like it.

Adding her groans to the mix, Lola sank into the pleasure, losing herself in the smell of the woman's perfume, the taste of her intimate sweat, the salty ambrosia of her sex. The woman's pleasure was hers too, and when her lover screamed out, thighs shaking, her sex pulsing under Lola's mouth, Lola's whole body clenched too, rippling against the sheets, just a breath from coming herself.

God damn…

The woman's shouts died away, and she collapsed on the bed, panting, eyes blinking up at the ceiling as if she was amazed at what just happened. She looked completely relaxed, completely taken care of. Like she could lay on those peacock sheets all night and not move until morning. But Lola was sure she didn't pay what had to be an extraordinary amount of money for only one orgasm.

Keeping an eye on the languid and completely relaxed creature on the bed, she went to the bedside drawer and took out the toy and harness she'd found there on initial inspection of the room. She had the toy buckled on her hips by the time the woman stirred from her stupor, bracing herself on her elbows in the bed and watching Lola with her tongue peeking from the corner of her mouth. Sweat made the woman's long body glow.

Lola's hands brushed soft thighs, and the woman sighed, her head falling back to give Lola access to the long line of her throat.

"This is all right, yes?" Lola knew how to make a question not much of one, just like a certain demanding woman she knew.

"*Sí.*" The woman breathed out a sigh. "*Sí, cariño.*"

Lola kissed her breasts and neck, whispering, "Now get on top. I want to watch you ride me."

The woman's breath caught in her throat, a delicate hitch Lola knew had nothing to do with fear or outrage.

Hesitating just a little, Lola second-guessed herself. Should she be this demanding? A big part of her had doubts. But since she'd bluffed her way into Agnes's circle, she could damn well fake confidence with a woman she was enjoying making love to.

She caught a soft earlobe between her teeth and gently bit down. "Come fuck yourself on my dick, goddess."

On her back and spread out with the thick blue dildo jutting up from her center, Lola held out her hand. The woman came to her. Red lips parted in a lazy smile, so very pliant and sexy, no hesitation, just her thigh thrown over Lola's hips, then she was sinking down onto the thick length with a sigh.

"That's right..." Lola loved that she'd reduced this amazing creature to wordless sounds and uncontrolled breaths. Hands on the woman's slender thighs now, she moved her own hips. "Now take what you want."

"How are you so perfect right now?" The crystalline head fell forward. Her body moved just a little. Then more.

Heat tripped through Lola, the base of the dildo bumping into her clit with each thrust of the woman's hips. Trying desperately not to drown in her own pleasure, Lola watched the woman, felt her, like a wave crashing relentlessly on top of her, breasts, belly, hips, all dancing in a sensuous choreography of sex.

Heat quivered in her belly, in her clit. Her nipples ached. Her body swam in desire. This lust was powerful. Its undeniable heat kept her hips moving, driving up into her lover. But she felt pride too at gifting this amazing creature a night she'd hopefully never forget.

"Do you feel that?" The woman twisted her hips, and the movement punched a helpless grunt from Lola.

"Fuck, yes..." Every moment of the woman's wild motions pushed the base of the dildo against Lola's clit, tapping an electrified bliss deep into her. Lola clutched slender hips and held on.

Though she couldn't properly see the eyes behind the mask, she knew they were on her, felt them on her, tracking her pleasure, watching her face, her body.

The woman rode Lola, her form rolling sensuously, the light hitting her mask in just the right way to throw sparks of brilliance from the crystals all over her bare body, heaving breasts, clenched stomach, and thatch of moist hairs guarding the place Lola pushed into. She threw her head back, and light scattered everywhere, reflecting from the massive mirror that showed how well the woman took control as she rode Lola.

Despite how boldly naked she was, how unashamedly bare in her enjoyment, something about the way this woman moved told Lola she didn't show off her body like this very often. But maybe Lola was just fooling herself, wanting to be special for a woman who probably did this kind of thing all the time.

Now wasn't the time to think about that. This encounter was what it was.

She was lucky she'd been assigned someone she was able to enjoy and connect with sexually. Sex for her was usually fun, but it was even better if she connected with someone. And boy, did she and this woman connect...

Electricity skittered up her spine as the woman skimmed firm thumbs over Lola's breasts, teased them in a circle that mimicked her motion on Lola's dildo.

"You feel incredible." The woman moaned, sliding fingers between Lola's sweat-damp breasts. "I could have you like this all night."

But the truth of it was that they couldn't and not just because Lola could feel her own orgasm barreling toward her at light speed, tightening all her muscles and spreading liquid heat through her belly and between her legs. Thankfully, her lover was losing it too, her hips moving faster, riding Lola furiously, her graceful rhythm gone. She cried out, a high sound of triumph, and shuddered gorgeously as she came. Only then did Lola let go.

Her orgasm, when it came, was like pulling a deep breath inside of her, then releasing it in a gasp, and the release was starlight and fireworks and everything that held light in the universe exploding out of her. All of that light hovered in the Peacock Room, obliterating everything but the woman on top of her, the heat of their bodies pressed together, the red mouth above her open on a laugh of exhilaration. Their heaving breaths were loud and heady.

Exhausted and completely satisfied, Lola closed her eyes.

CHAPTER 21

WHEN THE SEX WAS GOOD, Lola usually passed out right after coming. Which was the reason she woke up, groggy and boneless, alone in the luxurious bed. Her goddess was nowhere in sight.

She sighed in disappointment at the empty spot beside her. It would've been nice to wake up next to her mystery woman, to take off that crystalline mask and see each other completely naked for the first time.

Wait, what was she even talking about? This woman had paid for anonymous sex, not to have some newbie drool all over her with stars in her eyes, ready to plan the wedding.

You're such an idiot.

Lola indulged in a groaning stretch and sat up. Her orgasm blackouts, as she called them, usually didn't last very long. Half an hour at the most. But it probably wasn't a good idea for her to lay around the Peacock Room, naked and sticky from sex, like she belonged there. Where the hell were her clothes?

She could have sworn… There. On the other side of the bed. Her dress, the lynx mask, and the dildo and harness she'd used, all in a neat pile. Next to them lay a black envelope.

Lola drew a deep breath and felt something, a kind of ache, in her chest.

While making love to the woman, she'd sworn a connection sparked between them. Attraction that was more than just sex. But the goddess was a stranger. Lola was the hired help.

Any lingering high from her orgasm bled away. Lola forced herself into action, got dressed, and grabbed the envelope without looking inside. She was an asset now. She had a purpose. And it didn't involve falling in love with strangers and getting distracted from her target. Lola left the opulence of the Peacock Room without a single backward glance.

CHAPTER 22

AGNES RUSHED DOWN THE WIDE hallway, high heels sinking into the thick carpet runner, while trying to seem like she wasn't actually rushing. The phone in her hip pocket vibrated, and she snatched it up. "I'm on the way," she answered, not waiting to hear Whit say what she already knew.

"You said you wouldn't do this."

"I know." Voice lowering, she slipped past a pair of women whispering intently to each other near the stairs, grabbed the bannister, and picked up her speed. "Less than five minutes." She hung up.

It didn't take her long to get to the lowest level of the house, the sub-basement, her heart knocking in her rush, though more from her self-recrimination than the unexpected exercise. Her priorities were clear. She knew better. But it hadn't stopped what she'd done.

A pair of guards, anonymously dressed and with masks shielding their faces, met her at the bottom of the stairs where the short hallway began. The decor was more utilitarian than the 1920s decadence of the upper floors. Tiffany lamps and Klimt reproductions gave way to sterile white walls, a parade of sliding steel doors leading to small rooms equipped with the basic necessities. Beds, bathrooms, generic changes of clothes, one-way mirrors.

Whit stepped from the room on the end, a neutral look on her face that clearly hid her impatience. "Ready?" She handed Agnes a tablet with a name and the relevant data already queued up, and slipped a two-way bug in her ear. Agnes shivered. The bug was cold.

"Of course." Tablet in hand, Agnes followed her into the room, a larger version of the others, only this one had a long metal table in its center, a single chair (bolted to the floor) at each long end. A guard was already inside, standing just beside the one-way mirror. The ceiling-mounted cameras glowed red, already recording.

Seated, Agnes skimmed the list of names and the notations beside them. Whit had already processed the asylum seekers who just wanted to escape sex work, noted the organizations that treated the sex workers like garbage and the reasons those workers needed to be removed.

Whit had no tolerance for violence against the weak and often dealt with tormentors with a thoroughness that would've been frightening if Agnes hadn't often dreamt of doing the same thing. Scorched earth. Disappeared monsters. Gutted buildings.

Most of the people on that list, those who just wanted to escape the business, were already gone from the mansion and on their way out of town to their new lives. Whit was very good at her job.

This one case, though, was one Agnes needed to handle personally.

"Ready?" Whit asked through the earpiece. She was already in another room, watching from behind the one-way glass.

"One moment." Agnes slipped on the disguising mask Whit had left for her. For a moment, visions of her bed, warm and soft, where she would slide between the covers and re-live the best parts of her night, danced beneath her eyelids. With an effort, she opened her eyes. "All right, send him in."

A few minutes later, the door clicked open and one of the security men escorted in a shy young man. A boy, really.

Throwing nervous glances at his escorts, he crept in with caution. He wore the simple white shirt and pocketless pants left for him in his holding room to ensure no weapons or electronic bugs came in with him.

His skin was smooth, with not a wrinkle to be seen. If Agnes hadn't triple confirmed his age of twenty-two, she could easily believe him to be in his mid-teens.

"Come in. Have a seat." Agnes made her voice kind. Once the boy was seated and looked comfortable enough, she got started. "Tell me, what can I do for you this evening?"

"Hi, I'm Kevin Eubanks. But you probably already know that from the information I already gave."

Yes, she already knew that, but she dipped her head in encouragement and waited for him to tell her more.

"I want to work for you." His voice was just like him, delicate and soft-seeming, a breath of sound that invited the listener to lean close. "I'm good at what I do, and I want to keep doing it. For your house."

Like everyone Whit had already processed, Kevin had been checked out thoroughly, from his Social Security number to his school records, his acquaintances, and his family. Everything seemed legitimate, but Whit had doubts. Which was why Agnes was now interviewing him.

With his large amber eyes, curly hair, and graceful limbs, Kevin was a cliché of delicate and vulnerable. Fragility surrounded him like a halo, and every breath he took was a plea for someone to take care of him. Agnes could see why Whit was suspicious.

She couldn't help but compare the boy to Lola, the effortless appeal they both had, which was the currency they used in their attempts to penetrate The House's defenses. But unlike the boy, Lola had Agnes spellbound. With her strong and beautiful body, her challenging eyes. Delores Osbourne was a woman who, even as she twisted the truth to serve her own purposes, told the truth of her desire every time she looked at Agnes. And that desire, that unwilling honesty, was an aphrodisiac like no other.

Agnes shifted in the chair and refocused her attention on the boy in front of her. "Tell me, Kevin, what can The House do for you?"

"Keep me safe," he said immediately. His voice was as light as a butterfly's touch. He leaned into the table, and his scent, clean and crisp, drifted over Agnes's face.

So pretty. Such a beautiful liar.

"Why don't you feel safe now?"

"I-I just don't. My pimp can be cruel." He shuddered dramatically and bit his full lower lip. "Word among the houses is that people who work for you get a better deal. They get taken care of, and they get more money."

All true.

"Who's foolish enough not to treasure a gorgeous boy like you?" Agnes asked.

Pleased color touched Kevin's cheeks. He named someone she wasn't sure existed. "I just want a better situation." He hugged himself with one hand, long fingers draping artfully over his shoulder, his chin down.

Very, very pretty.

"That's what anyone who comes here really wants, Kevin." Agnes put aside her tablet, carefully watching Kevin's face. "They're with people who beat them, or take their children, or get them hooked on poison so they don't ever think of escaping the hell they're in." She paused. "Are you one of those, Kevin? Are you in danger? Do you need help? Or are you trying to take away sanctuary from people who really need it?"

As she spoke, her voice carefully soft, she sat back in her chair, keeping her posture open and nonthreatening. With each word, Kevin's pretty facade cracked just a little more.

"A young woman came to us tonight," Agnes said. "Her face was hurt. But her spirit even more so. Where do you think she would run to if we weren't here to provide shelter?"

His face flexed. He swallowed hard. "Shelter? What you mean is that you'd throw her in a dirty room somewhere and rent her out to people who don't care what her face looks like." A sneer tried to find a home on his face, but his beauty wouldn't let it rest there.

"No, Kevin. She's a woman who needs help. If she wants to leave the business forever, we can make that happen. If she wants to stay with us and work, she can. The house I represent has various types of employment opportunities. And we don't keep people against their will."

"Really?" Kevin's voice cracked. His bluster fell away, replaced with genuine surprise. Clearly, he'd been pumped full of lies before coming here. His ring finger had a gold band that Whit had let him keep. He twisted it.

Agnes sighed. She supposed this whole thing could have been worse. "Do you have any further doubts or issues I can clarify for you?" she asked.

"Um..." Kevin took his time answering before finally saying what amounted to nothing.

While he was talking, an image flashed on the surface of Agnes's tablet. "Excuse me a moment, please." She tapped it to activate the speaker. "What's happening, Julius?"

"We got a situation out here, ma'am. Some people were trying to breach the party from the rear of the house. We have them, but they're raising a stink." Which meant the trespassers previously had guns and now no longer had them.

"Are your people all right?" she asked, even though she suspected the answer.

"Yes, ma'am. What would you like us to do?"

"Deal with them as usual. We don't need anyone to interrupt the party. Thank you, Julius."

"Of course, ma'am."

Agnes disconnected the call, her eyes back on Kevin. His pale skin had gone paler, and he was compulsively licking his lips.

"Please don't kill me," he all but whispered, his voice hoarse and afraid. He convulsed, and the look on his face was like an angel facing a descent into hell. The chair he sat on rattled from his tremors. "I had no choice. Please!"

"We're not going to kill you, Kevin. And we're not going to keep you against your will."

"You're not?" A tear slipped down his bloodless cheek.

"Despite what you've been told, that's not how we do things here."

Agnes clasped her hands in front of her on the desk and watched a different kind of fear take hold of Kevin. Fear, she assumed, of the ones who'd sent him to her. Of what he'd go back to. The widening black of his pupils swallowed most of the amber and his damp lashes fluttered in time with his loud and trembling breaths. More tears fell. Pity stirred in her chest and she almost offered him asylum. However, if she did, she'd never be able to trust him.

So she offered him nothing.

An hour later, Agnes was done and Kevin was on his way back to where he came from. He'd been trying to infiltrate the house his group thought was "stealing" assets. When Kevin saw things weren't quite going his way, a twist of his ring had called for an extraction team. The security team around the grounds had done their jobs well, and Kevin was sent on his way. And not in pieces, as he obviously expected.

"That was well done." Whit propped her hip on the edge of the table.

Except for the security at the door, they were alone, most of the asylum seekers and transfers already dealt with.

"Thank you." Agnes took off the disguising mask she'd been wearing and put it aside. She'd nearly forgotten she had it on. "The key to getting an undercover asset to crack is to make them really think about who they're harming by exposing our operation—vulnerable people just like him. I'd bet every last dime that Kevin won't tell his superiors a damned thing I've admitted tonight. Because now Kevin's thinking, 'what if *I* need to escape one day?' It was in his eyes." Agnes sat back in satisfaction. "I like to think I do my job well."

"Well enough when it counts."

"Careful, I don't want all this flattery to go to my head." Agnes got up from the table, checking her watch. "I'll leave you to it. The mingling isn't going to get done by itself."

"Enjoy."

With a little wave, Agnes left Whit and headed back upstairs to the heart of the party. But leaving behind what happened in the interview room wasn't as simple as walking away. Her unseen enemy was getting bolder. Kevin was proof of that.

Whoever was helping Kevin could've caught her and exposed what she was doing to the whole world. This would've turned the Consortium against her as well as anyone attached to The House, leaving her isolated and without their considerable resources. But none of that had happened.

At least not this time.

Agnes snapped out of it when she bumped into someone. A woman.

"Excuse me," the woman said.

The thick of the party swirled around her, at least as thick as it got on the upper floor with its wide-open grand salon, Savonnerie rug, comfortable leather chairs in every corner, and watered-down jazz playing from hidden speaks. She didn't realize she'd wandered so far from where she'd started.

"My fault," she said, putting on her social smile. "I wasn't paying as much attention as I should have been."

The words came automatically, but as they spilled out, Agnes realized she knew the woman looking at her with calm expectation. She was undeniably gorgeous with her explosion of curly silver hair that gave her enough height to reach Agnes's shoulder, a dark dress hinting at her mature curves, and a pleased smile just below her mask.

"How rude of me." The woman pulled off her mask, and her eyes were warm and expectant.

She was one of the assets who wanted to come to The House, a woman as old as Agnes's mother who still had loyal clients. She wanted to join an organization she could potentially grow and retire with. An odd trajectory since she had chosen a profession that prized youth above most things. Then again, wasn't that all professions?

"I want to thank you," the woman said softly. With the music whirling around them, the low-voiced conversations, and the grand size of the room, they weren't likely to be overheard, but Agnes appreciated her discretion. "Not many would accept an older woman into their house."

"I'm not doing you any sort of favors," Agnes returned. "I know you're an extraordinary asset, and I already have a client in mind who would adore you. The benefit is completely mutual. It won't strain me to have a beautiful and experienced woman in my House."

A smile illuminated the woman's attractive features, and the lines at the corners of her eyes seemed like rays of light. Incredible. "Thank you," she said.

Something about this woman made Agnes fight her reluctance to touch strangers, and instead of backing away from her light perfume and gratitude, Agnes took the woman's square-fingered hand between two of hers and met her eyes.

"If possible, enjoy yourself tonight," Agnes said. "We'll see each other again very soon."

They exchanged another smile, and Agnes left the luxurious receiving room feeling lighter, less troubled than when she arrived.

CHAPTER 23

More and more, Agnes was turning out to be someone Lola had not expected. She headed toward the H Holdings high-rise with the money she'd made from the masquerade party a few nights before.

The sidewalk felt like a spring under her feet, propelling her toward Agnes and the building where she conducted her business. Anticipation buzzed in her veins. Words to a 1990s pop song she barely knew vibrated in her throat.

She hummed and memories of the woman she'd made love to—no, had sex with—floated through her mind like parts of the song. Unforgettable bits. The explosion of light over her skin. Her soft voice saying, breathlessly, "*Cariño...*"

Lola was such a fool to half-fall for a stranger. A stranger who paid her for sex and disappeared before she woke up. Annoyed, she blinked herself free of the memories and focused on where her feet were taking her.

To Agnes.

Vehicles rumbled past her on the early evening street, and from somewhere nearby came the indignant blast of a car horn. Rapid Spanish and friendly laughter poured out from the bodega she passed.

The goddess had spoken Spanish to her.

"Hey, *mami*!" a skinny kid called out, and she flashed him a smile on automatic, caught once again in memories of the woman who'd tasted like tart, forbidden things, and glittered like a jewel under Lola's hands.

At Agnes's building, Lola slowed her footsteps but didn't stop. Lola's bright blue Converse sneakers were silent against the lobby's expensive marble. The receptionist waved her toward the elevators with a smile. Once she was in the shiny car heading to the top floor, her heart began to pound.

She was being an idiot. Again. Because she'd seen something back at the mansion, Agnes touching the hand of an older beautiful woman, not with lust but with unexpected kindness. And the woman had obviously been grateful.

After Agnes had walked away, Lola went up to the older woman, chatting her up with smiles and asked who Agnes was to her. "The person who just might have saved my life," the woman had said.

Lola hadn't been able to hide her shock.

Now, in the tightly zipped inside pocket of her jacket, the cash from the anonymous goddess she'd fucked practically burned through the white T-shirt and into her skin.

When she'd followed Agnes, chasing after her like some pathetic puppy—although then she'd convinced herself she was looking for clues to something illegal that would at least make Jamika happy—the slippery coating of sex from her hour or so with the woman had slid against her flesh and gradually grown cold inside her panties. That reminder of the sex she'd had, that good sex, felt strange, almost disloyal.

But Agnes had been the one to send her to the stranger.

The truth didn't stop any guilt she felt.

By the time the elevator stopped, the mass of conflicted emotions hadn't become any less tangled. Lola let out a sigh and felt it down to the very soles of her feet.

If she could go back to her earlier self, the one spitting and carrying on about revenge as she left the medical examiner's office, she'd slap her hard and tell her not to do what she was thinking. That way, she never would've met Agnes. Which would actually suck.

Lola fought back another sigh. Why did things have to be so damn complicated?

The elevator doors slid open on Agnes's floor. To the left was a dead-end door marked "Authorized Personnel Only." In front of Lola stood a wide desk—a glorified guard booth—with two looming security guys. To the right was Agnes. But first, her guard dog, Clare.

One of the security men watched Lola get off the elevator and swipe the royal blue ID card against the electronic scanner on the desk while the other kept careful eyes on the monitor verifying who she was.

A stirring in the air behind her turned her around.

Her breath did something unnecessary in her throat. "Good evening, Agnes."

Agnes looked as if she'd just gotten off the elevator herself and was heading down the hall to her office. She turned and gave Lola one of those cool smiles that could mean anything.

"Is it evening already?" Agnes glanced at her narrow platinum wristwatch. "I swear I just walked in here a few minutes ago."

She wore a black pantsuit today, the slacks elegant and cut to show off her curves. The pink high heels and matching blouse that peeked from the open jacket didn't soften her even a little bit. Agnes maneuvered the small paper shopping bag she carried to take off the jacket and drape it over one arm.

"Technically, you did just get here. Which you can do since you're the boss."

"That's true." Her smile lit her eyes, a slow and gorgeous thing. "Are you here to see me, or have you come to ask Clare out on a date?"

Was Agnes actually making a joke?

Lola decided to go along with it, brushing aside her surprise. "Obviously. But Clare knows I'm fickle, so she won't be surprised if I get distracted from throwing the usual rose petals at her feet." Lola mimed throwing the petals, complete with a lovestruck look, then felt irrationally happy when Agnes looked one breath away from laughter.

"I'll make sure to tell Clare you said all that."

"That sounded suspiciously like a threat." Lola let her laughter free. "So, what's in the bag?"

"Nothing very sexy—" Which made Lola immediately imagine frothy lingerie and handcuffs. "—just some new Uno cards. Three packs."

Okay, definitely not sexy. Wait... "Uno cards. You mean the kid's game?"

"It's a fun game for adults too, but yes, they are mostly for Gretchen."

Agnes stopped, lips pursed, as if she regretted mentioning the kid. Then Lola could practically see the internal shrug. "She loves the game but somehow always loses cards all over the house. Now we have four decks. Hopefully she can keep these for at least the next month."

"It's good to be prepared." Lola purposefully didn't ask about Gretchen or any other obvious questions like, "Who the fuck is she to you?"

The slight tension she'd sensed in Agnes eased away.

They walked together toward Agnes's office, the only sound the sharp rap of high heels against the floor and Lola's nearly silent Converse sneakers. If that wasn't a commentary on just how different they were…

Not to mention, there was that whole madam who made a living off people's pain thing.

Maybe.

At Clare's desk, Agnes stopped to chat about something or other that Lola probably should've been paying attention to since she was supposed to be spying and all, but she just stood back as the two talked and cheerfully waved when Clare slid a cool glance her way.

When Agnes was done, she gestured toward her office. "Shall we?"

Her confidence, and the possessive way she put a hand on the small of Lola's back, left Lola tongue-tied. "Sure," she stammered.

"You can help me break in one of these Uno decks and prepare for when Gretchen launches her next attack." Agnes continued as if they were just having a friendly visit.

Lola was officially knocked off-balance, and she had a feeling Agnes knew it.

Agnes opened her office door, an almost-smile on her lips. "Come in," she murmured. "Promise I won't bite."

That's too bad. The thought slithered warmth into Lola's stomach, and she bit the inside of her cheek.

While Agnes held the door open for her, she ducked into the office, subtly inhaling Agnes's familiar and spicy scent as she passed. The door clicked shut behind her.

"Make yourself comfortable." Agnes hung her jacket on the coatrack by the door.

"Thanks." Lola's hands shook with nerves. She looked around the office, not quite sure where to stand. Or should she sit? She compromised by leaning against the arm of the sofa and tried to settle the buzzing under her skin that came from being alone with Agnes.

Other than a few exchanged text messages, she and Agnes hadn't spoken since the masquerade party. She'd thought of Agnes every day, though, and dreamt of her most nights. Those dreams confused her as much as they left her wet and wanting.

The touch of Agnes's lips morphed into the scorching slide of the goddess's skin against hers. Agnes's commands. Her client's effortless submission to pleasure. Moment by moment, touch by touch, her mind confused who was who until it was Agnes's name she cried out into her pillow as the dream-induced orgasm washed over her.

Skin flushing hot, she jerked her head to stare out the window and away from Agnes, the woman she was supposed to hate. But she couldn't keep her eyes off Agnes for long. Whatever excuses she had for it, Lola craved her.

Couldn't stop wanting her.

Couldn't stop thinking about her.

Couldn't stop filling herself up with the sight of her.

In slow, graceful strides that flashed the scarlet soles of her high heels and rocked the already hypnotic curves of her hips, Agnes crossed the room to firmly press on a section of the wood-paneled wall. A sharp click and the wall popped open to reveal a hidden door. Inside was a fridge, a small bar with gleaming bottles of liquor, and a high shelf neatly filled with small baskets of snacks.

"What would you like to drink?" Agnes filled two glasses with ice and put them on the bistro table set up in a windowed corner of the office.

Stop staring and answer the woman.

"Water, please." Lola cleared her throat.

Two glass bottles of sparkling water and a bowl of gold-wrapped chocolates joined the glasses on the table. Water, Uno, and chocolates. The setup looked very wholesome.

"What, no whiskey for you this time?" she dared to tease.

Agnes looked over her shoulder, eyes low-lashed and warm. "Every time I drink whiskey when we're together, you end up naked. That's not what I'm after tonight." Agnes paused. "Is that what *you* want?"

"I don't—maybe…" Lola stumbled over her words.

The heat from Agnes's eyes caught Lola on fire, and she nearly groaned out loud when most of that heat settled between her thighs. She scraped her teeth over her lower lip and took a quick, grounding breath. Did Agnes mean she wanted Lola again on another night? Her heart thumped heavily, anticipation and desire liquifying her brains and leaking it down her thighs.

But Agnes had already moved on. With a wave of her hand, she invited Lola to sit at the table, then took her own seat. "Did you enjoy yourself in the Peacock Room?"

Lola froze. A blush scorched her cheeks, and her stomach clenched from a sudden pulse of guilt.

Agnes had given her the room key and the order to sleep with that woman. She didn't have anything to feel guilty about. Yet the feeling remained.

Lola sat and pulled her chair closer to the table. "Yes, I did. My client made everything easy." An understatement if there ever was one. "That's actually why I'm here. To give you this." The envelope of money felt heavier than it should have when she took it out of her pocket and dropped it on the table. "For the night's work."

"Thank you." Agnes reached past the envelope for a gold-wrapped chocolate. "Do you stack your Draw Fours and Draw Twos or go by official Uno rules?" The dark chocolate disappeared between her bright teeth.

If Agnes was set on keeping Lola off-balance tonight, it was definitely working. One case of conversational whiplash coming right up.

"Uh…I've never been one to follow the rules." Lola watched Agnes neatly fold the chocolate's wrapper and tuck it back in the bowl. "But it's your house, so your rules. You decide."

A soft noise of pleasure left Agnes's throat as she chewed the chocolate. "You don't follow any rules at all?" She reached for the Uno deck already on the table and broke it out of its plastic.

"Some. Not many."

"Tell me then, are we playing by any rules now?"

Obviously, they weren't talking about Uno anymore.

Lola tried not to squirm under the unblinking regard. She couldn't afford to be weak in front of Agnes, not now. "Why? Are you afraid you're going to lose?"

"No. I'm worried you'll hurt the people I'm responsible for." Agnes's eyes searched Lola's, questioning. Demanding.

Lola's heart jumped high enough in her throat to nearly choke her.

A flash of memory came to her. The gray-haired woman at the mansion who'd said Agnes had saved her life. Her face had softened when she'd talked about Agnes, not like an employee toeing the party line but like a woman who'd gratefully stepped through a door to salvation someone else had opened for her.

Hidden under the table, Lola's fingers dug into her thigh, a bite of pain to force her to find some perspective. It didn't work as well as it used to.

Every passing day made it harder to see the Agnes she was getting to know as the cruel, power-mad woman Maddie had told her about. The Agnes who protected cute six-year-olds couldn't have helped her father treat other women like shit. A queen whose regular method of dealing with threats was "off with their heads" wouldn't have allowed Lola, someone she obviously suspected of having dangerous intentions, so close.

Lola loosened her clawlike grip on her own thigh. "You're not what I expected."

"And what did you expect?"

"Someone easier to hate." The honesty tumbled off her lips, and she could've bitten her tongue in two. Heat climbed up her throat and stung her cheeks. She looked up from the surface of the table expecting anger in Agnes's face. But it wasn't there.

"Thank you for giving me the truth," Agnes said after a small silence. Then she finished shuffling the deck and rapped the cards twice against the table. "Ready to play?"

Agnes won the first round, and Lola scoffed when Agnes won the second round as well.

"I thought you weren't any good at this." Lola tried not to sound like a sore loser, but it was hard in the face of the giant L on her forehead.

"Gretchen beats me every single time. I need the practice and the ego boost." With a self-deprecating laugh that still managed to sound kind of sweet, Agnes skillfully swept the cards up after her latest win and started shuffling them again.

For a few heart-stopping minutes, the warmth in Agnes's eyes distracted Lola from what she'd actually said. "A six-year-old beats you? Repeatedly?"

"She's five, but yes."

Lola couldn't forget the cute kid with her dimpled chin and clear adoration of Agnes in her surprisingly mature gaze. She and Agnes shared the same mahogany skin and straightforward way of looking at a person. It was that look more than anything else that had made Lola think Gretchen was a bit older.

"She must be a genius," Lola said, joking.

"Officially, yes. Her IQ is higher than mine."

"My God! Doesn't that scare you?" The question jumped out before Lola could stop it. Then she just kept going. "Imagine you as a kid but even smarter, ready to take on the world and damn what anybody else thinks."

Agnes breathed out a soft laugh, her hands flying as she dealt the cards. "When I was her age, I had more modest ambitions. All I wanted was my mother and a pony." She flashed a smile, but it seemed designed to minimize what she'd just admitted to.

"Your mom wasn't around back then?"

Agnes's long fingers organized her cards while Lola picked up her own. Her lashes guarded her eyes, and she spent so much time and care situating the cards that Lola thought she wasn't going to answer.

"She was around, but I wasn't," Agnes finally said. "Boarding school."

A five-year-old dragged away from home to live with strangers? Jesus. "That's fucked up."

"My father liked the idea of having a child, but he really had no business being a parent. So it was off to boarding school for me while he kept my mother here." Agnes's voice was matter-of-fact but didn't stop the pang of sympathy from throbbing in Lola's chest. "My mother tried to take me back a couple of times, but my father always found us."

Shock tightened Lola's throat. When Lola had done some digging into Agnes's life, she'd found that Agnes's mother had died in a car accident when Agnes was barely twenty. Now, though, Lola wondered if the car crash had actually been an accident at all or if Agnes's mother had just been desperate to escape her husband. *Or,* Lola thought with a sick lurch in her stomach, *had she been murdered?* From the picture Maddie had painted of Augustus Noble, that last option was very likely.

"I'm sorry." Lola wanted to say more but wasn't sure what words to use.

"Nothing to be sorry for. All that is in the past." Agnes dipped her head toward the spread of cards in Lola's hand. "Your turn."

But Lola didn't feel like playing anymore. And it wasn't—only—because she'd lost every game. "Let's take a break."

At Agnes's nod, she abandoned her cards and, taking her glass of water with her, drifted to the large bookshelf built into the back wall of the office. Her fingertips traced the spines of the books at eye level. Most were leather-bound classics with titles she recognized. Some were in French. Others in Spanish. Lola stopped at a copy of *Don Quixote* and imagined Agnes sitting on her leather couch, reading out loud to her genius child. She swallowed the thick lump in her throat along with a mouthful of water.

Agnes's revelations had unfurled a thorny sadness inside Lola. It stretched wide into her every crevice, where it pricked under her skin and made her too uncomfortable to just sit there and look into the face of the woman she'd come to destroy.

"Your mother loved you." She turned to face Agnes, who was still sitting at the table. Watching. "At least you have that. I was never sure of that with Mom. The drugs had her for so long that I don't remember her ever telling me she loved me. Or showing me."

God, shut up. But she couldn't stop talking. It felt important, urgent even, to give Agnes a bit of herself since Lola had taken advantage of her trust.

"My mother left me long before she died. And then my sister…my sister. Well, she's gone too, but she had so many secrets." Lola's mouth spasmed into an attempt at a smile. "It's like the version of her I knew wasn't even real." Her throat was dry, scratchy, and she had to clear it a couple of times, then drink more water to keep talking. "What I'm trying to say is, Gretchen is lucky to have you. I'm sure she knows, no matter what, you'll always be there for her. You'll always be her family. That's—that's important."

A smile ghosted across Agnes's mouth. She nodded, then reached out a hand, a clear invitation for Lola to join her.

They never did get back to the game. Instead, they sank into the leather couch and drank their waters, talking about what amounted to nothing much over the next hour or so. Gretchen was out of school for the week and was spending the time upstate on Agnes's horse farm with her best friend, which was Agnes's excuse for being in the office so late. She said this like it was a naughty secret. In return, Lola shared half-obscured details about Jamika, who she loved like family and was also a pain in the ass.

By the time Lola stepped out of the building and headed home, her head swam with victory, and she felt a little high from getting to know the real Agnes better, like she'd gotten a hit of the headiest, most forbidden drug. But she also felt like shit.

The last thing she wanted to do was hurt this woman she was coming to know. And love.

That pain, she also knew, was inevitable.

CHAPTER 24

LOLA HURRIED DOWN THE SIDEWALK toward the subway, shoulders hunched down in her jacket, eyes straight ahead. She moved through the light nighttime pedestrian traffic, feeling separate from everyone else.

She'd messed up. She was falling for Agnes.

No, that was a lie. She'd already fallen and was just waiting for the hard landing.

After she'd gotten over being nervous, being turned-on, being a liar who was there to take away everything Agnes had built, it was easy being in that office with her. Playing a harmless game. Laughing. Sharing pieces of herself she'd never revealed to anyone else.

The whole time, she'd wanted to confess the real reason she was there.

In the end, though, she'd kept her mouth shut. Zoe's killer was still out there, and she needed to find them. Needed to make them pay. So far, the only thing she was certain of was that Agnes wasn't the one who'd taken Zoe from her.

"Delores."

The sound of someone calling her name pulled her from her thoughts. No. Maybe they weren't calling her. Her name was as common as bodegas in New York. Speaking of which, she should stop and grab some chicken thighs. Her meat-loving household only had vegetables left in the fridge, and that was a crime Jamika would happily arrest Lola for. Since it would be her turn to cook dinner tomorrow, Lola could just throw the chicken in the oven with thyme, garlic, and chopped leeks while she finished up her assignment due at the end of the week.

"Lola."

Was that the same voice? She looked around, but no one nearby was paying her any attention. All the people in sight were looking at their phones, staring straight ahead with purpose as they walked, or, in the case of the obvious tourists, peering at street signs and landmarks to find out where they were or were going.

"Hey."

An arm bumped hers and Lola turned to see a slim figure—wearing an oversized hooded sweatshirt, tight jeans, and knockoff designer tennis shoes—keeping pace with her. The voice was low but somehow familiar.

"Do I know you?" she asked, irritated that she had to stop when all she wanted was to hurry home and unwind with Jamika on the couch.

The hooded head swung her way, and light from a streetlamp slashed across part of the female face hidden inside.

Lola stumbled. Her heart kicked savagely inside the cage of her ribs.

"Watch where the fuck ya goin'!" Lola barely registered another pedestrian's almost gentle words, the altruistic shove away from the street edge of the sidewalk. A car honked from too close by.

"Surprise." Her sister's face grimaced at her from under the dark hood. Her dead sister's face.

Lola reeled back in the middle of the sidewalk. Her gasping breath puffed out in a cloud of white.

"This is a sidewalk, not a side stop. Move ya blasted self out of the way!" Another shove from a stranger, this one not so nice, and Lola slammed into a newspaper box. Pain exploded in her knee, and she hissed.

The person with Zoe's face cursed and dragged Lola off the sidewalk to a quieter street. The hand around her wrist felt as cold as death.

Trembling, Lola shook it off.

"In here," the Zoe ghost said. "Come on. I don't have long."

The hood slid nearly all the way back to reveal most of the face—*Zoe's* face—and an expression tight with anxiety.

"Zoe?" Lola's knees trembled hard enough for her to need to grab out for the nearest thing, which turned out to be a filthy wall. Gross. She snatched her hand back and wiped it on her jeans. "You're—you're dead." Lola backed away, still unable to believe what she was seeing. "Oh my God. Oh my God." Something slammed into her back with a dull thud. A dumpster. Remembering the condition of the wall she'd just accidentally touched, she flinched away from it. "What the fuck, Zoe? What the actual fuck?"

Zoe's face under the hood looked older than the last time Lola had seen her, sharper cheekbones, a tighter jawline. There was a fresh-looking bruise near her mouth, and she wasn't wearing lipstick. But it was her. It was really her.

Lola reached out, fingers trembling, and touched Zoe's chin, her throat. She felt warm. Like she was really there.

Lola grabbed on to Zoe and held on. Even through their thick fall clothes, Zoe felt thin. Flimsy as if she would blow away on the next breeze. Lola squeezed her tight, felt tears on her own face. "It's really you…"

"It is." Light hands patted Lola's back, then gently pushed her away. "I can't stay, though." Zoe swept a fearful gaze around the alley as if she expected ghosts or worse to jump out at her any second. "I can't talk long. They'll realize soon that I'm missing."

"Who?" Lola grabbed Zoe's arm, fingers sinking in to never let her go again. Ever. Whoever had Zoe on the run, Lola and Zoe could face them together.

Zoe shrank down into her dark hoodie, shaking her head. "I escaped to find my baby. My daughter. She could be in trouble."

Lola drew in a shocked breath. "You have a *daughter*?"

"That's why I escaped. You have to help me. Tell me if she's safe or even still alive. House of Agnes took my baby girl—" She choked on a sob.

"Gretchen? She's yours?" Lola felt as if she was about to pass out. Everything she knew was a lie.

"She's mine!" Zoe looked up, her eyes bone-dry. "She's my kid. My responsibility." She grabbed Lola, and her grip was tight around Lola's wrist, grinding the bones together. Lola hissed in pain and tried to shake Zoe off, but Zoe held on. "I need to make sure she's safe!"

"It's okay. She's in the safest place she could ever be. Agnes would never allow anything to hurt her."

Zoe loosened her grip on Lola's wrist, her gaze narrowing to a laser-like focus. "Agnes still has her? You're sure? And she isn't saving her for one of her disgusting virginity auctions?"

Wrist throbbing from Zoe's rough handling, Lola took a step back. Damn, Zoe was strong. "Yes, I'm sure. Agnes is a good person. She's not what everyone says she is."

As she defended Agnes, Lola's throat grew tight with emotion. She believed what she said, had for a long time. Agnes wasn't kind. She wasn't some rainbows-streaking-out-of-her-ass type do-gooder, but she cared, and she was strong enough to protect the people she loved.

"Oh yeah?" Some emotion flashed across Zoe's face, too fast for Lola to catch. "Do you—do you and her have a thing?"

"No, of course not. She's just been really good to me." Embarrassed heat burst under Lola's cheeks, but she didn't look away from Zoe's probing stare.

"You should watch yourself. Even though you say she's not using my kid, Agnes Noble is not some lady knight in shining armor. She's a user and is only playing nice until she gets what she wants."

What could Agnes possibly want from me? It certainly wasn't sex or even loyalty. If anything, Lola was the one who'd been using Agnes to investigate—*fuck*. She stared at Zoe, sick realization surging up her throat.

Zoe's so-called death had drawn Lola to Agnes's House. To destroy it. Lola had been about to ruin an innocent woman.

The alley's dim light didn't hide the speculative look Zoe gave her. It reminded her of the times when Zoe, acting as a stand-in mother, had caught Lola in a lie and, instead of calling her on it, had made her stew in a mess of her own making until she confessed everything.

"Agnes doesn't want anything from me," Lola said finally. "*I've* been the one hounding her and—"

"Don't be so naive. Agnes is nobody's victim." Zoe's eyes skinned Lola raw, and it was like they shared the same home again and Lola was just a teenager, trying to keep the secrets Zoe found without even trying. "She's a predator, one of the worst. I'd heard this vague rumor about her, that maybe she was someone safe to go to for help. Turns out that was total garbage. Agnes *lies*. She said she'd help me and my baby get far from here and never have to worry about anyone hurting us ever again. But as soon as she heard that the pimp who had my contract was willing to start a war to get me back, she backed out of our deal and took my daughter with her." Zoe's head dipped, and her face disappeared into the shadow of her sweatshirt's hood. "They beat me so bad I almost died. Some days I wish they had killed me."

"No!" Lola gripped Zoe's arm in panic. "Don't say that." She remembered too clearly being flooded with grief while sitting in the ME's office and waiting to identify the things that belonged to Zoe. That wasn't something she ever wanted to feel again. "Just come back with me. Gretchen is safe, and now you can be too."

"I can't. They'll find me and rip me apart. I can't go through that kind of torture again."

My God. What had Zoe gotten herself into?

"Agnes will keep you safe."

Zoe choked out a sound of disbelief. "You're really gone over her, aren't you?"

Gone, no. Going, absolutely.

"It's because of your so-called death that I'm even near her in the first place." Lola pressed her lips shut. Zoe may not be dead but she sure as hell was in a shitty position. Lola had no right to snap at her. "Fuck, I'm sorry—"

"I don't have time for blame. They'll notice I'm gone any minute now. I have to go. I don't want them to go after Gretchen in revenge." Zoe grabbed Lola's arm again, and her grip was firm enough to hurt. "Keep her safe until I can get away for good."

A sudden sweep of light at the other end of the alley scraped panic through Lola, and she spun toward it, a hand raised to shield her eyes. It was just a single headlight, like one from a motorcycle. When it didn't come any closer, she breathed a sigh of relief and turned back to her sister.

"Zoe—"

But there was only empty space where she'd stood just seconds ago. Zoe was gone.

CHAPTER 25

With half an ear tuned into the sounds outside her bedroom door, Lola hit send on the last of the articles she had scheduled to finish for the day. Just in case the client didn't have any changes, she had the invoice ready to go. Between worrying about Jamika, who'd slammed her way into the apartment an hour before, and her worry for Zoe, Lola was lucky she hadn't been absentminded enough to just type out the ABCs in Comic Sans font and send them to her client by mistake. For now, she closed her laptop and followed the smell of popcorn to the living room.

The same night Lola had run into Zoe, she'd told Jamika what had happened. Jamika had gone absolutely nuclear, pissed that Zoe had been alive all this time and hadn't let Lola know. She was also suspicious as hell.

Why hadn't she contacted Lola all these years? Why crawl out into the light now? Jamika's words, not hers. What were they supposed to do about Gretchen, Lola's actual niece?

Plenty of questions but few answers. Lola had tried to get the answers, had tried to track down Zoe with Maddie's help, but had come up empty-handed. Zoe had proved yet again she was damned good at laying low.

And, because of the accusations Zoe had made that night, Lola reluctantly agreed with Jamika to keep going with the investigation into The House. But every single day since then, she'd wanted to stop and confess everything to Agnes.

Less than a week had gone by, and it seemed as if Lola wasn't the only one having some sort of crisis. For days now, Jamika had been acting weird. Lola was already tired of tiptoeing around Jamika's shitty mood and waiting for her to say what was so heavy on her mind.

After a quick detour to the kitchen for a bottle of sparkling water, Lola found Jamika on the couch. Popcorn, sweats, the Food Network, and a long face.

"What's going on, J?" She figured she'd waited long enough. It was getting harder and harder to see Jamika so obviously torn up and not say anything. Jamika was the type to keep quiet about what was bothering her until she was good and ready to talk, but every day she was getting more harried, a resigned look on her face replacing what had once been excitement about her job. Her official one—and what she and Lola were trying to do.

Jamika shoved away the bowl of popcorn. "I feel like such a traitor for saying this." But she didn't actually say anything else. Her lower lip, caught between her teeth, looked raw, as if she'd been chewing at it for days.

Lola hit the mute button on the cooking show, their universal sign for "serious talk ahead." She dropped the remote. "Tell me."

"You have no idea how it is there."

Since Lola had no idea where "there" was, Jamika was right so far. "Come on, J." She kept her tone encouraging and tried to suppress her worry. "Tell me."

"I am!" Immediately, Jamika's expression caved. "Shit. Sorry." She took a deep breath and curled into herself on the sofa, chin propped up on her knees. Her hair, pulled back in its usual ponytail, flopped over her shoulder. "At the station, a lot of the cops there are so self-righteous, talking about criminals needing to be taken down and not deserving to walk the same streets as decent people, all kinds of shit like that. But the things I see them doing when the world isn't watching... That's what's fucking criminal."

Jamika's whole face was a wince, a painful rictus, as if every word hurt. All her life she'd wanted to be a cop. She'd grown up watching *Law and Order*, had gorged herself on every cop show out there. When Lola had been floundering, trying to decide if she would even go to college, Jamika had been talking about her career as a police detective taking down bad guys.

Now she felt like she was working *with* the bad guys.

Lola squeezed Jamika's knee.

"They're doing so much fucked-up shit and right there in front of everyone's faces, like nobody's ever going to call them on it, and nobody does, Lola! It's nuts!" Jamika looked as if her whole world had fallen apart. "Every time I try to say something to the lieutenant or anybody higher up, they act like I'm the one doing something wrong."

Under her hand, Lola felt the tremors running through Jamika's knee. She scrambled for something positive to say, but she couldn't think of anything that wasn't a lie. People better than her were fighting to change things, but it was a long and dangerous road with no end in sight. "I'm sorry, J."

Like everyone else in America, Lola saw the videos of cops killing unarmed Black people and other ethnic folks in the streets, in their cars, in police stations, on social media, and she hated the system that allowed things like that to happen almost every day with no consequences for the killers. As for Jamika, she was one of the good ones, so Lola had hoped she could make a change from the inside. If even Jamika was giving up, what did that mean?

"I'm sorry too." Jamika rolled over until her head was in Lola's lap, her long body stretched out and feet rested on the opposite arm of the couch. She tugged on one dread, twisting and untwisting it around one finger, and stared in the general direction of the muted television. "With this thing that you and me are doing, it's like—it's like a real chance to do good, you know?"

"To balance out what the others are doing?"

"Yeah, kind of," Jamika murmured, though she sounded unsure, so much like the kid who'd climbed into Lola's bed when they were teenagers, crying from the depths of her soul after reading the note her own mother had left her before disappearing for good. "I have real cases on my desk—murders to solve, rapists to help prosecute—but it's hard to focus on that when my partner's screwing his confidential informant, and the wife of the guy I used to work with keeps calling my phone to get protection from him since calling the police on his abuse doesn't do any good. Fuck."

She rolled to her feet and ripped the hair tie from her locks. "You know what? Let me worry about all that shit at work. I've tried to stop a lot of it but…" Her hair flew as she shook her head. "Let's deal with something we can actually change."

Lola sagged back into the sofa, feeling helpless while the spot on her lap where Jamika had lain grew cold. "Um, yeah. Sure."

Right. Agnes. The House.

She'd already told Jamika about the older woman she'd talked to at the masquerade ball, the one who'd said Agnes had saved her life. They both agreed it was hard to square that with what Zoe had told her in the alley and with the endless stories Maddie had about Agnes being a creep.

"I'm going to see Agnes again tomorrow night. I'll snoop around the building before we meet up." Lola gnawed on her bottom lip, carefully weighing what she was about to say. "Honestly, though, everything I've seen so far says Agnes is working *for* her people, not against them. She may not take any shit, but she's not some Disney villain either."

Feeling a little guilty, Lola left out the little detail about playing Uno with Agnes the last week, sharing laughter and mineral water in the massive office overlooking the city, letting her suspicions rest for a while and feeling at ease for the first time in ages. Those evenings, few as they were, felt sacred and private. Lola wanted to keep them to herself for just a little while longer.

Jamika paced in front of the television, twisting the hair tie between her fingers while her locks flew around her shoulders and face with every turn. "So, if what you think is true—"

"I don't know," Lola said quickly. "We need to get more info."

Impatiently, Jamika shook her head. "If what you suspect is true, then this coldhearted madam—" Lola bit the inside of her cheek to stop her automatic defense of Agnes. "—treats her whores better than any of the guys I work with. And that's kind of messed up." Jamika stopped pacing and narrowed her eyes.

Lola said what Jamika didn't. "It makes you wonder if we're doing the right thing."

"Yeah. It does."

CHAPTER 26

"YOU'RE REALLY COZY WITH HER, aren't you?" Rox, the woman Lola had met in The House what felt like ages ago, stepped from the darkened hallway and strolled toward Lola, her hips rocking under a dark skirt. Behind her, the elevator doors slid closed.

Lola didn't know what had changed, but in the weeks since she'd become a "regular," Rox's attitude had done a complete one-eighty. The friendly, flirtatious woman with the welcoming smile had turned into a competitive bitch who snarked at Lola whenever they ran into each other.

"If you mean I'm friendly with her, then yes. She is my boss, *our* boss, after all." Lola shoved the elevator key card into the back pocket of her jeans.

Rox hummed in something that might have been agreement, but the look on her pretty face was too slick. "If I didn't know what a cold one she was, I'd swear you were fucking her."

Long-lashed eyes crawled all over Lola, and her skin pimpled up with discomfort at being the object of such a blatantly sexual and possessive stare. The potential clients Lola had met at the masquerade ball had nothing on Rox for making Lola feel like a convenient hole waiting to be filled.

Rox was gorgeous, and she knew it too. A couple of times, Lola had found herself wondering if Agnes was sleeping with her, but Rox had basically just admitted that Agnes had never looked at her as more than an employee. Or maybe that was the problem. Rox was just a spurned, jealous asset.

Lola dipped her head at the suggestion she was fucking Agnes. "But since you obviously know better…" She let Rox assume whatever she wanted from the open sentence.

Rox hummed again and pressed the elevator down button. "So I guess you two just play patty-cake up here all night when everyone's gone home?"

"Not patty-cake, but Uno."

A laugh of disbelief left Rox's red mouth.

"You should try it sometime," Lola said. "It's very relaxing."

"I'll take your word for it." Still laughing, Rox shook her head, her thick hair shimmering under the artificial lights.

Now it was Lola's turn to hum noncommittally. "Well, enjoy the rest of your evening." She headed away from the elevators with a wave in Rox's direction.

"I plan on it," Rox said. The elevator door chimed, and Lola looked over her shoulder in time to see Rox glide between the metal doors as if she were on a runway, all sleek skin and gorgeous hair. "You do the same."

Lola paused, wondered if she should be offended at Rox's snide tone, then dismissed her with a shrug and headed down the hallway toward Agnes's office.

"Good evening, Clare," she greeted as she took a seat in the waiting area.

Clare looked at Lola more sourly than usual, light glinting off the lens of her glasses as if she had Lola in the sights of a rifle. Lola knew Clare didn't like her, and as much as she'd like to challenge Clare—or, as Jamika had suggested, try to charm her—she'd bet Clare would find it easier to strangle her in a dark corner and leave her body for the trash guys than entertain any sort of cordial relationship with her.

"Ms. Osbourne." Clare gave her a sweeping glance, but unlike the one Rox had just given her, it seemed as if she was scanning her body for the most vulnerable parts to stick a knife in. "You can go right in. Agnes is expecting you."

How did she make Agnes's given name sound like a sign of respect while calling Lola Ms. Osbourne seemed like "eat shit and die"?

"Thanks, Clare. You're a real peach."

As expected, Clare didn't give a response. Lola slipped past her desk and to the door of Agnes's office. Even though it was open, she knocked and waited until Agnes looked from her desk, an invitation on her lips, before making her way in.

"Please," Agnes said, amusement crinkling the corners of her eyes. "Close the door."

The office looked neat as always, no hiding her anal retentiveness here, although Lola supposed it also made things easy to find. Across the indecently large space lay the high windows and breathtaking view of the city she never got used to. Whoever said rich people weren't truly happy probably didn't know any rich people. The room smelled faintly of Agnes's spicy perfume.

Agnes's dress today looked like some other designer label, forest green with short, fitted sleeves and military-style buttons down the front. As if anyone would ever forget who was in charge around here.

In her own faux vintage Jimi Hendrix T-shirt, jeans, and thrift-store leather jacket, Lola felt severely underdressed. "Looks like you're getting ready to work late again tonight." She went to the hidden mini fridge.

"Looks can be deceiving," Agnes said. "As of right now, I'm done for the night." As if to punctuate the declaration, she closed her laptop with a gentle click and got to her feet.

Lola stared. She couldn't help it. She might have even been drooling a bit. The dress turned out to be a skirt suit, proven when Agnes slipped out of her jacket and left it on the back of her chair. A pale green blouse, almost white, skimmed her lithe torso and tucked neatly into a high-waisted skirt. The skirt was tight enough to make Lola forget her own name. She swallowed and mentally replayed what Agnes had just said.

"Oh. I can come back or…" Lola wasn't sure what alternative scenario she was about to suggest. Her mouth wasn't either since it just hung open, waiting on coherent words to leap out. She toyed with the cap of a Perrier bottle.

Twist. Untwist. Twist.

"It's fine," Agnes said after a loaded silence. "I enjoy our games." With an eyebrow cocked, she glanced at Lola from the table with the cards and basket of chocolates already set up, a world of meaning in the single glance. "You make them fun."

"Well, to be fair, Uno is inherently fun. There's no way to make it terrible." Lola brought the glasses of sparkling water to the table and, after taking off her jacket and draping it over the back of her chair, sat down.

"Oh, you'd be surprised. Whit gets very aggressive once the Draw Fours come out."

All too easily, the memory of Agnes's Amazon guard came to Lola, the fierce scowl and the gun she didn't bother to hide as she came closer to Lola that afternoon in the park. Then she imagined that same woman scowling over a spread of Uno cards. Laughter snuck up on her, and she slapped a hand over her mouth.

"It's okay—you can laugh. It is kind of funny. Maybe one day you can join the three of us."

"Maybe," Lola echoed, internally freaking out. Was that an invitation to come to Agnes's house?

Okay. Calm down, Delores. This is not the time to lose your mind. God, why did being around Agnes turn her into a crushing teenage girl?

Across from her, Agnes put her glass of sparkling water to her lips. "Ready to play?"

"Yup." Lola picked up the cards and tried to pretend her hands weren't shaking.

Just as she started to shuffle them, the speakerphone on Agnes's desk burst with sound. "Agnes?"

"Yes, Clare?" Agnes tilted her head, a catlike motion, as she stared past Lola, listening.

It must be serious. This was the first time Clare had interrupted while Lola and Agnes were together. Lola heard a frenetic rush of noise from somewhere on Clare's end.

"There's someone here to see you." Clare sounded even more professional than usual. "It seems rather urgent."

A shuffling came through the phone. "They found me!" a woman screamed out, sounding breathless and afraid. "I thought—I thought you could protect me, but you can't. They're going to kill me. They're going to kill me!"

Agnes jumped to her feet, rushing out, and without thinking, Lola followed.

The usually unshakeable Clare was on her feet, leaning away from the pair of big security guards and a woman who would've been elegant and breathtakingly gorgeous if it wasn't for the fear twisting her face and the mascara tracks dripping toward her gaping mouth. Her hair was loose around her shoulders and flew everywhere as she twisted in the grasp of the two guards, babbling about someone coming to kill her.

"Why is she here?" Agnes demanded of the guards.

"She just ran down here, screaming her head off," one of the men said. "A team went up to the room to see what could've set her off."

Lola gaped at them all. She must have made some sort of sound because Agnes's gaze immediately landed on her.

A look that might have been regret came and went on Agnes's face. "Unfortunately, Lola, we'll have to continue this some other time."

"Oh! Of course. Sure." But Lola's curiosity burned. Who was this woman, and why was Agnes hiding her in one of the H Holdings penthouse apartments?

"Good," Agnes said. Although Lola got the feeling that she could've said anything and gotten the same response. Agnes had other priorities now. But then, she leaned in. "We'll speak tomorrow, all right?" She brushed a thumb across the inside of Lola's wrist.

Lola flushed as her whole body took notice, tingles racing from that point of contact to wrap around what felt suspiciously like her heart. This was the first time Agnes had actually touched her in front of other people. But the moment was short-lived.

Agnes pulled back. "Kyle, please escort Lola to the elevator and join me in the conference room when you return."

One of the security guards, who looked nothing like a Kyle in Lola's opinion, nodded briskly to Agnes, then placed a guiding hand at the small of Lola's back. "Come with me, miss."

With little choice, Lola threw a brief glance Agnes's way, but Agnes was already heading past Clare's desk with the crying woman and the remaining member of her security team. Clare sat back in her seat and rolled up to her desk, disturbance apparently already forgotten.

But Lola couldn't forget the terror on that girl's face. She was genuinely afraid that someone was going to kill her. And she'd come to Agnes for help.

Although Lola tried to hear what was happening behind her, Agnes spoke too low for her voice to carry, and besides, Kyle hustled her forward like he was in a rush to get rid of her so he could do whatever else his boss needed.

"Here you are, miss. When you get downstairs, just use your card to access the exit door as usual." Kyle swiped a black card across a glowing panel on the elevator, and with a sharp chime, the door opened immediately.

Wait a minute. This wasn't the elevator Lola was used to.

In their brisk walk away from the crying woman, she hadn't realized they were moving in the direction opposite to the lobby elevators. Instead, she was back in Agnes's office, the table with their abandoned Uno game several feet away.

Agnes had a private elevator. And Kyle had just taken Lola there because he assumed...whatever he assumed. Well, Lola wasn't going to look a gift security guard in the mouth. She was willing to bet this elevator let out somewhere only Agnes had access to, somewhere protected and private. Though Lola's motives for digging into Agnes's secrets might not have been the same as before, she still wanted to know them.

"Sure!" she said and hoped she didn't sound too eager. "Thanks a lot." Her hands prickled with nervousness. Any second now, she expected Kyle to realize his mistake and haul her out of the office, but he only stepped back and allowed her to get on the elevator. Pulse drumming loudly in her ears, Lola pressed the down button and bared her teeth at Kyle as the doors closed. He was already turning to rush back to Agnes.

Lola refused to squeal like she'd just gotten the best Christmas and birthday gift rolled into one. But damn, it was hard. Excitement fizzed inside her like soda in a shaken can. It needed an outlet. When the elevator opened after a long and uninterrupted journey into a brightly lit parking garage, she gave in and did a little dance. Just a tiny one.

Her excitement lasted for as long as it took her to realize she was trapped. And cold.

In all the craziness, she'd forgotten her jacket upstairs, which also had her phone in it. Wearing only her thin T-shirt and jeans, she shivered and cursed herself for being too impulsive for her own good.

Well, she might as well have a look around.

After a quick search, she realized she was trapped underground with three immaculate luxury cars and a motorcycle. To the left was a brightly lit tunnel, narrow and accessible only on foot, that ended at a person-sized steel door protected by some kind of electronic panel. Key card access point number one. To the right of Agnes's elevator, past the cars and bike, was a short driveway leading up an incline that also ended at an impassable door. Key card access point number two.

Naturally, The House access key card in Lola's back pocket was useless. No doubt there were cameras everywhere documenting her desperate back and forth wandering. No, she wasn't going to win any prizes for smart thinking today. Impulsiveness, yes, but that was pretty much every day. Now that she'd realized she couldn't muscle or dumb-luck her way out of this sealed underground tunnel, she had to *think*.

Jamika would probably laugh her ass off if she could see Lola now. Right after she asked Lola what the hell she was thinking by getting off what was basically an elevator to nowhere.

A shiver wracked Lola's frame, driving her into a corner between the sealed elevator doors and thick concrete wall.

Eventually, Agnes was going to come down, and Lola had to be ready with an excuse for why she was here. Although the real reason was good enough. Clueless Kyle and his assumptions. He obviously thought she and Agnes were a thing, that she had access to all Agnes's secrets. She didn't, though, no matter how much she wished otherwise. Everything she'd learned so far, she'd painstakingly dug up. Including the fact that Agnes was no monster.

None of the House assets Lola talked to wanted to leave. They were happy with how Agnes ruled her empire and wanted to stay. The ones who talked about leaving only longed for an escape to normalcy, cuddling with a wife or husband in front of Netflix, taking the kids to school, or just living alone with the luxury of solo baths and long nights spent reading without someone else's expectations of sex. Even when talking amongst themselves about Agnes, they joked about wanting to have sex with her, not about how scary she was or how she'd ruined their lives.

That girl upstairs had felt death coming for her, and she'd run to Agnes instead of away from her. Why? The girl's actions didn't make sense if what

Zoe thought Agnes was doing—exploiting vulnerable women—was the truth.

A draft of freezing cold air blew in from somewhere, raked its talons over Lola's exposed throat and arms, shoved icy fingers under her T-shirt, and dug into her skin. Shivering, she crossed her arms over her belly and pressed back into the corner. "Fuck..."

Outside, it had been a coolish autumn day, pretty with falling leaves and sunlight lapping at Lola's skin. This underground garage, though, was in the firm grip of winter. Lola didn't like it. But the cold forced her to think, to connect the dots.

The woman at the masquerade ball.

Agnes's protective attitude.

The frightened girl upstairs.

Zoe's resurrection from the dead.

Oh. Oh!

A shocked breath exploded past Lola's cold lips, and she stumbled, hands reaching out at her sides to steady her against the cool concrete. Her whole body jolted, like someone had just knocked her on her ass.

Agnes was saving women, not hurting them. And Zoe, obviously, didn't know.

How *could* she know? Zoe hadn't been able to escape, and she'd blamed Agnes. It seemed as if Agnes had saved a lot of women, though. Maybe some, like Zoe, couldn't be rescued without exposing Agnes's secret work?

Lola's mind whirled. There had to be more to this. But at the very least, Zoe could try again. Maybe this time Agnes could save her too.

This was huge. Lola had to tell Jamika. She reached into her back pocket and found—no phone. *Fuck.*

A sudden humming sound made her jump. The elevator. It was moving. Lola went limp with relief. *Thank God.*

Agnes was going to be less than pleased to find Lola lurking in her secret underground garage, but Lola would cross that bridge once she wasn't about to freeze to death. She huffed out a nervous breath and waited for Agnes to find her.

CHAPTER 27

AGNES UNDERSTOOD PANIC. SHE UNDERSTOOD questioning whether or not she'd made the right decision. That was why she calmed the woman, Natalie, the best way she knew how instead of allowing security to inject her with diazepam and drag her back upstairs to her room.

Natalie thought she'd wanted to stay in the business. She changed her mind and now was desperate to leave, and that was okay. With the PTSD she was obviously dealing with, complete with paranoia of being pursued, she needed more time to heal than she'd given herself. The House would help her with a new identity and whatever else she needed to move on from the horrors of the past few years of her life.

Agnes had done what she could for Natalie, and for others, but it never felt like enough. Every day, there were new monsters. New victims. She wanted to save them all yet knew she couldn't.

Weighed down with her thoughts, Agnes left her private elevator, barely paying attention to her surroundings. The situation with Natalie and all it represented were things she could never leave behind. She'd chosen this life when she stepped into her role as head of the House. But that meant she treasured the small pleasures of life even more. The Uno game with Lola, childish and harmless, was something she'd looked forward to all day.

When she'd first invited Lola to play at the beginning of the week, it had been a spontaneous offer that had leapt from her tongue, spurred by the loneliness of missing her little family. Now, though, Lola was gone, and with Gretchen and Whit still out of town, Agnes was on her way home to an empty apartment.

"You're not as awful as you'd like people to think, are you?"

A shocked inhale of breath cooled Agnes's throat. She spun, adrenaline surging, the slim knife normally hidden in her belt tight in her fist and ready to plunge into her attacker.

She froze.

Lola stood in the bright light of the underground structure, hands up, her face a mixture of challenge and fear.

"What the *fuck* are you doing down here?" Agnes's heart tripped and her blood raced. The unleashed aggression in her body yowled for an outlet.

"The—one of your guys let me down here. He probably thought I was meeting you here or something."

That meant Lola had been in the garage for at least an hour. She hadn't called for help at the intercom that was clearly marked, and she hadn't tried to get back into the elevator and head back upstairs.

"Don't make me repeat my question, Delores." Agnes's blood was hot, voice scraping against her throat in a threatening growl she couldn't control.

"I wanted to talk to—"

"And that's why you hid out here like some kind of sewer rat waiting to ambush me?" She'd known that Lola wasn't what she seemed from the first day. Her actions up to now had been no surprise—well, most of them anyway—so why did Agnes want to rip her to pieces? Nearly lost in a fog of rage and frustration, she crowded Lola against the wall.

"What—what are you doing with that knife?" Worried eyes flicked to the blade in Agnes's hand.

Impatient with the fear on Lola's face, Agnes slid the knife back into her belt. "Not a damn thing." She took a deep breath and drew in the tang of fear from Lola's skin. "But you already know that."

A pink tongue swept across Lola's full mouth, and with her back pressed against the wall, her eyes dropped down to Agnes's lips in a universal sign Agnes didn't want to ignore. She caged Lola with her body, her palms flat on the wall on either side of Lola's face. Her blood pounded with the desire for violence, or sex.

But she wasn't her father. She may not be much better, but she was at least different.

"Talk!" Agnes snapped. "What are you doing down here? What are you doing in my life?"

Words tumbled in a rush from Lola's lips. Something about being lost, being in the wrong place, not wanting to upset Agnes. None of it felt true. Lola's chest moved quickly under the thin blouse, the cold from the underground vents and chill autumn day above bringing her nipples to hard peaks against the material of her shirt.

Agnes wet her own lips. "Stop the lies. You haven't been honest with me since the day we met."

A flinch moved across Lola's face, the most genuine reaction Agnes had ever seen outside of when they were having sex. But it was a reaction, not the truth.

Agnes roughened her voice. "Tell me what you're really after—right now, right now—or I'm done playing nice." Her cold fingers tightened into Lola's shoulders, and Lola flinched again. Damn it, Agnes wanted to stop this and pull Lola into her arms and apologize, but that wouldn't get either of them anywhere. She really was done. Either Lola gave her the truth, or she'd really see the monster Agnes could become.

With an unknown threat breathing down her neck and Gretchen being potentially at risk, Agnes needed to show her strength. She needed to protect The House that desperation had forced her to build.

Against her, Lola trembled. Her eyes were wide with fear, and a question seemed to flash in their depths, a battle of whether or not to tell the truth.

Please tell me, Agnes wanted to beg her, but she kept her mouth shut.

Gretchen. The House. Whit. All the vulnerable people out there waiting for help. Everything was at risk. She couldn't afford to be weak.

"Lola..."

A harsh breath left Lola's throat. She squeezed her eyes shut and leaned her head back against the wall. "I'm an investigative reporter," she breathed out, her voice low, and Agnes almost sagged with relief. A reporter she could handle. "I'm doing a piece on The House and..." Her teeth sank into her lower lip as her words trailed away, obviously reluctant to say the rest.

"And what?" Whatever it was made Lola's tremors worse, and trepidation sank a ball of fear in Agnes's belly.

"I'm working with the police," Lola finished in a rush. She must have felt Agnes jerk against her, unable to hide her shocked anger, because she reached out then, trying to touch, but Agnes gripped Lola's shoulders, fingers digging in.

"No!" Lola gasped. "I just realized you're taking care of people in danger, not hurting them. The story isn't the same now."

"I don't want you to write *anything* about me," Agnes ground out. "And the only cops I want crawling around in my business are the ones I pay." Her anger at Lola's confession rolled inside her in scalding waves. Lola had barged into her life for *this*? To break some sort of five-minute viral exclusive?

All the reporters Agnes had ever had the displeasure of meeting were only interested in the sex and money of the business, not in supporting health care and safety for sex workers, not in rescuing those who'd been forced into sexual slavery and had no means of escape. Their morals ran only as deep as the next story.

As for any police who were sniffing around, Agnes could take care of that. The high-ranking cop she paid an indecent amount of money to every month would make sure to kill any investigation against The House in its tracks.

Agnes released her hold on Lola's shoulders and stepped back. "Is there anything else you're hiding from me, anything I should know?"

"No." Lola quickly shook her head. "There's nothing."

"All right then. You've confessed your dirty secret. Now you can go."

"No, don't send me away." Lola grabbed Agnes's hands and pulled her back, desperation clawing at the corners of her eyes. Her lower lip trembled. "Please. I'll kill the story and never mention it again. The investigation too."

Twisted up inside, Agnes frowned down at their joined hands and tried to pull away, but it only made Lola hold on tighter. "Do you have that authority, or are you just saying anything right now?"

"Yes, I do. I'm a freelancer. Look, I know I've been wrong, and I'll make it right. I promise." White teeth sank into Lola's bottom lip, and she glanced up at Agnes through her lashes, a ploy that had been tried on Agnes before, one she'd never fallen for. But she could feel herself melting now, her anger slipping away to reveal the truth of what she felt.

A betrayal that cut to the bone.

They'd been on the way to becoming something to each other, something genuine, Agnes thought. And only *now*, when Lola basically had no choice, did she offer to call off her dogs.

Lola squeezed Agnes's fingers. It hurt a little, but it also felt real. "I'll fix everything. I swear. Just please, please don't be angry."

"Don't be—" The pressure of the last couple of hours dropped down on Agnes like a hammer.

Still holding onto Agnes as if she thought she would escape, Lola crowded into her space. Agnes inhaled the scent of Lola's warm skin, her hot breath. And then they were just too close, and there was only one thing to do.

Agnes kissed her. And Lola kissed back.

Their kiss was full of anger. Hunger. Openmouthed and ravenous from the first touch of lips and a sobbing exhalation from one or both of them.

Agnes shivered and dove into the wet heat of Lola's mouth. It had been far too long since they'd done this. That thought, faint as it was beneath the onslaught of sensations from the press of their bodies, the meeting of their lips, crashed into memories of the last time they'd touched. The control she'd given up at the masquerade ball, the way Lola had selflessly pleased her and how *good* it had felt.

But that time was far away. Agnes had been pretending to be a different woman then.

This kiss now, a give and take, was them being naked to each other.

Reporter, spy. Businesswoman, infatuated lover.

Agnes owned that that was what she was as she feasted on Lola's delicious mouth. From the very first moment, she had tried to convince herself that this thing between them was an attraction she could control. Now that she knew everything Lola had to hide, though, Agnes could finally stop lying to herself and allow the storm of desire to overwhelm her.

The connection of lips and tongue tugged at all parts of Agnes, heated her throat, her nipples, the already hot space between her legs. She longed to take Lola someplace and just feast on her, allow the stress of the day to wash away in the tempest of their shared orgasm. The vibration of Lola's moan rippled through her.

If they didn't stop now, they were going to end up having sex in this tunnel, and Agnes very much did not want Whit's cameras getting that much of eyeful. Reluctantly, she drew back.

Thick-lashed eyes looked up into hers, open and bright, a dawning of realization in them. "You smell like her. You feel like her too." Lola brushed the backs of her fingers along Agnes's cheek, and Agnes shivered as much from the contact as the look on her face. "In the Peacock Room, it was you."

Before Agnes could answer, an electronic beep came from farther down the tunnel. "Not to kill the mood, ladies," Whit's cool voice came from the nearby speaker, doing just that. "Why don't you both come home to the apartment? It might be time for an actual open and honest conversation." She paused when a high, whining voice said something from nearby that Agnes couldn't hear. *Gretchen.* "Between *all* of us."

CHAPTER 28

LOLA'S KNEES WERE STILL TREMBLING, though not for the same reason as before. The shakes she had from confessing to Agnes what she'd done were long gone, and now, after a surprisingly short walk in the tunnel, she was in a glass elevator with Agnes by her side, riding swiftly up toward the apartment Agnes shared with Gretchen. Summoned by a firm voice that had both a tease and a threat in it. She had a pretty good idea who that voice belonged to.

Quiet hummed in the air between them. Not awkward. Not uneasy. Just a sort of waiting while Lola's mind spun around everything she'd just learned.

Agnes and her goddess were the same person.

In the tunnel, when the heat from their kiss grew, that crazy expensive perfume Agnes wore got stronger. That scent took Lola back to that night in the Peacock Room where she'd experienced a pleasure like never before. The goddess had surrendered everything to her. Despite the clues that she and Agnes were one and the same, their sex was so different from that evening in Vegas when Agnes wouldn't even allow Lola to touch her.

In her dreams, though, she knew the truth. It had just taken until now for her awake mind to be sure of it.

Agnes was her goddess, and Lola was in love with her.

The elevator slid to a smooth stop, and Lola, acutely aware of Agnes by her side, got a good look at a wood-paneled foyer, dark Italian marble floors, chandeliers, and classic-looking paintings and other knickknacks that screamed a luxury she could never afford before she realized a woman stood there—yes, the Amazon, in soft-looking gray pants and a matching shirt. She held a gun in both hands, muzzle pointed down. The elevator door opened.

"Nessa!" A child's voice screamed from somewhere out of sight. The sound was bright and joyous and made Lola smile, despite the sudden increased tension in Agnes beside her. "Whit said you had to work late, so I couldn't call you like I wanted." Then a figure came racing down the hallway. Jeans. T-shirt. Bright smile. She threw herself into Agnes's arms, and Agnes caught her effortlessly, sweeping her all the way off the floor and into a fierce hug.

"Gretchen, I told you to wait until I said it was okay to come down." The Amazon's gun was suddenly out of sight, although, to Lola, she looked just as dangerous.

"It's just Nessa. And a friend," Gretchen added, peeking over at Lola. Lola waved. "Nessa wouldn't bring anybody home who would hurt us."

The Amazon muttered something under her breath.

"It's not nice to say stuff out loud that other people can't hear," Gretchen scolded. She turned to Lola, baby teeth shining. "I remember you from the park. I'm Gretchen. What's your name?"

"My name is Delores, but my friends call me Lola." She solemnly shook Gretchen's hand, and though it should have felt awkward with Agnes holding Gretchen up and watching the two of them with faintly worried eyes, it felt fine. In fact, a glowing ball of warmth throbbed in the center of Lola's chest. This little girl, with her cleft chin just like Zoe's, was Lola's *niece*. Her family. And she was also the most important person in the world to Agnes.

"Hi, Lola. I'd like to be your friend. I don't have a small name, though. Everyone just calls me Gretchen."

"When a name is as cute as yours, you don't need a small name."

"Let's move this little party somewhere more comfortable, shall we?" The Amazon slid between the Agnes/Gretchen mass and Lola, and she wasn't as subtle about it as she probably thought. "Do you want anything to drink, Lola?"

"Yes, I do! But you didn't tell her your name, Whit!" Gretchen reached out to pluck at the Amazon's shoulder before she leaned back enough to look at Lola. "Her name is Whitley, but we all call her Whit because Nessa says she's so funny."

Lola blinked at the Amazon—uh, Whit—who looked as if she could break her in half or at least shoot her in the head without blinking.

"It's a pleasure to meet you, Lola," Whit said after a split-second pause. "Pardon my rudeness, please."

"Uh—that's okay. I'm sure you have other things on your mind." Like how to kill Lola and dump the body before Gretchen even noticed she was missing.

"I'd like a milkshake, please." Gretchen turned her mischievous look back to Whit.

"One glass of cold milk coming up," Whit said. "And what would you two like?"

Once Lola and Agnes told her what they wanted, Whit glided off somewhere, presumably in the direction of the kitchen.

"She's scary." Lola murmured, tracking Whit's movements until she disappeared around a corner.

Agnes gave a dismissive, elegant shrug. "Come on. Let's go out to the terrace. It's a nice night, and I feel like some fresh air. Whit will find us out there."

Lola followed Agnes, who had kicked off her heels and left them by the elevator. Agnes bounced Gretchen in her arms with each step, and Gretchen giggled.

"Will Whit really give me cold milk?" Held firmly in arms she obviously trusted, Gretchen held onto Agnes's neck and grinned at Lola, who couldn't help but grin right back. Cute kid. "I don't want to drink…" She rambled on while Agnes made occasional humming noises, probably to prove she was listening and not wondering what the hell to do now that Lola was in her space.

Not that Lola had any clue herself.

When she stepped out onto the terrace behind Agnes and her chatty kid, Lola stopped short. Rich people *really* were on some other level.

The terrace that Agnes had so casually led to, which was accessible through her home office, had easily one of the most spectacular views Lola had ever seen of the city. Skyscrapers glittered with light, like dark columns studded with crystals reaching for the galaxies above. The snaking river. The dark sky with its suggestion of stars that the city lights made it just about impossible to see. And they were so high up…

For all the beautiful views they had of New York, the terrace with its chairs and wide weather-hardy patio sofas felt absolutely private. Ringed in by tall trees and giant planters, it felt like they were in their own world. To her left, just beyond the trees and planters rippled the water from an infinity pool.

The things money could buy.

"Make yourself comfortable," Agnes invited as, next to her, Gretchen bounced on the patio couch like she was testing a mattress.

Between meeting her niece for the first time, Whit giving off murder vibes, and being surrounded by all this unfamiliar luxury, Lola wasn't about to be "comfortable" any time soon. "Um…thanks."

The terrace seating formed a U shape, with a broad table in the middle of the arrangement of chairs and sofas so someone could easily rest their feet or their drinks while enjoying the view.

Lola tucked her feet underneath her and leaned back in her chair, unable to keep her attention on only one thing. Seeing Agnes with Gretchen, obviously protective but also loving, revealed a facet to Agnes that Lola never knew existed. It was also sexy as hell. Who knew?

"Are you and Nessa good friends, Lola?" Gretchen crouched on the arm of Agnes's sofa, peering over at Lola, eyes wide and interested. "She needs friends." A quick look back and whatever Gretchen saw in Agnes's face made her sink back to sit in Agnes's lap. "Nessa's really great. If you don't like her already, you will."

Eyes meeting Agnes's, Lola said, "I already like her."

Gretchen clapped. "Good."

Luckily for Lola's melting heart, Whit came back just then with the drinks. She passed them around—hot apple ciders for Agnes and Lola, a warm milk that smelled of spices for Gretchen—before sitting back with her espresso.

"What did I miss?" Whit looked at Gretchen, and Gretchen laughed.

"Nothing, silly." Gretchen carefully balanced her mug of milk between her small hands before taking a sip. Her wide smile said she approved of the taste. "You were gone for zero time."

"Good. You know I hate being left out."

It was impressive how Whit managed to be playful with Gretchen yet effectively intimidate Lola at the same time. Lola would hate to have Whit as an enemy.

They talked about nothing concrete for a few minutes—favorite drinks, how nice the view was, when Gretchen would get to see Lola next—before Gretchen began getting sleepy. It wasn't long before she was sprawled out, half in Agnes's lap, half on the sofa, her nearly empty mug safely put away on the nearby table, eyelids drooping low.

"She's already had her bath and brushed her teeth before you came in," Whit said softly. "She just wanted to see you before she went to sleep."

"Okay." Agnes carefully lifted Gretchen. "I'm going to tuck her in. You two play nice while I'm away."

Then she and Gretchen were gone.

Once they were alone on the terrace, Lola looked everywhere but at Whit.

Whit, who kept a steady gaze on Lola—she didn't have to see those predator eyes on her to know where they were looking—didn't say a word.

After a few minutes of stilted silence, Lola blew out a slow breath. "Well, this is awkward."

"I'm fine," Whit said, showing her teeth. "It'll only get awkward if you screw us over, because then I'd have to kill you."

Lola didn't doubt she was telling the truth. "I'm not here to hurt you or Agnes."

"That's not what you said before."

Lola's head jerked up. "Before when?"

A pair of thick eyebrows rose.

Oh. Embarrassed heat rushed over Lola's skin like an army of fire ants. "You were listening to us that whole time?"

"Not the whole time but the alarm and audio-video monitoring devices in the tunnel are designed to trigger and contact me at the detection of any voices."

"Oh. Fuck. Me."

"I think Agnes can handle that," Whit said dryly.

And apparently Lola had spoken out loud. Face burning with the heat of all the suns, Lola jumped up from the chair and, nearly tripping over her own feet, rushed to the railing. The autumn breeze washed over her cheeks with a much-needed touch of coolness.

Nothing scandalous had happened in the tunnel. No panties had come off. But with the revelations crashing over her, Agnes's justified anger, and her own shameful confessions, those moments had felt unbearably intimate. Private.

Embarrassment flared up Lola's throat and into her face at the thought that Whit had seen it all.

"I hope you're not planning to jump."

Lola slowly turned at Agnes's voice. Agnes stood in the doorway between her office and the terrace, barefoot and still impressively tall with the artificial lights surrounding her unfair beauty like a halo.

Lola had kissed this woman. She'd made love to her. Twice. Her heart thumped powerfully.

"Not yet," she finally said in response.

"Good." A faint smile touched Agnes's lips. "I'm not ready to lose you." She left the doorway to sit in the chair opposite Whit. "Let's get to the business of why we're all here, shall we?"

"I feel like I've been dragged in front of the principal," Lola said with heat in her cheeks.

Yes, that was exactly what it felt like. Just because she was now a grown-ass woman who just happened to have made out with her crush in a public place didn't make this any less cringe-y. Was Whit going to put her and Agnes in detention?

"We can save the paddling for later." Whit froze Lola with her stare. "Are you really putting a hold on your plans to destroy us?"

Lola blinked. That was *not* the route she thought Whit would take. Brass knuckles and a scalpel seemed more her style, not dry humor and a threatening stare.

Whit stood and looked deceptively casual, even harmless, in her pale gray sweats as she wandered close to where Lola stood.

Lola's lizard brain told her to run, predator on the loose, but she stood still. Some would probably even say she froze.

"I heard what you said in the tunnel," Whit said. "You were going to write some 'tell-all' piece about The House and then sic the cops on us."

As if Lola needed a reminder that Whit had heard and seen everything she and Agnes had done to each other in that damn tunnel. She clenched a hand around the cool steel of the balcony railing and forced her feet to stay where they were. "But I'm not going to do that anymore."

"Yes, yes." Whit crept closer and finally Lola couldn't stand it anymore. She blinked first and backed up, moving along the railing and further from Whit, who was definitely stalking her instead of just having a regular damn conversation. She was like Jamika, who could face down criminals with guns and knives every day at work and barely blink. "But tell us about before that. Why did you set your pretty brown eyes on us in the first place?"

"Whit, stop scaring her," Agnes said.

"If she's not scared, she won't talk."

"I might pee my pants, though." Lola hated how breathless and, yes, *scared* she sounded. Her heart raced as if it were trying to escape her chest.

With only two feet of space between them, Whit stopped moving. "Okay. I'm not scaring you now. Talk."

A low sigh came from Agnes, then she was taking Lola by the hand and pulling her onto the sofa next to her. "You promised me honesty, Lola. I'm ready to hear it."

Lola's lips felt dry under the nervous swipe of her tongue. The truth. Just tell the truth. She took a long breath. "There are rumors floating around that you've had some of the girls working for you killed."

"Lies," Whit said, "but go on." She went back to her chair and fixed her stare on Lola.

It was hard swallowing past the lump of nervousness in her throat, but Lola managed. Barely. "Some say you get them hooked on drugs, make them dependent on you, then you destroy their lives or kill them if they want to quit."

"You've seen The House's assets." Whit's lips thinned. She obviously didn't approve of Lola's access to anything of theirs. "Do they look strung out and desperate to you? Unhappy to be where they are?"

They didn't. Most of the self-described assets wanted to stay at The House as long as their bodies could handle it. They loved the money. They admired and feared Agnes. Everyone Lola had talked to seemed content enough with what they were doing, even the ones making plans to leave the business later on down the line.

"No. Nothing is like I was told." Maddie had obviously lied to Lola, amped her up to hate Agnes and rush into the house for revenge. But did that mean Zoe had lied too? "There's a woman—"

A scalding curse from Whit cut off the rest of what Lola had to say. Whit looked down at her watch, then pulled a phone from her pocket, quickly tapping something on the screen. "We've got company in the tunnel. Lots of company."

Agnes stood, her face calm. "How many?"

Whit was already rushing toward the door leading back inside the apartment, and Lola followed, her heart starting its gallop again. "Too many to be friendly."

In the office Lola hadn't paid attention to before, a giant TV along one wall suddenly came to life. Whit had her phone in hand, and a quick look to the screen showed that the TV mirrored the phone's display. A small army of black-clad soldiers, at least a dozen of them, were rushing through the tunnel, their footsteps eerily silent. It looked as if they had guns strapped to every body part, and they said nothing, swarming through the Spartan space, their faces covered.

Oh God. "What's going on?"

"You tell us," Whit growled, and she pinned Lola with a lethal stare. "Who did you let into the tunnels, and what do they want?"

CHAPTER 29

"How should I know who these people are?" Lola backed away from the monitor, looking as if she was frightened the soldiers would jump off the screen and attack her.

"We've been safe all this time. For years," Whit growled, her eyes swirling with worry and anger. "Are you expecting me to believe it's a coincidence that we have a breach just as you worm your way in here?" She reached out to grab Lola, but Agnes stepped between them.

"That's enough, Whit. I'm scared too, but this isn't the way to handle it."

"I'm not scared. I'm *pissed*."

Despite the danger they were all in, Agnes rolled her eyes. "Of course."

Lola's hand settled on Agnes's back. "Quit jumping down my throat and call the cops," she said, her voice tense as she flickered her gaze between the army stamping through the tunnels and Whit's furious face. "We can't fight against an army like that on our own."

Whit let out an ugly laugh. "The last thing we need is the police. They'd sooner arrest us and snatch up the spoils of whatever these people—" She jerked her thumb at the screen. "—leave behind."

"We don't have time for this," Agnes cut in. "Whit, get Gretchen and go. I'll wipe the files and follow when I can."

"Fine," Whit growled. She looked anything but fine with it.

"And I need you to take Lola with you."

"No," Whit snapped. "Absolutely not."

"Wherever you go, I go," Lola told Agnes at the same time.

Whit growled again, and Agnes grabbed her arm. Her own temper snarled, ready to get loose, but she fought it.

Time was running out. The steel door between the tunnel and the elevator that would take the group of invaders directly to the penthouse apartment was strong. It would take powerful hacking skills or a big batch of C4 to get it down. But Agnes hadn't come this far by underestimating her enemies.

Whit's arm trembled beneath hers, and Agnes could practically feel the anger move under Whit's skin like a dangerous living thing. "Whit." She squeezed the jumping muscle under hand. "Go. I need to know Gretchen is safe. You're the only one I trust with her life. Please."

Whit spat out a curse, then rushed off to get Gretchen. They'd practiced this a thousand times. Whit knew what to do. They only had a slight change of plans.

Agnes helped a shaky Lola to one of the leather chairs. "Are you all right?"

"Yes, yes. But—" Lola looked around, as if she expected strangers to jump out of the hidden corners any second. "You've got to get out of here. I didn't have anything to do with this—this whatever it is. I promise."

"I know. It's okay."

"It's not okay. Even I can see that."

Agnes almost smiled. "A bit of comforting hyperbole then." She gently squeezed the back of Lola's neck before she jumped into action. After sending out the "go to ground" alarm to Clare and all the assets, Agnes started the auto delete for the files on her slim desktop computer. Her laptop, tablet, and phone went into a messenger bag along with stacks of cash and all her papers from the wall safe.

"When Whit and Gretchen come back, I want you to go with them." Agnes draped the bag over Lola's shoulder.

"No! I already said I'm not leaving here without you." Lola's eyes were wide. Her pulse visibly galloped in her throat. "It's not safe for you here."

"What do you think they'll do to me?" Agnes spared Lola a quick look as she opened up a hidden closet door, pulled out her go-bag and grabbed a handful of necessities from it. Jeans, T-shirt, boots, and socks. Leather holster. Gun. She quickly changed clothes, slid the gun into the holster, and pulled on one of the leather jackets hanging in the closet. Fear nipped at the back of her consciousness, vicious and slavering, but she couldn't afford to feel it.

Lola, though, looked at Agnes with all the terror naked on her face for anyone to see. "People like that," she said in a voice that shook, "dressed like they're going to war, they're only here to capture or kill the queen. *You.* Agnes, you can't stay here and allow them to take you."

Agnes couldn't argue with that, but there were more important concerns.

Whit appeared in the doorway, already changed into an outfit similar to Agnes's. She carried a sleepily blinking Gretchen on one hip as if she weighed nothing. Her go-bag, a lightweight knapsack, was already on her shoulder.

"Nessa?" Gretchen's voice wobbled.

"It's okay, sweet pea. Whit will take you somewhere for a while, and I'll join you all a little later." Although she was feeling far from soothed, Agnes rubbed Gretchen's back through her jacket and tried to project a calm she didn't feel.

"No dice," Whit said. "You come with us. Leave this one here." She jerked her chin at Lola.

"If I'm with you, then you all become targets. And I won't take the chance that they'll hurt her." Agnes pushed a resisting Lola toward Whit, but as soon as she let go, Lola moved out of reach.

"They'll hurt you, though, Agnes," Lola said. "Come with us."

"The emergency elevator only holds three hundred and fifty pounds." Or maybe less. "It won't fit all of us."

Agnes didn't know what she'd been thinking when she'd had that model installed—so small that it was practically useless. It had been a last-minute addition to the penthouse, a safety measure Whit had thought they needed.

"Then leave me behind," Lola insisted.

"Agreed." Whit's voice was hard. Uncompromising.

"For God's sake, Whit! What if they use Lola against us as a way to get to me? Be logical." Agnes's patience had reached the end of its tether. The enemy was coming. They didn't have time to argue.

Whit's head dipped in reluctant acknowledgment.

On the wide monitor, the soldiers approached the steel door at the end of the tunnel. Good. That should take them a while to get through. Then one of them took out a piece of paper and tapped a code into the electronic panel. With a series of welcoming beeps, the bolts loosened, and the heavy door began to slowly lift open.

Someone had given the soldiers the door code.

"What the fuck?" Agnes saw her own shock reflected in Whit's face.

The group rushed through the opening door.

"Take them out of here!" Agnes hissed at Whit. "We don't have time to debate this."

A low vibration came from Whit's large smart watch. "They're coming," she said. "Right now." The sounds of the main elevator rushing down to the ground floor filled the room.

Lola backed away from Whit, eyes fixed on Agnes. "I won't leave you!"

"Do what I say!" Agnes's fear made her voice cold and sharp, its icicles stabbing deep into her chest. For the first time since her mother had died, she was truly terrified. "Please."

It felt as if she'd just found someone who she could truly share her life with. The thought should have surprised her, but it didn't. Everything about it felt right. That was why Agnes didn't want to lose Lola now. She couldn't.

"Goddamn it." Fire blazed in Whit's eyes. "Go to the panic room. Don't come out until they're gone." She grabbed Lola's wrist and started to drag her away.

Gretchen whimpered Agnes's name but clung to Whit. She'd been taught a day like this might come.

"Keep my girls safe, Whit," Agnes said. "I'm counting on you."

With a last curse from Whit, they were gone, leaving Agnes alone with her furiously beating heart, her fear turning her stomach into a ball of ice.

When the main elevator slid back up from the garage with barely a whisper, she knew she'd run out of time. With her go-bag over her shoulder, she raced past the elevator and up the stairs, just barely making it to the panic room on the upper floor, the door closing behind her with a sharp click as the elevator chimed.

Her heart felt as if it were about to tear its way out of her chest.

Everything she'd built, everything she'd worked toward these last few years, was crashing down around her. She clenched her jaw, swallowing the scream of rage that wanted to erupt from her throat. Now wasn't the time for a tantrum. She needed to know who the fuck was doing this and why.

Agnes forced her breath to slow, sitting down at the desk with the spread of monitors above it. On one of the monitors, a familiar figure swaggered from the elevator as if she had all the time in the world. Agnes sucked in a surprised breath as white teeth flashed in a face she'd hoped never to see again.

Camille, her father's last mistress.

Dark-clad soldiers fanned out from behind her, seven of them, rushing toward the other rooms of the apartment with their guns drawn and boots thudding with loud menace across the marble. One stayed with her, an armed shadow, as she prowled around the apartment.

Like the soldiers, Camille wore black, but it was pretty stuff, leather for playing dress-up. And she wasn't armed.

Of all the dangers Agnes had sensed, that Whit had warned her against, this one was very much a surprise. The last time Agnes had seen her, Camille had been screaming nonsense over Augustus Noble's body. Why was this parasite back in New York?

Agnes narrowed her gaze at the screen, her mind running through the possibilities of who her father's ex-mistress could be working with, what she was after, and just how far her tentacles extended.

On the screen, Camille was just as beautiful as she had been the last time Agnes had seen her, but her face was leaner, as if she'd been working out. She'd also apparently been gathering an army together.

"Come out wherever you are, *Queen* Agnes." In Camille's poisoned mouth, the title didn't sound at all respectful. "I've come to collect what's mine." Her words were rounded, New England posh, nothing like the native New Yorker growl she'd had when she'd first made her way to The House and into Augustus Noble's bed.

"What do you want?" Agnes quietly asked Camille, even though the sick feeling in her stomach told her she knew exactly what Camille wanted.

Camille's beautiful face looked up, and the cameras caught her from every angle. Yes, it was undoubtedly her. When Camille had been with Agnes's father, Agnes had felt sorry for her, knowing she was only being used for her young body. But as she saw more of Camille's ambition, Agnes realized they were actually using each other, Camille and her father.

He used up her young body as much as the Viagra allowed while Camille flattered and fucked him, did everything for him to make her an equal partner in his business. But Agnes's father, as much as he traded in sex, had never allowed his dick to do the thinking for him.

For better or worse, Agnes was his heir, and no amount of cocaine-fueled blow jobs, supermodel orgies, or tattoos of his name on Camille's various body parts ever made him forget that.

"I know you're here, Agnes." Camille prowled into Agnes's office; her shadow had his gun drawn. "Come out. I just want to talk."

The armed man by her side made that a laughable lie.

A quick scan of the cameras confirmed that Whit had already gotten Gretchen and Lola out of the apartment. Agnes allowed a breath of relief to slide past her lips. If nothing else, they were safe.

Down in her office, Camille kept on talking. "You know what I want. All you have to do is give it to me." Her gaze went up, met the lens of one of the cameras, then keeping her eyes there, she swept a hand across the desk and sent everything on it tumbling to the ground. A crystal paperweight smashed. Pencils clattered across the floor.

Camille's pretty smile was a reminder of the two years she'd spent at The House, slinking around corners, alternately trying to seduce Agnes or get her in trouble with her father. "I should let him piss all over this office. Maybe that'll get you to come out. You always were a territorial bitch."

Although the man at her side was mostly stoic, a twitch at his jaw gave the impression that he wasn't happy about being potentially called upon to whip out his penis on request.

"Test me," Camille continued as she ransacked the office instead of acting like she was actually looking for something. "I'll let him do it."

Usually, men pissing in the corners of her home wasn't something Agnes would tolerate, but given the choice between allowing this man to let his bladder loose on the antique Elizabethan-style couch or ending up with a bullet in her head, the choice was clear. She just hoped Whit was doing what they discussed—getting herself and Gretchen to safety—instead of doing something hopeless and stupid.

Camille's men had methodically gone through the apartment while she'd been having her temper tantrum. Every room looked like a war zone, even Gretchen's, the mattress overturned, the cupboards yanked open and their contents spilled all over the floor. Did these men think Agnes had people stashed behind the shelf of kids' astronomy books or in Gretchen's toy chest?

Nearly all the men had some sort of machine in their hands that they used to scan walls and just about every surface they passed. They were looking for heat signatures. Looking for her.

Luckily, Whit had built the panic room into the ceiling, nothing obvious, and the door was too thick to emit any body heat. Hopefully.

One by one, Camille's men came back from the rest of the apartment to report back to her about what they'd found—nothing—then stood back in the office, hands on their guns, waiting for their next instructions.

"Whoever was here is probably long gone," one of the men said. "Maybe just monitoring us remotely by video."

"Fine." Camille leaned back against the desk, her arms crossed, plumping up her already impressive cleavage. "You want to play games with me, then let's really play." Another glance swept up to the cameras, and with dread crawling up her spine, Agnes felt as if Camille saw her there, sitting upright in the chair, her hands braced against the desk, waiting for the worst.

"Set it on fire." Camille tossed the words casually toward the men who waited around her. "The whole apartment. Every single room. If she's here, we'll burn her out. If not…" Her teeth flashed in another playful smile. "… oh well."

No. She'd never do that. If Camille was here for the reason Agnes suspected, it didn't make sense for her to burn down the penthouse. A breath of smoke curling from under the closed door of Gretchen's room killed Agnes's certainty.

Another camera showed the kitchen already half-hidden in a noxious gray cloud. Something inside the smoke shot sparks, probably some of the cleaning products catching fire and about to explode.

Camille wasn't bluffing.

With her pulse thudding hard in her throat, Agnes grabbed her bag, slid outside the panic room, and ran.

CHAPTER 30

LOLA ALMOST SUFFOCATED RIDING DOWN thirty stories in a tiny elevator with Whit, her huge backpack, and a softly crying Gretchen.

"I don't want to leave Nessa." With tears tracking down her face, Gretchen kept looking up as if she could see through the roof of the tiny elevator to where they'd abandoned Agnes.

Lola couldn't think of what she'd done as anything else. If she hadn't let Agnes's security guy take her into that private elevator, Agnes would be leaving now with Gretchen and Whit. She'd be much safer than she was now.

If Agnes died in that penthouse, it would be all Lola's fault.

The thought chilled her. She stumbled back against the cool metal of the elevator with a clink of the messenger bag Agnes had loaded her down with, earning her the stink eye from Whit.

The elevator slowed its rapid descent, then the doors were opening, and Whit gently shushed Gretchen with a hand on her back. "We have to be very quiet, love."

While her tone was soft, her gaze as it met Lola's was not. Whit's eyes were cold and unforgiving over Gretchen's bowed head. Yes, Lola thought Whit would gladly kill her if she knew Agnes wouldn't be upset about it.

Lola shrank back against the elevator wall, and Whit strode out, head already sweeping around to check what they were walking into. A cement-block room with yet another steel door. An electronic panel. Whit held up a hand in the universal gesture of "stop the fuck right there," and she listened, ear pressed to the door, hand making soothing circles on Gretchen's back, before swiping the card slotted into the wrist side of her gloves across the display.

The door silently slid open, leaving them in a well-lit underground garage that looked the same as any other in the city. It was nearly full, cars of all makes and models, and Lola could hear conversations coming from multiple parts of the garage. It was a public place.

"Let's go," Whit hissed.

Heart hammering like mad, Lola followed Whit's rigid back, aware she was darting nervous looks around the parking garage as if she were about to steal one of the Range Rovers nearby.

Thankfully, the car they were heading for was close, and Whit opened it, the lights flashing quickly without the dark Mercedes SUV making a sound. With the ease of obvious long practice, she buckled Gretchen into the car seat in the back and, after leaving the child with what looked like a bag of toys and books, slid behind the wheel.

As Lola watched Whit, her frantic mind drifted back to Agnes. What supplies did Agnes have in that panic room with her? Knowing her, probably a bunch of guns and a fridge full of her damn fizzy water. Was the room enough to keep her safe until rescue arrived? But, since Whit insisted they not call the cops, would rescue even get there?

"Are you coming?" Whit's growl dragged Lola's attention back to her own immediate situation.

"Uh…sure." Lola tumbled into the SUV. She arranged the messenger bag across her knees as the vehicle started up. Her knee jiggled as they slid quietly through the underground parking lot, passing a few people here and there but none who looked like they gave a damn who was in the late-model Mercedes with tinted windows so dark they looked black.

They could've been any one of a thousand cars in this part of Manhattan. Right? But that didn't stop Lola from peering closely into each shadow they passed and clutching the bag to her stomach as if it were some kind of security blanket.

Come on, come on, come on…

The breath she'd been holding for far too long rushed out once they were in the flow of traffic and moving smoothly down a busy nighttime street. Although it was hard to tell one set of taillights from another, it didn't seem as if they were being followed. Good.

As soon as that worry fell away, though, the one nipping at the back of Lola's mind presented itself front and center. Agnes was back there, trapped in that apartment with a bunch of heavily armed lunatics. Damn it, why did Lola leave her?

Because they would've killed you first as an appetizer, a voice that sounded a lot like Jamika said at the back of her mind. *You couldn't help her on your own.*

Still, Lola had to do something.

"What terrible ideas are you considering right now?" Whit's voice had the sharp edge of mockery to it, but Lola answered her honestly anyway.

"I don't feel right leaving her back there."

"You think *I* do?"

"I have no idea what you're thinking, but I do know driving away and leaving Agnes on her own is a sh—" Just in time, she remembered Gretchen in the back seat. "That's a terrible plan."

"Do you have any better ideas that don't involve me abandoning the most important job Agnes trusts me with?" A low sound of distress came from the back seat, and Whit reached back to touch Gretchen's sneakered foot. "You okay, princess?"

Gretchen looked up, her lashes still wet from her recent bout of tears. "I want Nessa," she said. "Where is she?"

"You'll have her back soon," Lola found herself promising recklessly.

"Okay." Gretchen bit her lip and went back to her coloring book and crayons.

Lola's chest ached for Gretchen and for herself. No matter what, she couldn't allow Agnes to be hurt. Gretchen needed her family to stay together, and Whit did too.

Of course, Lola didn't have a plan. But she knew someone who would.

"You know what? Let me out here." Lola gripped the bag in her lap for courage. "I can be more help here in the city instead of wherever you're going to stash the kid."

"Her name is Gretchen." The words were a growled warning, low and deadly, a dangerous predator protecting its young.

"Yes," she said softly. "I know."

Whit sighed, a sound faintly tinged with apology. "You're not going anywhere. Agnes said to keep you safe, and that's what I'm going to do."

213

"I'm getting out of this car one way or another." Lola grabbed the door handle. "So let me out, or I jump."

The car had automatic door locks, so it was mostly a toothless threat, but if Whit insisted on dragging Lola wherever she was heading with Gretchen, Lola was going to make damn sure Whit knew she wasn't happy about it.

Whit didn't look very concerned. "You know that going back is a bad idea, right?"

"I know you don't care, so spare me the sound advice."

"That's not very nice." Gretchen picked that second to chime in from the back.

"Sorry, honey bunny." Lola gave the girl what she hoped was a reassuring smile. "But your Auntie Whit is being a pain."

"She's just Whit, not Auntie anything." Gretchen knocked the heels of her sneakers against the car seat. "But 'Auntie Whit' sounds nice. I'll ask Nessa about that when we see her."

A lump the size of all New York jammed itself into Lola's throat. She desperately wanted there to be that next time when they could talk about titles and why Whit should be 'Danger Auntie' maybe instead of plain 'Auntie Whit.'

God, Lola sounded delirious, even in her own head. Was this what unrelenting fear did to a person? "That's a great idea. For now, though, I have to go. I'll see you all later, okay?"

"Okay. Maybe we can have a milkshake for real then."

"I'll do my best to convince your Nessa and not-Auntie Whit to make milkshakes for both of us." The smile Lola turned toward the back seat felt forced, but she couldn't do anything about it. Fear for Agnes twisted in her belly like a pinned snake, frantic to escape and do *something*. Lola put a hand on the door latch and gave Whit a more savage version of that grin. The "let me out or else" was strongly implied.

A few seconds later, the SUV slid to a stop next to a delivery van, double-parking. "Here you go. I'll make sure to tell Agnes that you forced me to kick you out of the car."

"You don't have to sound so happy about it," Lola muttered, climbing out of the truck.

Whit grunted.

Only when the dark SUV had disappeared into the sea of other cars on the wide avenue did Lola realize she still had Agnes's messenger bag.

Well, shit. Nothing to be done about it, though.

Now that the presence of Whit too close to Lola in that tiny space wasn't making her seize up with anxiety, she actually started thinking. The bag. Agnes had swept a bunch of things off her desk into it. Including a damn phone. Lola stepped under an awning of a closed electronics store to root around in the messenger bag. She fist-pumped when she found the phone.

"Hey, it's me," she said when Jamika answered after the first ring.

"Good," Jamika said. "I'm glad you realized my call was an emergency. So, what's your choice?"

Having been prepared to jump immediately into the reason for her call, Lola stuttered. "Uh, what?"

"Pineapple and chicken on the pizza or fried eggplant in white sauce?"

"How about Agnes is being held at gunpoint in her own apartment and we need to help her out?"

"I don't think I like that flavor."

Lola started in the direction of the subway and told Jamika everything that just happened. "I know she's not one of your hero cops, but she doesn't deserve what's happening to her."

"Fuck. Okay. Come on home. I'll have a plan together by the time you get here."

Lola sagged with relief. "You're amazing, you know that?"

"I haven't done jack shit yet. Plus I don't even know if whatever I come up with is going to work."

"I know. But you don't have to help."

"What kind of best friend would I be if I let your crush die before you get the chance to do it in a real bed?"

"You're such an ass."

"Yeah, yeah. But I'm the ass who's going to save your girlfriend's ass. Hopefully."

CHAPTER 31

AGNES CREPT OUT OF THE panic room. Silently, she dropped down from the opening hidden in the ceiling and landed in a crouch. Above her, the door slid closed with a sigh. Smoke roiled at each end of the long hallway, snaking toward the ceiling. But it smelled strange, a slightly chemical odor that made Agnes's nose twitch.

She didn't have time to linger and analyze what made it so different. The clock was ticking. All she had to do was avoid Camille's men and make it to the emergency elevator without getting caught. Easy. Maybe.

The rest of the building sounded like chaos. Booted feet stomped across the floors. The sound of heavy things crashed against the marble. No voices, though. Camille and her little army were disconcertingly quiet in their destruction.

And the smoke kept coming.

Agnes cursed and yanked a handkerchief from her pocket, wishing she'd taken the time to wet it, and put it over her face. Silent, she crept down the smoke-filled hallway, hugging the wall. When she stepped over scattered pieces of a shattered vase, the go-bag thumped awkwardly against her back. She adjusted its weight and tightened the straps.

"Good to know you're as predictable as ever."

Agnes froze where she stood, her heart dropping to her boots. *Fuck.*

A grinning Camille emerged from the smoke, her steps unhurried, as if she didn't have to worry about the fire currently consuming the penthouse and threatening everyone in it. Clouds of gray swirled around her, and Agnes heard a hissing sound as if a den of snakes had been let loose.

One of the security men ripped the bag from Agnes's back and threw it aside.

The smoke. It didn't smell as if anything was burning. It didn't smell like real smoke at all. Angry and embarrassed heat flooded through Agnes, and she curled her hands into fists.

"Did you figure it out yet?" Camille actually threw her head back and laughed. "Clever, right?" But she didn't wait for Agnes to respond. "You two—drag her back downstairs. The rest of you, put out that smoke."

A pair of soldiers grabbed Agnes's arms, gloved fingers digging in deep. She didn't fight them, even when they yanked her faster than she could walk, deliberately jogging her through the smoke-filled hallways.

The apartment wasn't destroyed.

There was no fire.

Heart racing, she allowed them to propel her through the building, the boots of her captors thudding along beside her quieter ones, and she saw a few men sucking out the smoke with some kind of vacuum machine as they pulled her toward their destination. Whit's big, open office.

The door connecting the office to Whit's bedroom was wide open. Camille hadn't trashed either room. A notebook lay open on the desk, as if Whit had just stepped out for a coffee and would be coming right back. The men threw Agnes down into a chair.

"Now, we can talk face-to-face." Camille flashed a lot of teeth. "Isn't this much better?"

"I don't know about better. I was fine where I was, to be honest."

"Good thing I didn't ask for your honesty." Camille sank into the chair behind the desk while the two men who'd dragged Agnes in stood behind her as if they were posing for a photo.

The image was striking, Agnes had to admit, Camille in her black leather romper with its many unnecessary zippers, cleavage plumped up, and her lipstick a dark red. The armed men behind her were impressive accessories.

Breathing evenly and deeply, Agnes took in Camille's posturing, emotionally distancing herself from the danger of the situation and giving her racing heart a chance to calm down. Survival was important here, and if that couldn't happen, she needed to keep Gretchen and Whit safe.

Lola's face also flashed across Agnes's mind, her fear and desperation to stay behind and protect Agnes. They'd just reached a place where they were honest with each other, had admitted there was something between them other than just sex. Agnes's heart squeezed tight. She wanted more of that. This fucked-up evening, trapped with Camille, couldn't be the end.

Agnes swallowed thickly against the panic trying to claw its way up her throat, then crossed her legs in a deliberate show of nonchalance.

"So…" Camille's chair sighed as she leaned back, her fingers linked across her stomach. "Where is she?"

For a wild moment, Agnes thought Camille was talking about Lola. Then she got her head back in the game. "If you think I'll tell you, you're more deluded than the last time we saw each other."

"Why are you hiding her from me? She's my darling child after all."

"Your darling? Right." Agnes scoffed. "Do you even remember her name?" Her father had named Gretchen after his favorite childhood nanny, then had promptly forgotten Gretchen even existed. To say Camille had been disappointed that her great gift to Agnes's father hadn't been as well-received as expected was an understatement. Up until that moment, Agnes had thought only children threw temper tantrums.

"Her name doesn't matter much, but Lola reminded me of it just a few days ago." Agnes tried to hide her surprise, but from the smirk on Camille's face, she wasn't very successful. "Ah, yes, I know about your precious Lola. I got Gretchen's name from her the same way I got the code to that overrated gate you have in the tunnel." She flashed her teeth again. "By using the people you *think* are loyal to you."

Her words landed a solid punch to Agnes's stomach. Lola knew Camille and had never said a word. Was Camille saying that Lola was the one she'd gotten the code from?

No, that was impossible. The trust between Agnes and Lola was new, but Agnes felt, deep down in that place reason couldn't touch, that Lola wouldn't betray her in this way. At least not knowingly.

"Now, back to what I was saying." Camille rapped her knuckles against the desk's surface, attention-getting, as if she knew the mental rabbit hole Agnes had fallen into when she'd mentioned Lola. "Tell me where the kid is."

"I already gave you the only answer you're going to get from me."

"Fine. I'll just go fetch her myself. And just so you know, my guys won't be gentle." Camille turned to one of the men behind her. "Take two of the others with you, and follow the tracker we have on the kid and her bodyguard." She smiled the whole time, her look playful, while Agnes blanked her face and gripped her hand into a fist, trying not to react.

Camille was bluffing. Just as she'd bluffed about setting the apartment on fire. More than that, Agnes trusted Whit not to take anything with her that would leave a trace. But maybe, just maybe, they'd managed to plant a tracker on Lola.

The fear Agnes had been keeping a tight hold of broke loose. "You don't have to do that," she said after the man strode out to get his friends.

"Oh, why is that?"

"She's a child who doesn't mean anything to you."

Camille was the least motherly woman she'd ever met. Other women would stop chubby-cheeked babies passing by in their strollers to baby-talk and give compliments, while Camille had just dumped her own baby with a convenient nanny, then set out to get her pre-pregnancy body back.

After it was clear that Augustus hadn't left anything for her in his will, Camille had just disappeared. She'd abandoned Gretchen with a frightened nanny who'd promptly brought Gretchen to Agnes.

"You won't get any leverage over me if you bring her here," Agnes said. "She'll just get in the way."

"I doubt that very much. You *love* her," Camille sneered. "You care about her. When Lola told me you and the brat were busy playing Mommy and Me while I was being cheated out of what's rightfully mine, I knew I had something on you."

Fear bounced Agnes's thoughts all over the place. When had Lola talked to Camille? Why? Was Camille really going to hurt Gretchen despite the blood they shared?

Calm down. She forced herself to keep that unaffected pose, legs crossed, face blank. "I'm not sure what Lola said to you, but she's wrong. Gretchen may be my father's child and my sister, but she's also a potential rival. There's no leverage there."

"Really? So you wouldn't mind if I dig her out of whatever little hidey-hole you stuck her in and sell her to one of your daddy's old friends?"

Agnes's face twisted as nausea sloshed around in her belly. A sound rose from the very depths of her soul. A growl.

Camille let out a bark of laughter. "Jesus! You're such an easy mark. So soft when everybody's been fooled into thinking you're some untouchable bad bitch. Queen Agnes, my ass." The contempt written all over her face was nothing Agnes hadn't seen before, but it mixed with something else. Hatred. Frustration. A hint of jealousy. "When I started this whole thing, I was going to take over The House and make you disappear. But I changed my mind. Someone like you needs to be dragged down into the gutter with the rest of us.

"You don't make proper use of all your resources," Camille continued. "Rox says you have dozens of potential, big-money clients you don't take on because of some stupid moral code. Lola is practically on her knees, ready to do anything for you, but you never put her to work. And you're holding on to that kid like she's some kind of treasure."

A look of disgust turned Camille's mouth ugly. "At least Philip has the right idea. Unlike you, he doesn't have any emotional weights dragging him down. He's ready to cut his father's throat, take over Rake Enterprises, make use of anything or anyone—including your little princess—who can make him some money."

Philip Rake.

Geoffrey Rake's son.

Had Geoffrey known where the threat was coming from? Of course he had. He'd warned Agnes at the Vegas meeting because he didn't have the courage, or resources, to destroy his own son. He'd wanted her to do it for him.

A fierce hunger burned from Camille's eyes, and Agnes watched her, listened to her, with dread pooling in her stomach. Every revelation was a bombshell, a dirty secret freely given. Resting half-hidden in her lap, Agnes's hand curled into a fist.

"But." Camille raised a finger. "There is one thing you can do to make this all go away."

Of course there was. "And what's that, Camille?"

"I'll give you complete and uncontested custody of the kid, and you two can disappear wherever losers go." She paused, her pretty smile a frightening thing made of red lips and sharp teeth. "All you have to do is sign The House over to me. Every hidden asset. Every fucking cent. I said I was coming for what's mine, and I meant it."

CHAPTER 32

JAMIKA'S IDEA FOR AN AGNES Noble rescue, as she'd explained it to Lola at home, was simple. They'd sneak into the penthouse using some architectural plans they'd found crammed in the messenger bag along with a bunch of other documents Agnes had tossed in from the safe. Then they'd locate Agnes, record any damning conversations between her and her assailants, and call in the cavalry, rescuing Agnes in the process.

The sneaking in had been slow but effective, using the small escape elevator Whit had used to get them out.

They'd managed to avoid any of the armed men in the penthouse, slip behind one of the many hidden walls in the apartment, and follow the maze of hallways and rooms to the sound of voices. Behind the walls lay a whole other world. A world of evenly spaced monitors, small lockers packed with snacks, changes of clothes, even weapons. It even had its own separate ventilation system and power source. Whoever had upgraded the building was the most paranoid asshole who ever lived.

Lola and Jamika had their phones out and on dark mode and used their notes app to communicate instead of talking out loud. They'd crept behind the walls and waited, expecting to surprise soldiers from a rival house or something that Lola could maybe understand. But all her expectations had been blown far out of the water when Lola looked up at one of the monitors and saw who was actually holding Agnes captive.

Lola stared in shock. The woman who had Agnes prisoner was there. With armed soldiers.

And that woman was Zoe.

Not a stranger. Not some crazy criminal Lola didn't recognize.

Zoe rampaged through the house, ripping paintings from the walls, throwing glass everywhere, stepping over the shards as if she expected someone else to clean up after her. And then she started goading Agnes.

"So, you wouldn't mind if I dig her out of whatever little hidey-hole you stuck her in and sell her to one of your daddy's old friends?"

Lola felt like her whole world was exploding in front of her face and the pieces were blowing back into her body, ripping her into bloody shreds. She met Jamika's eyes to see that Jamika looked as shocked as Lola felt.

"What the actual fuck?" Jamika mouthed.

Lola wanted to rush out and confront Zoe. Or this stranger who was wearing Zoe's skin. If only things were as simple as "my sister got replaced by a skin walker and now she's evil." Lola was sure there was an exorcism for that. And at least that way, the Zoe she'd mourned for years would be dead and Lola could still grieve.

Zoe would not have transformed into a creature who thought it was okay to sell her child. Someone who hurt Agnes and threw Lola under the bus by claiming Lola had let her into the penthouse.

Lola crouched, her thighs burning, though the pain in her chest was much worse, and she nearly cried at the touch of Jamika's warm hand on her back, comforting and heavy, in the same way that Jamika had wordlessly comforted her in the medical examiner's office.

This latest blow was an absolute kick in the tits.

Jamika was quiet, giving Lola time to absorb the pain before they kept going and did what they broke into the penthouse to do: observe, get some dirt on the attackers, call for backup. Free Agnes.

Then Jamika typed out something on her phone and showed it to Lola.

I don't think she's going to let Agnes go.

Lola didn't think so either. She had to change the plan before it was too late. Because in the "capture or kill the queen" scenario, it sounded a lot like Zoe preferred the *kill* option.

Lola's entire body flushed hot. All she could do was feel. Anger at Zoe. Anger at herself for getting caught up in a game of revenge designed to do nothing but hurt an innocent woman. Breath coming quickly, she stumbled back from Jamika and felt for a latch she'd seen a few minutes before.

A hand darted out to grab her. Jamika's.

"No!" Jamika whisper-shouted. "We're not ready yet."

They didn't have time to get ready, though. When would it be the right time? When Zoe had a gun to Agnes's head and was about to pull the trigger? When Agnes, who Lola was pretty sure she loved, was on the floor and bleeding out while Zoe ran away?

No. Lola couldn't stand there and do nothing. Her fingers found the latch and she pushed, felt the click as the door gave, and then she was out in bright light.

"Camille!" A male voice shouted a warning.

Lola blinked to get accustomed to the light that was very different from the cool gray of the hidden space. "Zoe, you can't do this."

Rough hands grabbed her, pinning her in place. One of Zoe's goons.

"What the fuck are you doing here, Lola?" Zoe snarled.

"Lola, you shouldn't be here!" Agnes jumped up from the chair as another man grabbed Lola's arm.

"Let her go," Zoe snapped to the man holding Lola. "For now." She stalked from behind the desk, coming toward Lola with anger lighting up her face. Zoe's fingers sank into Lola's shoulder, and she winced. "Look and see who else is in that damn wall," Zoe shouted to one of her men.

But just as he got close enough to do as she demanded, Jamika climbed out with her gun raised.

"NYPD. Back the fuck up." She flashed the badge dangling from the chain around her neck. "I have a van-load of other cops on their way, and they better find all of us in one piece."

Other cops? When did she call them? Or had she?

"What? You brought a cop with you?" Zoe's narrowed eyes examined Jamika like a bug under a microscope. "Aren't you Lola's little friend? The little dyke she used to run around the neighborhood with?"

"This little dyke is now a cop, and I'd suggest you and your asshole friends put your hands up," Jamika snapped, obviously annoyed.

Fuck. Lola took in Jamika's combative posture, Zoe's narrowed eyes, and Agnes's tense face. This was falling apart. She knew she'd messed up the way Jamika wanted to do this, but now it was as if they were stepping onto a lit powder keg. This thing could go in any direction. Her belly clenched with fear.

"This isn't a game, Zoe," Lola said. "Give up."

"Zoe? Who on earth is Zoe?" Agnes demanded.

"Her." Jamika jerked her chin toward Zoe. "Her real name is Zoe Anders, and she's Lola's sister."

"Fuck me…" Agnes muttered, looking between Zoe and Lola. To say that the look on her face was one of betrayal and anger was an extreme understatement. "Has this been your game all this time, to soften me up for when she came calling?"

"No! I'd never do that." Lola choked out and took a step toward Agnes, only to be brought up short by the anger on Agnes's face. "It's only been a couple of days since I found out she's even still alive. I didn't know what she was doing. I swear. And I never gave her the code to get in here!"

"I want to believe you," Agnes said.

"Then believe me!" Lola burst out before Agnes could say the "but" that was clearly coming.

"My *God*," Zoe groaned. "Don't be so pathetic. I thought you'd at least grown some spine since I left."

"What?" Lola stuttered and stumbled back from the unexpected spite in Zoe's voice.

"You heard me. Even before Mom died, you were always so fucking needy. Everything had to be about babying you and making sure you were taken care of and safe. And you were always there, sucking up the attention, taking up time and money we didn't have to spare. Nobody ever cared that I was giving up my childhood or my life for you."

At her side, Lola's hand tightened into a fist. She felt pummeled into the ground, battered by Zoe's attack, but she was nobody's punching bag. "What are you talking about, Zoe? I was a *child*!"

"I was too!"

"That's enough!" Agnes snapped. She stepped between Lola and Zoe, the heat of her back to Lola's front. Never in her life had Lola wanted so much to cling to anyone for shelter and never let go. "Not every person in your life has to be an unresolved grudge, Camille."

Lola heard the name but didn't even try to correct Agnes. This woman was truly a stranger. The sister she knew and missed would never—

Her vision blurred, and she blinked, looked away from Zoe so she wouldn't see her tears and use that as another excuse to call her weak.

Despite her resolution to at least appear strong, a pair of renegade tears leaked from her eyes. She roughly wiped them away.

The sound of a gun being cocked jerked her head up.

"Do not fuck with me, son," Jamika said, cold as ice, staring at a soldier with his hand bare inches from his holstered pistol. "Pull that gun and you're dead." She raised her voice without looking away from the soldier. "Zoe, I've been recording everything since you threatened to kill Ms. Noble here. The tape from before has already been e-mailed somewhere secure, and I'm still recording now. You and I both know what that means."

Zoe scowled at Lola and took another step back, nearly bumping into the desk in the center of the room.

"That's right," Jamika continued. "Demanding Ms. Noble's enterprise in exchange for custody of your child? Threatening said child with sexual assault? I can take your ass to jail for blackmail just as an appetizer. You get me?"

"I get you just fine, you little shit," Zoe growled.

There was something else going on, something that had Jamika's eyes flashing a feral fire.

"It seems as if everyone knows what's going on but me," Agnes murmured.

Lola shook her head. "I don't know what's going on either." She knew Zoe was scared, though.

From in front of the desk, Zoe watched Jamika warily. "Before you make any sudden moves, cop, consider what I can offer you if you just let me get out of here and pretend you never saw me."

"You do know I'm still recording, right?" Jamika raised an eyebrow but kept her gun steady.

"Recordings can be erased."

"But this one isn't going anywhere. If your plan is to impress me, you better talk fast. My colleagues will be here any minute."

The soldiers had been getting restless, watching each other with obvious worry. At the sound of frustration Zoe made, the one closest to the door ran out. Three others followed right after him.

Zoe took a jerking step, as if she was about to run after them, but Jamika got in her way. "Talk, don't run," Jamika snapped. "What do you have for me?"

"I'll tell you everything you want to know about Philip Rake and Rake Enterprises. They're the ones funding my little operation, including supplying these thugs. I'll give you information to back it up. I'll be your informant if you get any possible charges against me dismissed. You get a big bust, and I get my freedom. Everybody wins."

"What about Gretchen?" Agnes cut in. "I want to be sure she's completely safe from you."

Of course, that was all she ever wanted, Lola thought. Agnes wasn't even thinking about Zoe's threat of taking over her business. If they'd waited long enough, she would've probably given Zoe everything she wanted just to keep Gretchen safe. This was what Lola had done, brought this danger to Agnes and to Gretchen. She swallowed the acid burn of regret.

"You heard the cop; it's all on tape. I don't have a leg to stand on with regard to that kid. You're safe from me," Zoe sneered.

"As safe as we can be with you alive and causing trouble." Jamika fished handcuffs out of her pants pocket. "Agnes, put the cuffs on her, would you, please?"

"With pleasure." Agnes snapped the cuffs onto Zoe, and even Lola could tell they were too tight. "All this is well and good," Agnes said as she hauled Zoe tight against her, her taller frame looming, "but right now, I need you to call your dogs off Whit and Gretchen."

"Fine," Zoe ground out. "You don't have to be so rough."

With all of them listening in, she made a call to her goons, telling them to stop tracking Whit and Gretchen and head back to Rake Holdings.

By the time she was done, the four of them were the only ones left in the penthouse. Agnes checked on the monitors to be sure.

Lola tried to catch Agnes's eyes, but Agnes refused to look at her.

"All right then." Jamika broke the awkward silence. "I'm taking Zoe downtown to get her statement while you two, uh…chat."

"What about the cops who're supposed to be on their way to get me?" Zoe grumbled.

"Don't worry about that. I'm much nicer than they are. Just be grateful they're not here yet." She yanked Zoe out the door. "See you at home, Lola," she called out as she left.

A heavy silence blanketed the room after their footsteps faded away. Lola, feeling a little ridiculous now in her black-on-black penthouse-infiltrating outfit, squirmed where she stood, wanting nothing more than to run away and hide. But if she wanted to rescue this relationship the way she and Jamika—mostly Jamika, really—had rescued Agnes, she needed to stay and fight.

"I'm sorry," she finally said to Agnes, who stood behind the heavy desk, watching Lola with hooded eyes.

"I know you are." The acid in Agnes's voice told Lola almost everything she needed to know about her chances for forgiveness. Agnes's blank face told her the rest.

She couldn't just accept that, though. She had to try. "Agnes, please—"

A sudden vibration of the phone in Lola's waist pack stopped her groveling from getting too bad. She rushed to answer it. "Hello?"

"It's Whit. If you're with her, tell her we're safe."

The sudden flood of relief nearly made Lola dizzy. Whit was enough of a badass to take on any number of gun-wielding nutjobs, but it was still good to have proof she was all right. "You should tell her yourself. I don't think she trusts me." Worrying her lower lip between her teeth, Lola turned slightly away from Agnes's sharpened gaze.

"But you are with her, correct?"

"Yes." As if she'd be anywhere else.

"Good. Repeat after me: the crèche is secure."

Lola frowned, but she repeated the words. Instantly, Agnes was on the other side of the desk and snatching away the phone, but from her repeated "hello, hello," Lola knew Whit had already hung up.

An explosive sigh left Agnes's lips, and she dropped her head low, chin nearly touching her chest. She squeezed the cell phone tightly. "They're okay."

"Yes, and now you are too."

"That's relative, isn't it?"

"I'd say it's damn good. At least my sister can't hurt you anymore." *Although she can still hurt me all day long*, Lola thought. Echoes of Zoe's spiteful words still rang in her ears and would, she suspected, for a long time to come.

"Yes, about that." Agnes looked up, all the softness bleeding from her face. "Just who the hell are you really?"

Lola's heart dropped.

CHAPTER 33

AGNES KEPT HER GAZE LEVEL and waited for an answer to her question, although it had been a mostly rhetorical one. With Camille's explosive revelations, she knew perfectly well who Lola was.

"After what happened today, I'm not so sure I know who I am," Lola replied after a tense silence.

Although she kept her face expressionless, Agnes internally winced on Lola's behalf. Camille had said some hurtful things, things that had obviously hit Lola hard. The mouthy, flirtatious woman she'd come to know over the past few weeks had withdrawn into herself and seemed like one big bruise.

"Camille is your sister, and you worked your way into my House to get back at me for hurting her, not to write some exposé." Agnes didn't make it a question.

"It was both at first. Zoe disappeared when I was a teenager, and it almost felt worse than when I lost my mother. At least with Mom, I knew she was going. I knew she loved the drugs more than she loved me." Lola lifted her head, and the overhead lights caught the pain dragging down the corners of her mouth, the new sadness in her eyes.

"One day, Zoe was there, helping me with my homework, and the next, she was gone. I thought she was dead. The police found a body. The penknife with your House initials pointed straight to you, and because I was told it was my sister, I had to find out what happened. Whether there was a newspaper story at the end of it or not, I was determined to know who hurt Zoe and make them pay. Everything I found out up to that day that I arranged to meet you at your club convinced me you were a terrible person.

"Then we met, and I started to have doubts. I started to fall for you." Lola's voice broke, and although she didn't want to feel it, the agony in it echoed in Agnes's chest. "I fell, actually, very fucking hard." Lola cleared her throat a couple of times. "Then suddenly, there she was, telling me you hurt her and that you stole Gretchen.

"Something she said that day made me doubt she was telling me the complete truth, but all this?" Lola shook her head, and her sadness appeared on the verge of leaking from her eyes and spilling down her cheeks. But, with a frantic fluttering of eyelashes, she seemed to pull herself together. "I had no fucking idea. She's a stranger. She's the real monster she accused you of being."

Lola looked gutted. Agnes wanted to go to her, to hold her. Instead, she clasped her hands behind her back and stepped away from the source of temptation. The anger she'd felt at what she'd thought was Lola's betrayal had simmered and bubbled, blistering her with its heat before evaporating, finally, into nothing.

"You didn't know she worked for my father and then became his lover?"

"No!"

Agnes took a badly needed breath and held it. "Why did I miss that you lived with a policewoman in your background search?" There were so many things she'd missed, although she'd thought she was being thorough.

"Your guys aren't as good as you think?" A smile flashed briefly across Lola's face. Then the smile died. "I'm not on the lease with Jamika. My credit is crap." She shrugged. "Poor impulse control in Williams Sonoma."

"That's...very specific."

"And true. I love to cook and bake. Our little apartment has two closets full of pots, pans, and bakeware. Who needs clothes?"

"Your wardrobe does seem limited."

"Fuck you."

An image exploded in Agnes's mind. Lola from that evening in the Peacock Room, the dildo strapped to her hips as she lay on the bed, her lips wet from Agnes's pleasure as she invited her to climb onto her and take what she wanted.

Agnes cleared her throat and slid her eyes away from Lola. The truth was, Agnes wanted that again. This time, no masks, just the two of them in one bed, sharing pleasure, touching each other without games, without holding back, just two women intensely into each other, having fun.

She didn't think it would happen, though. Not after today.

"When I asked you before if you were holding anything else back from me, you said no." Agnes captured Lola's eyes.

Lola bit her lip and looked down. She crossed her arms under her breasts, her expression wounded. "Yeah." Her voice was barely a whisper.

"You lied."

The vulnerable line of Lola's throat moved as she swallowed. She hugged herself, keeping her head down, her face turned away. Agnes thought she saw a tear slip down her cheek but wasn't sure. Her feet wanted to take her closer to find out. Her arms wanted to pull Lola close. Her heart wanted to keep Lola inside it for as long as they both could stand it. But Agnes's head was what ruled.

"I appreciate you coming back for me—" A sharp cry cut through the room, Lola's, but Agnes kept going. "—but I can't trust you. I gave you the chance to be honest with me, and you pissed on it until I stumbled into the truth on my own." The lump in Agnes's throat wouldn't go down, no matter how much she swallowed.

"I understand," Lola choked out. She looked up, and Agnes's stomach dropped. Lola's face was wet, her chin wobbling. "I'm sorry." Then, after a wild glance around the office, she fled.

CHAPTER 34

THE NEWSPAPER WAS ON THE kitchen table when Lola finally dragged herself out of her room in the late afternoon. She glanced at it because, of course, she was only human and was proud of the story, even if it wasn't under her real name.

Back when Lola had first started her career, Jamika had suggested she use a fake name, not just for safety but to throw off those editors or readers who'd ignore her work because of all the things her real name revealed about her. Because of that, Lola was AD Burne whenever her work appeared in print.

Raked Over the Coals of Justice: The Betraying, Ambitious Son Who Almost Brought a Brothel Empire to Its Knees

Lola reached into the nearly empty fridge and took out the bottle of pineapple ginger juice she'd made the day before. The world could end, and she'd always find time to make something in the kitchen.

From the little basket near the microwave, her phone vibrated. She'd left it there for the past few days, not wanting to deal with much of the outside world.

She sat at the table with her glass of juice and pulled the newspaper to her. It whispered across the plastic tablecloth.

Lola was rereading her own words in print, sipping the juice, the only thing she'd been able to keep down for the past few days, when she heard the front door open.

"Are you finally out of bed, girl?" Jamika banged her way inside the apartment, loud as always, and entered the kitchen, frowning down at Lola, just a few minutes later. "You smell," Jamika said after eyeing Lola's outfit, the rainbow onesie she'd been coincidentally wearing all week.

"No, I don't." Lola got up and showered every day and *then* crawled back into bed, thank you very much. The onesie only went on for her brief trips into the kitchen. "You, however, have smelling bad pretty much covered."

Jamika was in her running clothes, hair in a high ponytail, sweat dripping everywhere. "This is the sweat of a hard morning's labor, my friend." She dropped her gym bag in the corner and grabbed a glass of water before joining Lola at the table. "Guess what?"

"Chicken butt?"

"Ha ha, so mature." Jamika braced her arms against the table, her smile obscenely brilliant in the afternoon sun coming through the window. "You going to guess or what?"

Lola gave her a look.

"Okay, fine." Jamika rolled her eyes. "Because of the amazing job I did bringing down that little creep Philip Rake, I will be getting a commendation."

That broke through Lola's cloud, drawing a tiny smile out of her. "That's great."

"Yeah…" Jamika's enthusiasm leaked out in a sad little sigh. "But that's not going to get you out of bed and back to the real world, is it?"

What would at this point?

Every day since Agnes told her to fuck off had buried Lola under a steadily growing weight of depression. The very thought of eating tightened up her throat. Her sleep was restless, both too short and too long. Even cooking didn't bring her the same comfort it used to.

"Don't worry about me. I'll be fine. You got a big-time bust out of this whole thing with Agnes, a commendation, and maybe even a raise."

Jamika's help bringing a stop to Zoe's madness had been a big win for everybody. Zoe's fear of ever seeing the inside of a prison had her singing like a canary, and every dirty little secret had come out. The bust had dragged the cockroach Philip Rake out into the light, rescuing victims from the sex trafficking network he'd been running through his own father's business, according to an insider source—aka Zoe. The story had been high profile enough to take over the news cycle for a few days and gain Lola a front-page story.

But the things she'd lost because of this whole mess couldn't compare. The sister who she'd thought had loved her. A niece she'd never even known existed. And Agnes—Lola swallowed as Jamika's features blurred in front of her eyes. She'd lost Agnes before she'd even had the chance to really have her.

"Please stop that." Jamika scowled.

"What?" Lola looked up, but a drop of wetness slid down her face and plopped onto the newspaper, creating a dark circle.

"That. The chick was cool but nothing to have a whole depression over." Of course Jamika would say that. All her own relationships had been quick, easy, and forgettable. Just as they had been for Lola before.

From the other side of the kitchen, her phone vibrated again.

"You going to get that?" Jamika asked.

"No."

"Come on. It's been almost two weeks. You can't cut yourself off from the world forever."

"I'm not. I just need some time." How much, she didn't know exactly. Maybe until she didn't feel so bruised anymore.

A muttered curse fell from Jamika's lips. "This so isn't you. You're not the moping kind of chick."

"Maybe I am now."

"That Agnes must really have the bomb pu—"

"Don't."

Jamika rolled her eyes just as the phone started again. "Oh my God." The chair scraped against the floor as she pushed back from the table and reached for Lola's phone.

"Leave that alone!"

"If you really wanted me to ignore it, you should've put it on silent." She grabbed the phone from the basket. "Hello, Lola's phone. Can I help you?"

Lola had the half-assed idea to snatch the phone from Jamika, but even the thought of it was too much effort. Sighing, she shoved the newspaper away and drank more juice.

The money for the story was already in Lola's account, and because of it, she'd had a few potential new clients reach out by e-mail, but she wasn't ready to go back to work just yet. She could still pay her half of the rent for a few months plus afford the mint green KitchenAid mixer she was lusting after.

"Yes, I'll let her know," Jamika was saying as she scribbled something down on a piece of paper. "Yeah, she'll be into it." A few seconds later, she hung up.

"I told you not to answer my phone. Whatever it is, I'm not interested."

The smile on Jamika's face was smug and annoying. "Oh, I think you'll be interested in this." She slapped the piece of paper on the table right next to Lola's juice, making the nearly empty glass jump.

The name written on the paper thickened Lola's throat. "What's going on?"

CHAPTER 35

THE DAPPLED GRAY PONY'S HOOVES thudded against the packed dirt as it carried Gretchen around the white-fenced paddock. Agnes adjusted the thick scarf around her neck and leaned on the fence, carefully watching.

"I'm okay, Nessa. Promise," Gretchen called out.

"I know you are, love. I'm just admiring how well you're doing." Agnes's breath plumed out into the chilly air.

"I *am* doing great!" And she was.

Gretchen had definitely been on an independent streak lately. Agnes was sure when Gretchen was ready to fly away from home and do her own thing, she'd be far from ready. But if the world waited until humans were ready for change, there'd never be any progress.

Agnes drew in a deep lungful of the crisp November air, clean and fresh and far away from the city with its smog and noise. It had been Whit's idea to leave the city for a while, take Gretchen out of school for the week and escape the madness. Clare was holding down the office just fine, and Agnes had let her know she was only a phone call or short helicopter ride away.

Gretchen's delighted giggles sailed across the paddock as the pony sped up at her urging.

"Be careful, love," Agnes said.

"I am." Another trail of giggles. Gretchen made another circle, her smile flashing, then she stopped, looking at something behind Agnes. "Hi!" She waved. "Come watch me ride!"

Assuming it was Whit, Agnes didn't look away from Gretchen. Beyond the paddock, the fall colors of the trees surrounding the property flashed their deep oranges, burnished coppers, and brilliant yellows, which had been a big selling point when she'd bought it. The farmhouse itself was a boring white, but it had a gigantic barn with a hayloft she and Gretchen loved to climb up into and watch the world pass by.

Agnes felt a movement behind her just as she smelled something sweet. Chocolate. Not just chocolate. German chocolate. She turned. Her booted foot slipped off the railing.

"Hey."

Lola stood next to Whit, nervously pressing her lips together. She held a cake carrier in her gloved hands, her fingers curled around the edges and, it seemed, holding on for dear life. The breath exploded from Agnes's parted lips, and her heart did a little runaway gallop in her chest. She hadn't seen Lola in two weeks and had missed her every one of those days.

"I brought cupcakes," Lola said.

Agnes drank her in, from the multicolored knit beanie pulled down over her ears to the thick yellow parka that seemed a bit excessive for the relatively mild fall weather. Close-fitting jeans hugged her thighs, and black army boots covered her feet.

She looked good. And nervous.

Something about the way she stood, clutching the cake carrier and meeting Agnes's eyes with a mixture of defiance and fear, reminded Agnes of that first day Lola had come to her office. Her offering back then of whiskey-laced sweets had made Agnes leery, but that hadn't stopped her from eating them, even the one Clare had refused with a look of suspicion. Each time she'd eaten the desserts—and she'd drawn out the experience over two days—the taste of cream, cherries, and the subtle flavor of alcohol had kept Lola on her mind for hours.

Gretchen trotted over on her pony, pulling Agnes out of her mini stupor. "I like cupcakes. Can I have one?"

Lola cleared her throat. "It depends on what your Nessa says."

"What—what are you doing here?" Agnes could barely get the question out, probably because she was so busy staring.

Whit, in riding clothes she hadn't been wearing less than half an hour before, patted Agnes on the back hard enough to make her stumble. "She's here to deliver cupcakes." To Gretchen, she said, "You can have one later, sweetheart. I'm going to saddle up and join you while Agnes has a chat with Lola."

"Are you going to stay until I'm done, Lola?" Gretchen was being sweet, but her eyes strayed tellingly to the cupcakes held in Lola's arms like a baby.

A shaky smile shaped Lola's lips. "I hope so."

"Okay." Whit thumped Agnes's back again, this time a little harder.

Although Gretchen was closely watching them all, Agnes was very tempted to push Whit into the railing.

"Have fun chatting about cupcakes, the two of you," Whit added. "Gretchen and I will see you later."

Agnes nearly stumbled when Whit turned her around and nudged her in the direction of the house. "Don't fuck this up," Whit murmured after giving her a final pat on the shoulder.

On legs that were rubbery but more or less functional, Agnes led the way to the house, white and two-story with a wide porch.

Clutching her cake carrier like a lifeline, Lola walked alongside Agnes. *Kitchen.* Lola had cupcakes so that meant the kitchen. Right?

Once Agnes got to the kitchen, though, she didn't know what else to do. She stood in the sunlit room with the smell of fresh coffee from the automatic coffeemaker in the air along with faint traces of that morning's French toast and eggs.

Lola seemed similarly at a loss. Cake carrier clutched to her chest, she looked around the airy room.

Agnes couldn't help but notice Lola was like a bit of sunshine herself in the bright jacket that came down to her knees.

"I can go if you don't want me here." Lola cleared her throat again.

"No!"

"Oh…" Blinking rapidly, Lola started backing out of the kitchen. "Sorry."

"No, I mean. I don't want you to go. Ah…" A pair of coffee cups turned down on the sideboard to dry caught Agnes's attention. "Would you like some coffee or tea?"

Lola hesitated. "I'm not a huge fan of either one, to be honest. Do you have any cider?"

"Yes?" Whit was the one responsible for their groceries, so Agnes had no idea what they had. Luckily, a quick search of the fridge and cupboard yielded a jug of cider. "Do you want me to heat it for you?"

"Sure." Lola shrugged.

It gave Agnes something to do, fussing with the saucepan, cinnamon sticks, and mugs while being hyperaware of Lola behind her in the kitchen. Although Agnes wasn't watching (very closely), Lola eventually relaxed enough to put the cake carrier on the dining table, take off her jacket, and sit down.

When the cider was done, Agnes, her heart beating wildly in her throat, brought the two mugs of cider to the table.

Lola grasped the mug Agnes offered and brought it to her nose, sniffing deeply. "Thank you." She hesitated before taking a sip of the drink while all Agnes could do was stare.

It had been a long two weeks and four days of thinking about Lola and wondering if she'd made the right choice. Second-guessing herself wasn't something Agnes indulged in much these days, but watching Lola walk away from her that evening, she'd felt the crushing weight of the decision she'd made. Agnes had missed her, had wished she or Lola had made different choices.

Now, here Lola was. In Agnes's home. With cupcakes.

"Apparently, you weren't expecting me," Lola said after a long silence filled by the sound of their tandem cider sipping.

"I was not." But she was glad Lola was there. Her wide eyes and soft-looking skin, that vibrant youth of hers that both challenged Agnes and made her feel, every once in a while, like a dirty old woman. Although only thirteen years separated them.

Only.

Disbelief threatened to make Agnes think this was all some wild fever dream. Whit, who'd mistrusted and maybe even hated Lola from the beginning, had invited her up here. It didn't make sense. Then again, the whole time since Camille had been carted away and they had settled back into the scrupulously cleaned penthouse, Whit had been casting worried looks Agnes's way, not exactly asking what was wrong, but doing small, caring things that were out of character and, to be honest, a little scary.

Now, Lola was here. The fact that Whit seemed to trust her, and wanted to invite her into their small family, was nothing short of mind-blowing.

"You don't want me to leave then?" Lola asked with a faintly hopeful look.

"Not before Gretchen eats one of your cupcakes, no. She'd forgive a lot of me but not that."

"Oh." Lola's eyes fell into her mug of cider.

"I don't mean it like that." Agnes reached across the table, and suddenly their fingers were tangled together. Agnes looked down, felt the warmth that had seeped into Lola's fingers from the mug leak into her own normally chilled hands.

Lola's skin was soft, her fingers long and her nails almost painfully short, as if she'd just clipped them. Her hand trembled. Agnes squeezed it before letting go.

"Whit called and told me to come," Lola blurted out. "I don't want you to think I'm stalking you or anything like that."

"I didn't think that. This place is very secure, and Whit had to be the only reason you're here. Not to mention, if you'd managed to sneak up here somehow, I doubt she'd be as welcoming."

"True." Still avoiding Agnes's eyes, Lola scraped a thumbnail against the handle of her mug. "I-I was really glad to get Whit's message. I mean, I was shocked because she pretty much hates my guts, but I was glad too." She worried her lower lip between her teeth, eyes steadily down. "Although Zoe is gone, I'd love to have some kind of relationship with Gretchen. She's the only family I have left."

Disappointment landed solidly in Agnes's chest. "Is that the only reason you're here?" Although she couldn't blame Lola if it was. She'd been the one to sever their fledgling relationship. Lola had struck her as many things during the short time they'd known each other but a glutton for rejection wasn't one of them.

"No." Lola put the mug to her lips.

The liquid sound of that pointed sip took over Agnes's ears, and she leaned back in her chair, waiting for the rest. But Lola didn't say anything. She'd made the first move. They both knew it.

At this point, it was up to Agnes whether or not she would make the next one. She swallowed and toyed with the handle of her own mug.

"Your article was good," she finally said. "I could practically smell Rake's blood on the paper."

Although Camille had been mostly absent from the page, it was obvious in the article where she'd fit in. While certain of her victory, Camille had given up the pawns she'd been using to close her trap on Agnes.

There was Rox, who'd spied on and tried to seduce Agnes for her boss, not to mention supplied the penthouse's door code to Camille's army. Some woman named Maddie, who'd manipulated Lola and gotten her inside The House. Also, Camille had had someone trailing Lola all over the city. There had even been something about a large amount of money Camille had deposited into Lola's account, but no one knew if that was to set her up for something later, or if it was just a careless gesture of financial support from a woman who didn't *exactly* want her sister to starve to death in an expensive city.

Everything that wasn't laid out in the news story, Agnes had gotten from Lola's policewoman.

Jamika was an interesting person who seemed to be on the way to forming a dangerous attraction to Whit. The two women were odd together. The cop and the killer. Although some would say they were one and the same.

"Thanks." Lola put down her mug. "I'm glad things turned out the way they did. I—" Her lips that were slightly chapped and swollen from being bitten and exposed to the cold pressed nearly flat. "I'm sorry about what happened. Zoe manipulated me, but I should have done my own research. I shouldn't have allowed myself to be led like a sheep."

Agnes had had enough time to stew in her own anger and regret. The anger was gone now. Camille was persuasive and focused. If she wanted someone to do something, it was only a matter of time before it happened. Agnes had seen that in her own father. Such as the way he had taken in a young Zoe and, unlike all the other women since Agnes's mother, elevated her to heights that made Zoe dizzy with power…and assumptions.

"It's no crime to trust someone you love," Agnes said.

"Unless that someone makes you commit actual crimes." Lola's mouth twisted.

"But you didn't, did you? Instead, you tried to fix something you thought was wrong." Agnes barely stopped herself from reaching across the table once again for Lola's hand. "Your sister knew how to lead the most cynical people by the nose. You didn't stand a chance."

Lola's head jerked up, and Agnes caught the flicker of something in her eyes. Was it hope? But then she looked away again.

The sound of Gretchen's joy floated in through the kitchen's open windows, and Agnes lifted her head toward it, breathing in the scent of domesticity left over from the happy morning they'd all spent together making French toast and planning their next few days.

"I'm glad you came." The truth tumbled from her lips.

It felt like such a big confession, admitting to missing Lola, who Agnes had thought was a liar and couldn't be trusted, when it turned out that maybe it was Agnes's head that couldn't be trusted and that her heart had it right the first time. Lola was someone worth trusting, worth having, worth loving.

She was a coward, though. If Whit hadn't lured Lola up to the farm, Agnes didn't know if she would've had the courage to reach out on her own.

But Whit did always say that each of them had their strengths. Agnes's initial impulse was to save everyone first, then sort herself out *if* she had the time. Whit, however, made the hard decisions and put them into action.

With her help, everything had been sorted out. Rox was now gone from The House. Camille had been expelled from Rake Enterprises where she'd been sowing lies and plotting to take The House from Agnes. Because she'd done the unforgivable—turned informant by giving Philip and Rake Enterprises to the police—Camille had burned *all* her bridges. The last Agnes knew of her, she was in South America somewhere, friendless and too scared to come back to the United States.

With all that business put to bed, Whit had made a decision, then acted.

Agnes couldn't help but feel relieved.

"I'm glad I came too." Lola said. Her eyes came up, and this time they stayed, gently smiling at Agnes from across the table. "You want a cupcake?"

The offer felt loaded with more than just carbs. Maybe an offer to deliver on what their kisses had promised in the underground garage all those weeks ago.

Agnes's tired heart turned over in her chest. She wanted those promises. "I'll take it, but only if there's a German chocolate one in there."

"There absolutely is."

They each took a cupcake, and feeling vulnerable yet bold, Agnes invited Lola on a tour of the house.

Lola accepted.

Agnes slowly ate her cupcake as she meandered at Lola's side through the two-story farmhouse, showing off the massive stone fireplace in the living room, the sprawling views from upstairs, and the bedroom Lola could use if she wanted to spend the night. Lola gave Agnes a look from beneath her lashes as she said this, although Agnes gave nothing away about her own feelings regarding what the night would bring.

As for the cupcake, it was a moist wonder, the chocolate rich and dark. The frosting, Lola told her, was a mixture of not just the usual shredded coconut and pecan pieces but shredded carrots too. Agnes may have moaned a little at the first taste.

"Is it weird that I miss the sound of cabbies honking their horns and swearing at me?" Lola asked.

She and Agnes were perched together on the attic balcony, backs pressed to the wall as they stared out to the wide expanse of fall-colored trees, green grass, and blue sky. The cool air pricked Agnes's cheeks. "It *is* weird. I'm a city girl, and even I don't miss that."

"You're not a real city girl then." Lola breathed out a laugh. She ate her last bite of cupcake slowly and with obvious pleasure.

Agnes had long ago finished hers.

They sat close enough together that she could smell the chocolate on Lola's breath, the scent of the wool beanie pulled low on her head. She didn't know when they had drifted so close, only that suddenly they were. Their thighs pressed together, and their eyes looked over the same grove of trees. A feeling of peace settled over Agnes, and she exhaled a quiet breath.

The air between them shimmered with possibility. Yet Agnes couldn't follow that glimmering thread until she said something that had been weighing on her for weeks.

"About before, what I told you in the apartment." Agnes paused to gather some courage. "I lied. I *do* trust you." A trembling smile shaped Lola's mouth, giving Agnes the strength to keep going. "I've just never allowed myself to want something like this, a life with someone—with you—this badly."

Lola's fingers gently gripped hers and tugged her from the miasma of her doubts. "Even if you really don't trust me, I can't blame you," Lola said softly. "All I want is the chance to prove that I can be worthy of your trust and, hopefully, your love."

"You're worthy of both those things."

Lola dipped her head, and Agnes caught the tremor of her mouth, but when Lola looked up, she was smiling.

"I want to kiss you," Agnes said.

"Then kiss me." Smiling, Lola licked a bit of chocolate frosting from the corner of her mouth and tilted up her lips to receive what Agnes desperately wanted to give her.

Agnes leaned in, staring into Lola's warm brown eyes that glowed with affection and desire.

"Just to warn you, though," Lola said. "I want more than one night this time."

"I'll consider myself warned." Agnes smiled against Lola's soft lips and fell deeply, dizzyingly, into their kiss.

OTHER BOOKS FROM
YLVA PUBLISHING

www.ylva-publishing.com

A CURIOUS WOMAN
Jess Lea

ISBN: 978-3-96324-160-4
Length: 283 pages (100,000 words)

Bess has moved to a coastal town where she has a job at a hip gallery, some territorial chickens, and a lot of self-help books. She's also at war with Margaret, who runs the local museum with an iron fist. When they're both implicated in a senseless murder, can they work together to expose the truth?

A funny, fabulous, cozy mystery filled with quirkiness and a sweet serve of lesbian romance.

REQUIEM FOR IMMORTALS
Lee Winter

ISBN: 978-3-95533-710-0
Length: 263 pages (86,000 words)

Requiem is a brilliant cellist with a secret. The dispassionate assassin has made an art form out of killing Australia's underworld figures without a thought. One day she's hired to kill a sweet and unassuming innocent. Requiem can't work out why anyone would want her dead—and why she should even care.

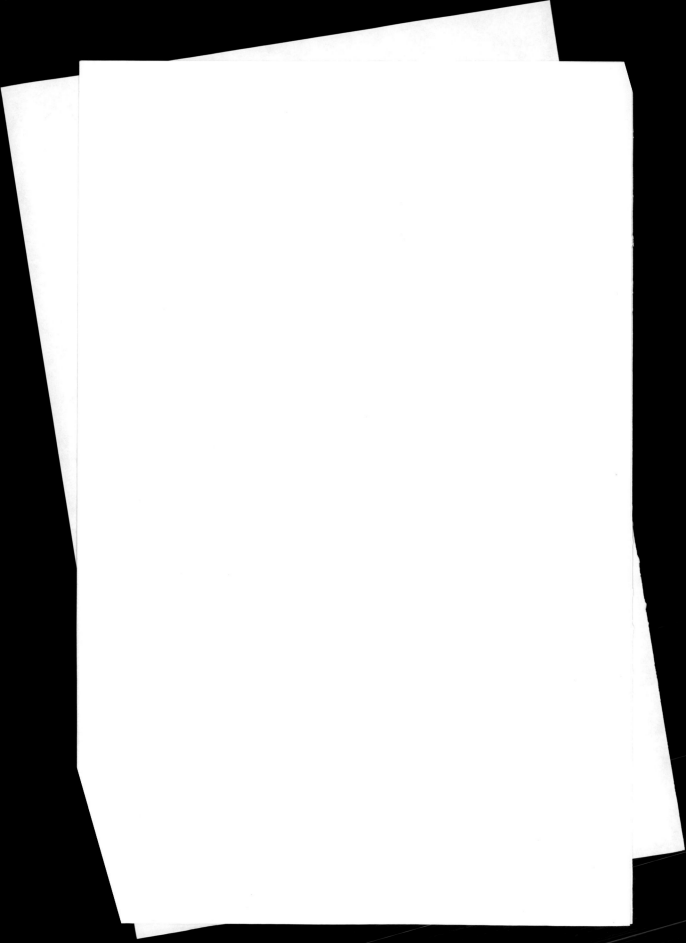